Deadly Magic

by

Joy Brighton

This is a work of fiction. Names, characters, places, and incidents are either the product of the author's imagination or are used fictitiously, and any resemblance to actual persons living or dead, business establishments, events, or locales, is entirely coincidental.

Deadly Magic

Cover Art by *Kristian Norris*

The Wild Rose Press, Inc.
PO Box 708
Adams Basin, NY 14410-0708
Visit us at www.thewildrosepress.com

Publishing History
First Fantasy Rose Edition, 2016
Print ISBN 978-1-5092-0419-9
Digital ISBN 978-1-5092-0420-5

Published in the United States of America

Rattles shook,

and she pulled the rough wool blanket closer. Even though the sweat lodge was stifling, she shivered. "I can't do it, Grandfather. I can't see the way forward."

"It is never easy to forge a new path," Grandfather coaxed. "Sometimes you must falter first. Trust and the vision will come."

Breathing deeply, she focused her thoughts again, feeling the packed earth under her. She slowed her pulse to match the cadence of the drums. White light and shadows danced, and the drumbeat faded until all she heard was her own heartbeat.

Then she was transported to a new place, a round, Southwestern kiva, tucked inside a limestone cliff. A narrow shaft of sunlight penetrated the fissured rock, highlighting dust motes in the hot, parched air.

A sun-browned man stood before her, armed with a flint knife and holding a staff that coiled and twisted in his hand.

They were alone, but she wasn't afraid.

In the dimness, she recognized his pale brown, gold-flecked eyes. The elder she'd seen before. A beautiful turquoise amulet shaped like a jaguar's head hung on his bare chest. His long, black hair, crested with silver, had been braided with leather thongs and an eagle feather. Shaman.

She lowered her eyes and sensed his radiating strength. A very ancient, but very powerful spirit.

Setting down his staff, he folded his legs and sat before the smoldering fire.

Kudos for Joy Brighton

2010 Linda Howard Contest—1st Place
~*~
2010 Silicon Valley RWA Gotcha! Contest—1st Place

Dedication

In 1943 John MacGregor, an archaeologist, discovered the ancient tomb of a Singagua man. Located in the Ridge Ruin Pueblo in Walnut Canyon, Arizona, the tomb held a vast array of precious goods from the time, a treasure. He was named The Magician.

When I read of this discovery in the course of my research, the nine-hundred-year-old Native American inspired my ghost, the Magician, and the preservation of his magnificent treasure became the goal of my human characters.

Only recently, I learned the Magician has been returned to his tribe and secretly reburied.

I would like to dedicate *DEADLY MAGIC* to this ancient man and his ancestors. May his spirit rest in peace.

Acknowledgments

Countless people have contributed to this book, more than I can possibly name. I'd like to mention a few, without whose help *DEADLY MAGIC* would not have been possible.

Most importantly, I want to thank my family. My wonderful husband, Dave, supported and encouraged my writing efforts and believed in me and in my writing career when few others did.

A huge thank-you to my fantastic critique group, the Armadillos: Teri Bradburn, Linda Hill, Anne Maragoni, and Janet Periat. The book would not have been finished without your help and support. You are all very special, very talented and insightful women.

I'd also like to thank the Silicon Valley chapter of the Romance Writers of America. I learned the writing craft through seminars, workshops, and the graceful and gentle mentoring of fellow SVRWA members. You're an amazing group of writers, and lots of fun.

My special thanks go to the Los Gatos Monte Sereno Police Department and the Santa Clara County Sheriff's Department for ride-alongs, fly-alongs, and answering what must have seemed to be endless questions. Thank you to she-who-must-not-be-fully-named, FBI Special Agent Julia. Any errors in procedure or weaponry are mine.

Thanks to my web designer and web mistress, Rae Monet. Your designs for the website are amazing.

Thanks to other friends who read part or all of various versions of this manuscript, including Dan Baxter, Celeste Dyer, Andy Fischer, Deb McKenzie, Susan Miller, Deb Mumper. I owe you lunch.

Prologue

South Central Los Angeles, One Year Earlier

The pit bull turned in a slow circle and finally collapsed, its huge jaw drooping onto its paws. Two more dogs dozed nearby with stomachs full of sedative-laced sirloin.

Norah Redfox eased from behind the garbage cans and crept through the dark, littered alley. She inched closer. No noise from the dogs.

No barks.

No growls.

With a wobbly hand, she reached out and rattled the chain link fence.

The animals didn't stir. She heaved one shaky sigh and then another.

Grasping the rough metal, she scrambled up the fence. When she swung over the top, her shirttail caught on the raw, twisted ends and jerked her off balance. She ripped free, dropped to the ground, and darted across the dead grass.

Crouched low in the shadow of the back porch steps, she paused to catch her breath. Her spirit guide nagged in her mind, *"No time! Get them now. Hurry!"*

A chill shuddered through her despite the stifling August heat. The drug bust would go down in less than ten minutes. She had to rescue her sister Laverne and

1

niece Amber before Ray murdered them. She couldn't bear to identify their battered, bloody corpses in the morgue. Again.

Her belly smoldered like she'd swallowed a stick of dynamite with the fuse lit. She'd already failed to change tonight's events once when the vicious guard dogs had stymied her. Each attempt became more dangerous. A third history-twisting journey back through time could be fatal.

From inside the rundown, 1930s bungalow, she sensed fear and pain radiating from her sister. Rap music blared from open windows, but Ray's angry voice boomed above the pounding bass. Why had Laverne married that sadistic, hyped-up son-of-a-junkie? Norah clenched her jaw. Love? No. Lust. Lust that was deaf, blind, and brainless.

Norah slipped into the pool of light spilling through a screen door. Holding her breath, she stole up the cement steps and slid a screwdriver into the crack where the warped bottom gaped away from the peeling doorframe. She jimmied the tool upward and strained but couldn't budge the hook.

Her clammy hands slipped, and the sharp metal sliced one finger. She hissed a breath through her teeth at the pain and wiped off the blood.

Using all her strength, she forced the screwdriver up, and the latch released. As she eased the door open, metal screeched against metal. Her heart jumped hurdles inside her chest, but she licked her parched lips and stepped onto the cracked brown linoleum. Edging past a rust-speckled washer and dryer, she peered around the corner and down the shotgun hall.

In the living room doorway, Ray stood with his

back to Norah, dressed in droopy jeans and a wife-beater with a red sweat rag tied around his shaved head. He loomed over Laverne, ranting and waving his tattooed arms.

She whined something Norah couldn't hear over the loud music and cowered, shielding her face with her hands.

His shoulder muscles bunched. He grabbed Laverne by her long, dark hair. "You got shit for brains? You stupid whore!" He smashed his fist into her nose, and she screamed.

Laverne's pain seared through Norah, and she staggered back a step, gasping. Although her hands shook, she couldn't afford to wait. She had to act now. Wiping the sweat from her brow, she inched toward the living room, hugging one wall.

Seconds later, the door across from her opened. Eight-year-old Amber shuffled into the hall, wearing a faded, oversized T-shirt. The child rubbed her sleepy brown eyes with her knuckles. "Momma?"

An ache twisted Norah's heart, muffled her voice. "Shush, sweetheart. It's Aunt Norah."

The child's gaze jerked up.

Norah clamped a hand over Amber's mouth and yanked her flat against the far wall. A flurry of gunshots erupted, and one splintered the doorjamb where Amber had stood.

Norah sensed Laverne's spirit flicker, and her life force snuffed out.

Agony ripped through her as she choked back sharp tears and glanced toward the living room. Laverne's body lay crumpled on the floor, her dark eyes wide and frozen.

Numbness clogged Norah's throat and turned her blood to sludge.

Too late. She was too late, forever.

Whimpering, Amber squirmed against Norah's hand. She scooped up her terrified niece, turned and ran.

"What the fuck? Who's there?" Ray yelled. His footsteps pounded after them.

With her pulse thundering in her ears, Norah slammed out the door and raced across the backyard. She dove into the shrubbery and shielded the child's body with her own. Think invisible. Think absolutely still, but each breath snagged, shaking her body, and each heartbeat throbbed in her cut finger.

"Aunt Norah?" Amber shifted her head. The scent of baby shampoo dueled with the tang of fear.

"Hush."

Ray appeared in the porch window. Even in the dark, his aura quivered with rage, chromium yellow streaked with muddy brown. He thumped down the steps and bellowed, "I know you're out there. Show yourself, you coward."

Light from the kitchen window glinted off his gun.

Norah ducked her face as bullets exploded. Puffs of dirt and shards of Bermuda grass flew against her hair. Squeezing her eyes closed, she swallowed a sob.

In the distance, sirens spiraled closer.

"Go ahead and take the fucking brat. Never wanted that whiny little shit anyway." He fired one more shot into the dirt.

The screen door banged shut, and he disappeared from view.

"Come on, sweetheart." Bruised and numb, Norah

struggled to her feet and dragged Amber toward the fence. She'd failed to save her sister, but at least she had her niece.

Using her free hand, Norah scrambled up while half carrying Amber. To the screech of sirens, they hurtled over the top and tumbled into blackness.

Chapter One

Sereno, California, Present Day

Norah hustled into the Silicon Valley Fast Mart. "Go get the drinks, Amber, while I wait in line."

When Amber flashed a cocky grin and raced off, her soccer cleats smacking the floor, Norah moved toward the counter, keeping her niece in sight.

At the cash register, an adolescent boy, maybe eleven or twelve, slouched beside a brawny man with thick, blond hair. The man leaned close to the high school girl behind the counter and drew his hand through his perfect hair. He smiled a perfect smile, showing his perfect teeth.

When Norah stepped closer, all the fine hairs on her body stood on end. Her grin evaporated into a shudder. The man's handsome features couldn't disguise the menace that rolled off him in waves, like a jarring shock from two-twenty current. Her nostrils burned from his psychic stench.

The man stuffed a roll of lottery tickets in his pocket. "Damn it, Josh. Quit whining." He grabbed the boy's shoulder and squeezed.

Josh stiffened. "Yes, sir."

Her power hummed, and she brushed a hand over the prickles on the back of her neck. Spirits clamored in her mind, urging her toward the boy.

As if sensing her, Josh turned his head and sucked in air. His razor sharp cheekbones and stick-straight, black hair mirrored her own. When he looked up, his sherry-colored gaze pierced hers.

Her handbag slipped from her fingers, and the clasp broke on impact. Coins jangled onto the floor, and her carved stone fox skidded beneath the candy display. Heat rushed over her face. Stooping, she groped for the small statue.

Josh wrenched free of the man's grip and scrambled toward her. Crouching, he reached under the shelf. His hand fisted around the carved fox, and he opened his eyes wide. "A shaman with white braids and black eyes that can bore a hole through you."

She shivered. "How do you know?"

He raised his chin. "Your spirit guide's a fox," he said in a high, rapid voice.

Leaning back on her heels, she opened her mind to the boy, and her breath caught. Pulsing energy, red and violet with cinnabar streaks, swirled around him. Intriguing. Unique. Ancient.

The man turned and glared at her. An unlit cigarette drooped from his cruel mouth. He stomped toward the boy, yanked him upright, and snatched the reddish stone. "Take care of your own shit," he snarled and pitched it at her.

The carved stone hit her cheekbone, dropped, and shattered. Norah covered her bruised face, and furious tears stung her throat.

Josh straightened and glared at the man. "Don't hurt her."

The man clenched his huge fist, then glanced overhead at the surveillance camera and smiled. He thumped the boy on the back. "She's not your problem, runt."

Norah jumped to her feet and reached for Josh. She'd seen too many abused children at work and couldn't let this go. "Leave him alone," she yelled, her voice like the slam of a gavel.

The man loomed closer, his light blue eyes iced steel, the bulky muscles in his arms and shoulders taut and bunching. "Butt out, bitch." He grabbed the boy and elbowed her hard in the center of her chest.

Pain arced through her ribcage, bowed her back. She landed on her rear, stunned and gasping.

"I'm calling the cops!" the blond clerk shouted from behind the counter.

"Come on." The man gripped Josh's arm and dragged him outside.

Her spirit guide penetrated her dazed consciousness. "Help him. Two boys are in danger."

Norah lurched to her feet and shook her head, but couldn't clear the gray spots clouding her vision. She staggered toward the storefront windows, moving slowly like fighting through chest-deep mud.

Alone in the parking lot, the man cuffed the side of Josh's head and heaved him into a battered white truck.

Hoping for a glimpse of the license plate, Norah stumbled toward the door. The engine roared, and the man backed out.

The pickup skidded onto the street and stopped at a signal down the block. The light flashed green, tires squealed, and the truck disappeared from view.

She paused in the doorway and doubled over, swearing under her breath.

Pressing her fingers over her eyelids, she struggled

to remember the number on the plate when she'd driven past it in the parking lot. A California plate?

No. A cactus. Arizona. But she could only picture three numbers.

Wide-eyed and ashen, Amber peeked around the candy display, clutching a six-pack of neon green bottles. "That man yelled at you. Did he hurt you?" She set down the sports drinks and hugged Norah's waist.

Norah wrenched herself back to the moment and stroked Amber's dark hair. The child had seen far too much violence in her short life and didn't need to hear about more. "I bumped him, and he got mad, but I'm okay."

Trembling, Amber looked up. "What about the boy?"

Cold fingers squeezed Norah's heart.

****

Norah crossed the busy road holding Amber's hand. The sky had clouded over during soccer practice, and a brisk wind whipped at Norah's French braid.

Amber chattered, tugging her toward the crowd waiting to enter the Fall Festival at Sereno's community center.

Just inside the gates, a tall man sat on a worn sleeping bag and played an oboe. Cash littered the open instrument case beside him. His denim shirt left strong, tanned forearms exposed. Heavy, masculine stubble shadowed his lean cheeks, but those black dreadlocks looked unnatural hanging over his impressive, I-can-dead-lift-an-elephant shoulders.

The smoky, mellow tones of the jazz ballad he played glided through Norah. Warmth spread, lured her closer, and she slowed to listen.

9

When he glanced up, their gazes locked. A half-grin crinkled the corners of his dark gray eyes, triggering a quick jump in her pulse.

Norah tucked a loose tendril behind her ear, and he winked.

"Aunt Norah!"

With a start, she re-focused on Amber's anxious face. "What did you say?"

"Hannah and her mom are playing ring toss. Can I go, please?"

Norah picked their friends out in the crowd and waved. "Okay, if you stay with them until I get there."

"Can I play, too?" Amber wiggled in place, shifting from foot to foot.

"Have fun." She handed the girl a bill, and Amber skipped ahead. Soccer had done wonders, helped Amber work through her fears and recover some of her spunk. Even the nightmares had eased.

Norah leaned against the wall, rubbing her bruised cheek. Grandfather nudged her mind. *"Both boys are in danger."*

Acid churned in the pit of her stomach. *"You've given me a mandate, but what can I do? Tell me how I can help."*

No answer.

She huffed out a breath, unable to shake a gnawing sense of urgency. Why had he mentioned two boys? She itched to be safe at home finding the answers, but she'd promised Amber time with her friend. Grandfather would have to wait.

The last notes of the jazz melody meandered through the air. Norah swallowed the strange lump in her throat and dug in her purse, tossing a single into the instrument case.

The street musician's gaze brushed over her and tingling heat branded her neck and face. "Thanks, beautiful," he said, his voice deep and triple-chocolate rich. "Are you okay?"

Norah dropped her hand from her cheek, flicked a surprised glance at her fingers and grinned crookedly. "I'm…I'm fine. Close encounter with a soccer ball."

He flashed straight white teeth and began a new song. His powerful, long-fingered hands raced up and down the oboe, playing a lilting Shaker tune.

Captivated, she sank onto a nearby bench. When her tender backside met the hard stone, she couldn't stifle a wince, but she closed her eyes and let the song wash over her.

He played with such purpose, each note pitched clear and true. The knot in her shoulders loosened as the bewitching melody painted pictures of spring in her mind. Immersed in the magic of his music, she could almost smell the sage blooming at Grandma's cabin in the Black Hills. A totally unexpected yearning ignited. She swayed forward and something untouched within her stirred.

Trembling, she studied his full lips where they curled around the reeds of his oboe. Her heart beat faster, her blood coursed hot beneath her skin. The notes swirled in a tight spiral of sensation, and a warm ache radiated low in her body.

****

"Come on, Josh. We gotta job to do." Kenny Swank flicked his cigarette butt out the truck window, where it hissed into the overflowing gutter.

Hunched in the passenger seat, Josh stared at the

floor. "But we should go home. Mom will be worried."

Kenny wanted to punch the smart-mouthed brat but cracked his knuckles instead. Just his luck the other kid flaked out. Now he was stuck with Gina's whiny nephew. But he'd seen the runt in action with that interfering bitch yesterday. The kid had real talent, if only he'd play along.

Gritting his teeth, Kenny drew his lips up in a curve and softened his voice until it was as smooth as a fat Cuban cigar. "You want to help your mom, don't ya?"

Josh's head bobbed. "Yes, sir."

"This old lady just wants some info on an old gun and powder horn she inherited. Thinks it belonged to a Revolutionary War soldier named Ephraim Lee." He wove a threat into his tone. "Give her what she wants."

The runt shrank back, stuttering. "I n-n-never know what I'll see until I touch something."

"What's wrong with you?" He shoved his face up close to the kid's. "Doesn't matter what you see, stupid. And for fuck's sake, don't tell her it belonged to some horse thief."

"No." The boy's eyes widened, showing white all around.

"Put on a show. Moan and groan. Then feed her a fancy fairytale." Twisting the runt's shirt in his fist, Kenny raised him off his seat. "Be sure you call the guy Ephraim. Ya got it?"

Color draining from his face, the boy shriveled away from Kenny's hand. "Yes, sir."

Kenny's pulse spiked, and he sucked in a breath through his teeth. Good. He'd scared the runt enough to control him for a while. "Come on. Let's get 'er done."

He jerked Josh out into the downpour and frog-marched him along the sidewalk.

When they turned up the flagstone path, Kenny eased his grip. Might be a camera at a McMansion like this. He slapped on his stupid-hick grin and poked the buzzer.

A pudgy woman in pearls opened the door. Kenny removed his cap and shook off the rain. Widening his smile, he wrestled his gaze off the bling glittering on her stubby fingers. "Evening, ma'am."

"Mr. Swank. Will you and Joshua please take off your wet shoes and leave them on the tile." She fluffed her poufy gray hair, twittering like a fucking canary. "Everything is in the kitchen."

"Yes, ma'am." Kenny cased the joint while he kicked off his shoes. A suitcase-sized purse sat open on the dining room table, inviting him to take whatever he wanted. He sucked on his tongue to find some spit. What a rush. The runt better not blow this. He grabbed hold of the kid's collar. "You're lucky we could fit you in. Josh has talent, powerful psychic talent."

She patted her hands together and gushed, "I'm so excited to hear what he sees."

"Once he does the reading, you'll have the true history. Absolutely bona fide." He grinned at his mark again and caught a glance of himself in the mirror over the fireplace. He clenched his molars and pulled his smile even wider. "You sure got a nice place here." The kind of place he deserved.

Beaming, she led them into a huge kitchen. Her exhaust trail of sickly-sweet perfume gagged him.

From the granite counter, she lifted a beat-up old powder horn with a metal band around the rim. A dirty green cord hung from both ends. "My great aunt left this to me."

Josh's gaze fixed on the piece. "May I hold it?"

"You didn't tell me he had to touch it." She stepped back and eyed the boy suspiciously.

Kenny pitched his voice low, like he didn't give a shit. "You want a vision?"

Her lower lip jutted out for a second, but then relaxed. Something in the kid's dopey look must have made her cave. Damn good thing.

"Okay, but be careful. The horn's very old and valuable. Sit down so you don't drop it."

Josh obeyed and took the piece with both hands. His eyes rolled back, and he swayed in his seat, moaning. In a singsong voice he said, "I see a ram, a ram in the mountains, and a man walks through the forest, and the trees are red and golden, and he works at night, by firelight to make the powder horn for his son." His voice drifted lower, and he began to mumble.

Tensing her fists, she leaned closer. "Who were they? Do you know their names?"

Kenny's mouth watered. The old bitch was buying the kid's patter. Come on. Get the fucking name right.

Josh's eyes snapped open. He twitched like a butterfly with its wings ripped off. "Yes. Lee. The son is Ephraim Calvin Lee. Ephraim for his grandfather and Calvin for his father."

A shiver grabbed Kenny by the balls. Creepy. Maybe the runt really did see stuff.

Her mouth gaped wide in her flushed face. "Here. Touch the musket," she squeaked.

Josh laid one hand across the wooden gunstock and froze. "Ephraim's a soldier."

"Where? When?" She stared at the kid, twisting her hands together.

The runt was a natural. Kenny bit his cheek to keep from laughing and slid away from the pair.

Easing into the dining room, he rifled through the purse and silently opened a zippered compartment. Better leave the cash. She'd notice when she paid 'em. He lifted a couple credit cards, slipped them into his jacket, and glanced at the overloaded hutch. What could he swipe she wouldn't miss right away? A jeweled egg on the top shelf sparkled.

A few minutes later, Kenny patted his jacket pockets and slipped back into the kitchen. Josh still had the old bitch hooked.

"Ephraim's on lookout, wearing the horn." Josh's head jerked. "A shot. He sees a scout and fires. There's blood, blood on the scout's red uniform." With his face white as a line of coke, the runt stared blankly.

"Joshua?" She tugged on his arm. "Tell me where."

"What? Where? Hub…Hub something." Josh shuddered and set the horn on the table with shaky hands. He rubbed his forehead, sighed and keeled over.

****

Adrenaline spiked Kenny's nerves. He felt pumped up, electrified, but smelling the Chinese take-out was making him drool. Juggling three grocery sacks, he shoved a gallon milk jug into Josh's arms and laid a twitchy hand on his shoulder. "Don't say nothing about the job. Don't want to worry your mom."

Eyeing him, the kid shrugged, and his hair flopped forward over his eyes. He pushed open the unlatched door to the apartment. "Mom? We're home."

"We're in Stacy's room," Gina called.

Kenny lugged the plastic sacks into the kitchen, pushing aside piles of his sister-in-law Stacy's crap to make room on the ugly orange counters. He twisted a beer can free and shoved the rest of the six-pack into the refrigerator, cramming Stacy's insulin into the back corner. "Josh, put the milk in the fridge and show your mom the shoes you picked out."

Josh pounded down the hall, yelling, "Mom? Guess what, Mom? We got dinner! Wanna see what Uncle Kenny bought me?"

Popping the can open, he guzzled half the cold brew. What a set-up. A hundred bucks for food, and a pile of junk from Wal-Mart. He'd charged everything to the old bitch.

He chugged the rest of the beer. When he crushed the can in his hand, a sharp corner nicked his palm. He sucked on the cut, tasting nicotine and blood.

Tonight he and Gina would drive to Vegas to see what Charlie could get him for the goods. He'd clear eight or ten large off the runt's work today, maybe more. Man, the kid would make him a mint when they got back to Arizona. But first, he'd pry both the journal and the runt out of Stacy's paws. Whistling softly, he strutted toward the bedroom.

Gina sat next to her sister on the double bed. She glanced up at him and leaned forward, showing her cleavage. He flashed his sexy grin. Later he'd show her the loot he'd swiped. Money always put her in the mood to fuck.

Gina's sister, Stacy, sat propped up in bed, covered with an old quilt, her dark eyes bloodshot in her puffy face. She pushed back her limp, black hair and looked up at him with a wan smile. "You know, I wasn't sure what to expect when you came to visit, but I appreciate your help, Kenny."

The kid crowded next to her and hugged her arm. "We went to see one of Uncle Kenny's friends, and I told her about this soldier—"

Kenny's stomach cramped. He pinched the back of the runt's neck and leveled a cold stare at him. "We weren't going to tell your mom I took you along while I fixed that computer."

The damn kid's gaze darted upward, but he turned back to his mother, shielding his mouth behind a fist. "Anyway, um, remember, I did a report about the Green Mountain Men in school last year? She had a musket like the picture in my history book."

Stacy's eyes narrowed, and her lips thinned. The bitch must have seen the runt's tell. Kenny pushed out his chest and put on his suck-em-in face. She was nothing but another fucking mark. "Yeah. Then we got shoes and a new coat for Josh."

"Uncle Kenny said we'd found a treasure, so we went shopping with the gold."

When Gina and Stacy grinned at each other, a surge of possessiveness twisted his gut. He hated the tie between them, but maybe his idiot wife could wheedle the journal from her idiot sister.

"We used to go treasure hunting in Arizona as kids. Remember?" Gina asked.

Stacy's eyes lit briefly, and she brushed Josh's hair behind his ear. "I remember using Great Grandma's diary as a treasure map."

Gina bent toward the kid. "Before she died, she drew pictures in her journal, clues to a treasure buried near the Reservation," she said, shading her voice with an I'm-gonna-share-a- secret hook.

Stacy propped her chin on her knees and gave Gina another sappy look. "We spent hours poring over her sketches, dreaming we'd find the lost gold."

"Wonder whatever happened to that old diary?" Gina tapped a nail against her lip.

Jaw clenched, Kenny stepped closer to the bed. *Come on, bitch, blab.* He flexed his hands and cracked knuckles gone bloodless.

Stacy focused on his face for a split second and then dropped her gaze. One finger traced a spiral on the quilt. "I'm sorry. Can we talk later?"

Gina winked at him on the sly. "No problem. Tell me where you keep the diary. We can check out the pictures while we eat." She giggled and patted her sister's arm. "It'll be fun."

"Sorry, maybe later." Yawning loudly, Stacy squeezed her lids shut and pulled up the quilt.

Kenny turned his back and glowered at the ceiling. *Fuck. Shoulda been on the road by now, with the journal and the brat. Time to take control.*

"Do you want some almond chicken?" the runt asked his mom.

She hugged him and kissed his forehead. "Chinese? You really did splurge."

"I'll bring you a plate, Stacy," Kenny said. A cold thread of violence curled around his heart, but he hid his snarl behind a grin.

****

Norah unclenched her fist from the medicine bundle and shook the stiffness out of her fingers. She glanced around her dimly lit kitchen—3:00 a.m. already?

No point in trying again. She'd failed twice to send herself back in time. Zero results.

Shoving her palms against the round oak table, she stood to stretch and lit the gas under her teakettle. Nausea jarred her belly, leaving a throbbing pain, and she swallowed hard to keep from being sick. What had blocked her attempt to change the past?

A shiver crept through her. Grandfather insisted she could help Josh. She'd spent most of the night trying. Her gift had always worked before, but for some reason she couldn't twist history tonight, couldn't change what she'd done in the store.

She rested her head against both hands and rubbed her temples. If she couldn't free Josh, what would he face at the hands of that sociopath?

Still frowning, Norah plunked a chamomile tea bag into her favorite cup and poured in boiling water. Herb-scented steam curled up from the liquid, tickling her nose. She drew in a deep, calming breath and slumped back in her chair.

There had to be another option. She scratched at a spot on the tablecloth with a fingernail. Grandfather Redfox had said boys, plural. What if her gift hadn't failed? Sitting straighter, she sipped her tea. What if she had to find Josh and send him back? What if Josh had to alter the past in order to save some other boy?

Norah's senses hummed, and a vision engulfed her. Her kitchen transformed. She stood in the open doorway of a smoky, dirt-floored lodge. Drums echoed into the night.

She knew this place. Her spirit had traveled here many times. Easing the door flap shut, she planted her feet and centered, sensing the solid earth beneath her.

The sharp smell of sage cleared her thoughts. A crackling fire ringed by smooth stones beckoned. She walked forward unafraid. Now she'd find some answers.

Burning sweet grass and ritual tobacco caught in the back of her throat. Her sight blurred. She blinked away tears, but her pulse slowed and kept time with the steady drumbeat.

Behind the glowing embers of the fire, a fox sprawled on an old patterned blanket. She sank to the ground opposite the creature, folded her legs and opened her mind.

The animal licked a paw, rose and morphed into a familiar old man. Grandfather gazed back at her. Firelight reflected from his sharp black eyes, still the eyes of a fox. His craggy face was lined and brown, parched like the Lakota reservation. "You must act, child. There is much at stake."

A bitter taste filled her mouth. "I understand, but I couldn't twist time and go back to the store. I tried."

"No."

A diamondback rattler wriggled near his feet, and the vision wavered. Tension coiled inside her, and she frowned at the intruder. Nothing felt quite right. "Should I send Josh back?"

"You cannot change that past," Grandfather said in a grim, flinty tone. His aura swelled, purest indigo shading into brilliant white. He grabbed the snake and raised it over his head. Thrashing and twisting, the reptile glowed with power. Then the snake stiffened and petrified into a shaman's staff.

Adrenaline burst through her veins, and icy fingers traced her spine. She struggled to keep her voice soft and even, but panic clutched her throat. "What? What must I do?"

A faint flute melody swelled and threaded through the pulse of the drums. Stern-faced, Grandfather cocked his head toward the music. "It's time."

"Time? Time for what?"

"For many changes, child."

The vision flickered again. She surged to her feet, concentrating furiously on her grandfather's scowling face, but opalescent sheets of color shimmered through the air, distorting the scene.

Spirits in traditional buckskin danced behind the old man. Bow on his back, a bronzed, broad-shouldered hunter towered over the other dancers. His long, muscled legs stamped with the beat and sent the fringe on his boots flying. In the firelight, his taut abdomen and naked chest rippled. As he danced, he held a bone flute in his big hands, raised the instrument to his lips and played a melody, sweet and lingering.

Her heart skittered and damp heat pooled low in her body. In the wavering light, the hunter looked familiar, and she strained to see his features.

"Time for many changes," Grandfather repeated. "This quest will affect more than the boys' safety. Even I do not yet see the full consequences. Go with great care, child." He lowered his eyes and held up a hand to dismiss her.

Frustration wrenched her insides. Her muscles knotted, and her mind churned as she tried to find words. "Wait. Who's the man? The hunter?"

Grandfather slammed the staff on the ground. Sparks flew.

A fox leaped over the fire and vanished.

Norah slumped forward, sloshing cold tea onto her hand. She shook off the moisture and stared at the pale gold puddle in the saucer. Who was the hunter? His image kept dancing through her thoughts, and the haunting melody he played nagged at her memory. She pursed her lips. Grandfather had been cryptic, as always, and direct questions were worse than useless.

Around her, the house creaked, buffeted by the wind. Rain pounded on the tile roof, jangling her nerves. She stomped into the living room, plopped onto her chair, and snatched a throw to cover her legs.

At first, the sweat lodge vision had seemed familiar, but where had the snake totem come from? She'd learned early in her training to beware of malicious supernatural powers. Had a spirit from the Southwest invaded Grandfather's sweat lodge? She shivered and pulled the blanket closer. No, too soon to panic. In the Hopi tradition, snakes also opened the portals to the spirit worlds.

Rubbing her scratchy eyes, she leaned her head back against the cushion. Whatever the vision foreshadowed, she had to find Josh fast. The spirits had made her assignment clear.

Chapter Two

An out-of-season storm hammered Silicon Valley with gale force winds that matched the spirits battering her consciousness and demanding action. Shivering, Norah yanked the parking brake and switched off the windshield wipers.

"Find the boy," Grandfather yammered in her mind again.

She jammed a loose pin back into her chignon. *"I'm trying. I've done everything I can think of to find him. I grilled the store clerk, searched the databases at work. I even drove around in this blasted weather, hunting for that beat-up truck."*

"Find help, or soon one boy will be lost." Grandfather's voice was strident, as if crammed through a funnel.

"That's why I'm here. Now cut the commentary so I can think." Earplugs. She'd sell her soul for a pair of mental earplugs.

Norah forced open her door against the blustery wind. Holding her raincoat hood, she dashed between puddles and up forty-seven slippery steps to the police station entrance.

Inside, a trainee seated her in Captain Nate Kapulani's office. Norah curled her shaky fingers around a cup of hot coffee, soaking in the warmth and comforting aroma.

Built on a rise, the Spanish style building sprawled above Sereno. Today the wind gusted, pounding gray sheets of rain against the picture window and obscuring the view of downtown.

Her friend's husband, Nate greeted her and eased his tall frame into the chair next to hers. Dressed in a crisp dark blue uniform, he looked comfortable in his own, very dominant skin.

A trickle of adrenaline elevated her heart rate. Norah shifted in her seat, twisting her silver and turquoise earring. How could she convince this savvy, clear-headed cop to listen?

As her silence lengthened, his brow furrowed over deep brown, almond-shaped eyes, but his expression held no fear or suspicion. Yet.

She lowered her mental shields and studied his aura. Blue-green. Solid. Radiating warmth. Squaring her shoulders, she met his shrewd gaze. "I need help, Nate, but I'm not sure how to explain."

He tapped an unsharpened pencil against his wide gold wedding band and cleared his throat. "Jana told me how you helped her."

The heaviness in Norah's chest eased, and she nodded.

"Don't understand how, but I believe you stopped, or, uh, reversed a murder." He hesitated. "Mine."

"Jana did."

"She called you a catalyst."

Norah slid a smile into her voice. "Close enough."

He ran a finger around his collar. "I'll help if I can. Guess I owe you my life."

"Thank you." She took a long, deep breath. "A boy is in great danger."

"What's his name?"

"The man he was with called him Josh."

Nate sat silent for two heartbeats then frowned again, his nostrils flaring. "That's it? No last name?"

"I can give a good description." The clamor in her mind doubled. Her nerves knotted. She turned her bruised cheek toward Nate, angled so she'd catch the light. "The man might look like a film star, but he's evil. I tried to stop him when he abused the boy, and he elbowed me."

"What?" His mouth a fierce line, he rose in his seat and examined her face closely. "Damn it. That creep hit you."

"He knocked me down."

"We'll get the details and send a uniform out to the store."

"The ditzy clerk wasn't much help, but the store owner said he'd cooperate."

"Anything else you can tell me?"

"I remember part of the license. Arizona plates on a ratty, white Ford pick-up with a camper shell."

"An out-of-state partial?"

"Yes. And the parking lot camera wasn't working."

Nate combed his fingers through his dark wavy hair and slanted a questioning look at her. "What about your department? Child Protective Services any help?"

She laid both hands on her lap, palms up-turned. "Not without a full name."

"Fill out an incident report anyway. We'll track down the scumbag." Settling back into his seat, Nate tugged on his ear. "The truck or the boy could match an APB. We'll check, but for now, I can hook you up with vehicle ID."

"Thank you." Finally, Grandfather quieted.

"Hold on a sec." Nate reached for his phone.

She closed her eyes and replayed the scene in the store one more time. The fear on Josh's face, the way he'd cringed sent shivers coursing through her again. She released a fragmented breath. Grandfather insisted she could help, so there must be a way. She'd never forgive herself if she failed.

Nate finished a second call and turned back to her. "Gonna start you off with the department artist. Sometimes security camera photos aren't worth much."

"I'd better get moving. I only have an hour." She grabbed her raincoat and opened the door.

"Great. Blake's waiting to sketch Josh and the man. He'll take your incident report."

A uniformed cop paused in the doorway. "Hey, Captain."

She noticed his blues and build first. Tall, with a granite chin and light-years-wide shoulders. Just another gorilla cop.

"That disguise worked great." He tossed a dreadlock wig onto Nate's desk with easy precision.

Norah looked up into his tanned, clean-shaven face. Heavy-lashed, deep gray eyes captured hers. Her jaw dropped, and her pulse bumped.

He grinned at her, and a troupe of butterflies invaded her belly.

She shook her finger at him. "You're the oboe player."

"Norah Redfox, Sergeant Jackson Marino," Nate said. "He heads our undercover unit."

Jackson trapped her hand in his long, warm fingers. "Pleasure," he drawled in a low, rumbling, come-to-

Jesus voice. As her skin tingled with awareness, a quick thrill shot up her arm. She discovered her knees were shaking, and something odd gripped her throat.

Jackson's gaze, a little too confident and far too intimate, roamed over her, spreading prickles of warmth and an uncomfortable awareness of his masculinity. With that face, he probably thought all the women in the world should swoon.

She extricated her hand and returned his wolfish grin. "Great disguise, Detective. I never imagined you were a cop." She flashed him even more teeth. "But I didn't buy tramp, either. Your big, toothy smile gave you away."

He let out a throaty laugh, and the freaking butterflies turned somersaults. A blush flamed her body from her toes to her cheeks. Her hands curled into fists.

"Thanks, Nate. Sergeant." Nodding curtly at Jackson, she pivoted and marched away.

She'd lose her gift if she ever had sex. Who needed it anyway? She refused to let this cop, this charmer, this tomcat-on-the-prowl breach her defenses.

****

Jackson rubbed his chin thoughtfully. Friday, she'd looked good in sweats, but today in a short skirt and heels, she sizzled. "You know the lady?"

"Norah? She's an attorney, an old friend of Jana's." The captain returned to his desk and picked up a folder. "Very interesting woman."

"I'll say." Jackson leaned against the doorjamb and enjoyed the view as the graceful Ms. Redfox negotiated the long corridor. Her jacket emphasized her tiny waist and ended just above the fine curve of her hips.

One corner of his mouth lifted. Snazzy green shoes

did amazing things for her long, sexy legs. When she allowed a rookie to open the door for her, Jackson whispered, "Look at me."

She turned to profile with a bright smile aimed at the kid. She must have felt his gaze because another blush raced across her cheekbones. She firmed her mouth, but her dark eyes glowed.

The lady was skittish, but very aware. He grinned fully and formed his lips into a silent whistle. He needed to run his hands through her hair and touch the soft, black strands.

Nate cleared his throat. "Marino." A commanding note snapped through his voice.

He dragged his attention back to the captain.

"Fill me in on the drug bust," Nate said, enunciating each word precisely.

"Oh, yeah," Jackson fumbled his way back to the case. "Arraignment's set for tomorrow. DA says the evidence looks good." He glanced over his shoulder. She had slipped between the doors and disappeared. He wanted to track her down, but the hunt would have to wait.

Eyebrows arched, Nate followed his gaze and shook his head. "Don't usually see you so distracted, buddy."

"No kidding." Couldn't remember the last time he'd drawn a bead on a woman that fast. "She prosecuting a case?"

"No. Filing an incident report for an assault."

A gush of anger fisted his hands. "Good. She said she was fine on Friday, but I could tell she was hurt." An unwelcome thought surfaced. "Boyfriend?"

"No. Stranger. Wrong time, wrong place." Nate

pulled the office door closed and then steepled his fingers. "Marino, Norah is different."

Jackson flashed another glance at the door.

The captain's face went horizontal. Narrowed eyes. Tight mouth. Lined forehead. "Her Amber plays soccer with my daughter. Norah's assistant coach."

His stomach twisted, but he didn't let the disappointment show. A kid? "Got it."

"Good." Nate handed him a report. "Hustle over to the Medical Center. Unidentified juvenile came in Saturday night."

"Who brought him in?"

"A woman. She skipped out, but they caught her on camera. Talk with ER and Marty in security."

A painful lump rose in his throat. "Kid gonna be okay?"

The captain's brow wrinkled again. "He's in bad shape. Been abused."

****

Seated in the hospital's darkened security office, Jackson looked away from the monitor, flexing his fingers. "Run the film by me once more."

"Marty" Martin, a wiry wise-ass with a salt and pepper crew cut and bright blue eyes, replayed the hundred and forty-second segment for the third time.

Jackson squinted at the grainy image. "Still can't make out the details here. The ambulance blocks the whole ER dock."

"Lousy parking job, but you can kinda understand with that storm." Marty tapped the screen. "There she is, over by the beat-up white truck. She's carrying the boy."

The kid's head drooped over her arm. He looked

like a stringless puppet. Jackson winced and watched her struggle toward the entrance. The wind whipped back the hood of her sweatshirt. "Can you zoom in on her face?"

"We get a better look from the other camera." Marty hit a few keys, and the fluorescent-lit emergency room appeared.

On screen, an orderly looked up and pushed a gurney through the crowd, calling for help. The woman eased the boy onto the sheets. Suddenly his back bowed and stiffened, his eyes widened. A gurgling sound escaped his throat, and his body twitched.

Jackson's chest tightened. He'd seen seizures before but had to clamp his lips together to repress a grimace.

The orderly reached down to steady the child, shoved the woman's hand away, and rushed the gurney though the automatic doors.

Her protest was garbled. She followed for two steps, hesitated, and then pivoted. For a split second, she faced the camera full on, but recoiled, her expression a terrified mask.

Marty slowed the speed to one frame a second. "You think she's surprised?"

Her expression made Jackson's hackles rise. "No, she's scared. Scared of the camera." Sure enough, she jerked her hood over her stringy dark hair and ducked away from the front desk. "But we got a good look. Five-five, one ten, brown, brown. Around thirty." Her low-rise jeans revealed a taut strip of belly licked by a tattoo.

"Yeah. That's the best shot. She's skinny, but her sweater sure covers a nice rack." Marty chuckled.

"Too nice. Implants?"

Marty restarted the action. "Yep, not much jiggle."

Slouching in the far corner, the woman drew a pack of cigarettes from her jacket pocket, shook one out, and flicked the lighter. Inhaling deeply, she glanced both ways and hurried out the door like the devil himself had her in his scope.

Marty backed the machine to the clearest frame and clicked print. "The orderly heard her call the kid Tyrell. No last name. No ID in the kid's effects."

Shaking his head slowly, Jackson picked up the sheet and studied the blurry face. "Gutsy, wasn't she? Did another camera get a better angle?"

"Want to see 'em again?"

"No. Give me all you got. I'll see if our guys can clean it up."

Marty punched keys and handed Jackson the disc. "I'll call if she comes back."

"Fat chance." With a half-assed salute, Jackson headed out. He wandered along the hospital corridor, slapping the flat plastic case against his hand. Damn little to go on.

Outside the crowded ER, a paramedic shouted, "Coming through," and powered a gurney past Jackson, while doing CPR on the run.

"Hey, Marino."

Jackson turned toward a tall man with spiky blond hair and green eyes.

Dr. Drew Carlson gave his hand a powerful squeeze. "You here about Tyrell?"

"Did you call a report in?"

"Yeah. Listen, a string of nasty wrecks kept the ER hopping all weekend." Drew waved a stack of paper.

"Give me a second to drop off orders, and we can talk."

He followed Drew to the nurses' station outside the ICU and leaned against the wall, flipping through the shots Marty printed. He couldn't see the woman's features clearly, but she looked brassy, overdone, like a weathered barn with too much paint. But with those bones, she might be Native American.

Norah Redfox had the same cheekbones, but her lush, smiling mouth and rich chocolate eyes promised more. Damn shame she was off limits.

He glanced up. Drew, his carousing buddy since college, had handed the charts to a petite, curvy nurse and turned on the charm. That guy could sweet talk crumbs from an ant.

After a couple minutes, the nurse left smiling.

Drew clapped him on the shoulder. "Where do you want to start?"

"This is what we have so far."

Drew checked out the pictures, twisting the stud in his eyebrow. "Never saw her. Took twenty-four hours to register no one was coming back for Tyrell."

Scowling, Jackson jabbed his fingers through his hair. "Can I see him? I need to straighten this out."

"Won't do much good. He's sedated, on a ventilator."

Jackson sucked in a harsh breath. "Will he make it?"

"Hard to say." Drew leaned back, resting his shoulders against the wall. "Dehydration screwed up his kidneys, but if the pneumonia clears, he'll have a chance. Starvation complicates the prognosis."

"Starvation?" His gut churned. "Jesus."

Drew heaved himself forward. "See for yourself.

Poor kid hasn't had a decent meal in months."

They pushed through the doors into the ICU, and Jackson's skin crawled like a million centipedes had just hatched in his armpits. The whir of the ventilator and constant beeping of the life support system sent his blood thundering at his temples. Anger burned his insides, and his fists jerked. He forced back the bile oozing past his tonsils. The poor kid all but disappeared in the white sheets and tubing.

Drew lifted the boy's eyelids and listened to his frail chest. "Weirdest thing. Before we sedated him, Tyrell kept raving about ghosts."

****

The persistent drizzle and her client's poor-me, gripe-and-whine attitude pushed Norah's already gloomy mood deeper into Slugville Swamp. She sighed and focused all her senses on the challenging fourteen-year-old girl facing her in the children's shelter interview alcove.

Casey's attitude left a sour taste in Norah's mouth. Not surprising. The girl had never had a strong, positive authority figure or consistent discipline.

A power spike surged against Norah's awareness, and a shiver skated up her spine. Her head snapped toward the disturbance. Josh, the kid from the convenience store, shuffled across the room and hunched into a corner window seat, steering clear of the other children in the airy playroom. She shut her gaping mouth. What was he doing in the shelter? This was the very last place she'd ever imagined finding him.

Norah squinted at his muddy aura, shot through with jagged, dark brown streaks. Blood pounded behind her eyes. She rubbed a hand across her forehead and shut out his deep pain.

Casey huffed out a breath that morphed into a snort. "Yo. Remember me? We done here?"

Norah wrenched her attention back but shifted in her seat to keep Josh in view. She cleared her throat. "Where did you and your boyfriend go Thursday night?"

Casey rolled her eyes and let out a disgusted noise. "I already told you. I haven't seen him since they locked me up in this dump."

"That's a lie," Norah bit out before she could stop herself. She tempered her tone. "The guard caught you sneaking in."

"Bullshit."

"I watched the surveillance tape."

With a glare that could freeze methane, the girl ruffled her spiky blue hair and locked her arms across her chest, but didn't meet Norah's gaze.

Norah grimaced at the cobra tattoos winding around the fourteen year-old's wrists and gave her a frigid nod. "You're underage. He's twenty-seven and on probation. I'll have to report him to the police." One predator would be headed back to jail.

"Whatever." Casey flounced across the room to a low-slung industrial couch and glowered at her around a worn magazine.

Norah checked the time and bit her lip. She had to talk to Josh. Her schedule was already overbooked, but she had no real choice. She'd have to risk Judge Pascal's wrath.

Josh didn't notice her approach until she crouched in front of him. Her eyes ached when she looked at him, but she forced herself to study his profile. His aura pulsed sluggishly. "Josh?"

He raised his head and blinked. Above his lean cheeks, his bloodshot golden eyes looked red and puffy. He picked at a hole in his ragged jeans, his fingers in constant motion.

"I'm Norah Redfox. We met at the store last Friday. Are you okay?"

A quick smile flitted across his lips. "I remember. I held your fetish. You're the shaman."

"I am, but not many people know." She settled into the window seat next to him, projecting calm and warmth. "How can I help you?"

He sat silent, his gaze averted, and chewed on a dirty thumbnail.

How could she reach him? She took three deep breaths to quiet the tremors racing through her. Wind gusts swirled soggy autumn leaves past the plate glass windows. "I like the rain. Sometimes I put on rubber boots and stomp in the puddles."

Tilting his head, he glanced out the rain-splattered window. "Me, too."

"My Grandfather spoke to me again this morning. He's worried about you. So am I."

"My mom used to worry about me."

Norah's heart squeezed. "Used to?"

"She's dead." His lower lip quivered and grief radiated from him in chaotic waves.

The misery in his words stung like the winter wind howling off the Black Hills. If she sent him back in time, would this pain be prevented, too? "What happened to your mom?"

Josh scrunched his eyes shut, and his aura shrank and darkened. "I found her. I went to wake Mom for breakfast and she was—dead," he croaked out the word.

Norah swallowed, but a sharp edged lump clogged her throat. "I'm so sorry, Josh. That must have been awful." Her hand twitched toward him, but she stopped and rested it on her knee.

He rubbed his palms up and down his thighs. "The police talked to me, but I couldn't even say anything."

"Was there anyone there to help you?"

"Mrs. Rittenberg came over from next door, but the policemen said I couldn't stay with her. Aunt Gina left on Saturday after dinner. They couldn't find her. I don't know where she went, so they brought me here."

Her chest filled with bruising pain. "It must be hard to have so many strangers pressing against your mind."

Josh glanced around the room before he dropped his chin and whispered, "It's not just the people. Everything I touch holds anger and sadness."

"Can you sense what has happened to an object, see the people who've used it?"

Although his eyes were cast down, he nodded sharply.

Poor kid. Leaning forward, she offered him her hand. "But the visions aren't always pleasant, are they?"

The muscles in his tense face relaxed, but his fingers trembled in hers. "You understand."

"I don't have the same gifts you do, but I can help you learn more control."

"Really?" He almost smiled.

"Yes. But first, can I help find your aunt?"

His lip drooped again, and he huddled into the window seat. "I'm not sure I want to. Would I have to live with my uncle?"

"Is he the man in the store? The man who hurt you?"

"Yeah. Uncle Kenny." Josh rubbed his head and winced. "Aunt Gina's okay, kinda funny sometimes. But Uncle Kenny scares me."

She frowned, unsure how much of what she'd sensed about that psychopath she should explain.

Her phone rang, and she jumped. "Shoot! Why didn't I turn the thing off?" She glanced at the caller ID and rolled her eyes. "Sorry, Josh, it's a judge. I have to answer this."

He turned away, put his finger to the fogged window, and followed a large drip down the glass. The drip sped up and disappeared onto the leaves below.

"Ms. Redfox, be in my chambers in an hour," Judge Pascal demanded in a clipped voice.

"I…" Norah fumbled.

"It's the only time available, counselor. Otherwise your case will be bound over until next month."

Damn. "I'll be there, your honor." Norah clicked off her phone and glanced at Josh. "I'm sorry. I have to go, or three young children will be sent back into an abusive situation."

He tucked his knees under his chin, his bleak aura pulsing only inches from her.

"I understand why you don't like the shelter, but you'll be safe here until lunchtime."

Josh didn't respond.

"Can I bring you anything?"

He sat quietly for a moment. Then he lifted his head and said in a hesitant voice. "I feel like a baby, but could you get my mother's quilt? The one with a sun on it. It's on her bed."

"I'll see about the quilt and be back as soon as I can." Wishing she could hug him, she tried her best to give him a reassuring smile, turned, and hurried toward the exit.

"Norah, hold up a minute." Dr. Dennis Milligan, the shelter psychologist, called from his office doorway. With an earnest expression in his light blue eyes, he pushed up the sleeves of his maroon Mr. Rogers' cardigan.

She hesitated.

"You're the first person Joshua has spoken to since he arrived Saturday afternoon."

The boy was so sensitive, no wonder he hadn't communicated. She swallowed a tiny pang of guilt. "I need to report this officially, but I witnessed Josh with an abusive man he identified as his Uncle Kenny. Whatever you do, don't let that creep near the boy."

A frown lengthened Milligan's already thin face. He rubbed his balding head, and a few stray hairs stood on end. "Makes sense. Poor kid had bruises, but wouldn't explain."

"I'm not surprised." She glanced back through the glass wall at the playroom. "What's Josh's last name?"

The furrows lining his forehead deepened. "Kwail. Single mom. Only child. Police brought him in. At first we suspected her of the abuse."

"I don't think so. He seems to have loved her very much. Was the mother ill?"

"Diabetic. She went into a coma." He tugged on one of his oversized ears and shook his head slowly.

"Josh mentioned his Aunt Gina."

"Yeah, Gina Swank, the mother's sister." Dennis opened the front door and ushered Norah out. "We're trying to contact her, but no luck. The only info we have is a disconnected Arizona cell phone and a Phoenix address."

Her shoulders knotted, and she exhaled an exasperated breath. No time. "Just keep Josh away from her husband, Kenny."

"I'll put a note in his file."

She glanced back again, but Josh wasn't in the window seat. At least he'd be safe from his uncle. Norah jingled her keys. Taking him home with her would skirt the rules, even though she needed him to change the past. She turned to Dennis. "Would you do me a favor? Josh asked for his mother's quilt. Can you e-mail me the contact info so I can follow up?"

"No problem."

"I'll call later today. I have a hearing with Hermione Pascal." Norah checked her watch, ignoring the tremors rocking her stomach. "In forty-three minutes."

"You'd better run. Don't worry, Josh isn't going anywhere."

Chapter Three

The coroner hadn't returned her call yet. Norah frowned and tapped her nail against the keyboard. She needed the details to pick up Josh's quilt before she returned to the shelter. She'd wait another five minutes, but no more.

Squinting at her computer screen, she zoomed in on the limestone cliffs covered with sooty patina. She enlarged the petroglyphs, images of hunters and wild game etched throughout the Southwest a thousand years ago. Tall and prominent, a shaman figure held his staff high as he trailed a snake toward a crevice in the rock. She could almost hear the magician chant as he journeyed into the spirit world.

She studied a diagram of grave goods from Walnut Canyon. That Magician's staff was different from the wriggling serpent in Grandfather's lodge. There were carved eagle totems, but no snakes.

A cough broke her concentration, and she looked up at the tall, solid man filling her office doorway. He stood off center with a charcoal sport coat hooked over his shoulder on one finger. Even with her shields solidly in place, she smelled his testosterone. Damn he was hot, but why had she even noticed?

She clicked off the screen and met smoky gray eyes framed by sinfully lush, black lashes. "No dreads today, Sergeant?"

"Cute." His smile cut a dimple into one cheek. "Hope I'm not interrupting. Didn't see anyone in the outer office, so I came on in."

"My secretary's at lunch. I was just surfing while I wait for a call." She had to ditch this guy and leave quickly. Making a show of checking her watch, she stood. "Oops. Sorry, but I'll be late unless I hurry."

"Won't keep you long." Jackson settled onto the chair in front of her desk and flashed her another broad grin. Despite her curiosity, she refused to open herself enough to read his aura, but earthy red-oranges leaked through. The damn man oozed sex.

Her lower body felt warm, almost liquid. Heat rose on her face, and Norah dropped into her chair. She swallowed quickly, shuffling the papers on her desk to give herself a mental breather. Why did he trigger these crazy sensations?

Rolling his shirt cuffs over his well-muscled forearms, he stretched out his long legs and surveyed her private office, stalling briefly on her landscape of the Black Hills. "Nice space."

Her gaze skated across his broad shoulders and hard chest, but snagged on his full lips. Her stomach jittered. Those damn butterflies were turning somersaults again. She grabbed her iPhone and added an impatient edge to her voice. "Thanks. Do you want to make an appointment, Detective, or is this a social visit?" She stared at her calendar. What a stupid comment.

One dark eyebrow quirked with humor, and his smile lit his eyes. He rubbed a big hand along the crease in his slacks. "Business first. We can make it social some other time."

Damned if her heart didn't do a back flip. She pinched her lips together. Ridiculous. "I can come by the station later this afternoon."

"Captain sent me over about the boy."

She straightened her shoulders and spine. "Josh? What have you learned?"

"Probable hit on the truck." He handed her a photo.

"I think you found it. I remember the dented fender." She studied the background of the grainy shot. "But that's the hospital."

He passed another photo, scrutinizing her. "A boy was admitted Friday night. First name, Tyrell. Recognize him?"

She shook her head. The atmosphere in the room had sharpened, almost as if she'd been shoved under a high-powered microscope. She tried not to squirm. Why had he transformed into an interrogator? She sneaked a peek at his aura. Sure enough, the orange glow around his head and shoulders was capped by a glacial blue-green.

Feeling like a bug he'd dredged from a mud puddle, she shifted in her seat. To hell with it. Let him read her body language. She folded her arms over her chest and crossed her legs. "Will Tyrell be okay? He looks very ill."

His frown answered her question.

"This woman brought him in." The next shot zipped across her oak desk. His eyes narrowed, pinning Norah in place. "Know her?"

"No."

He gathered the pictures into a pile and zoomed in on her face with a higher magnification.

A queasy feeling gripped her insides. Boys in

danger. One will soon be lost. The blood left her face, and she leaned back in her chair, cradling her forehead.

"Help them now," Grandfather bellowed.

Damn. Where were those mental earplugs? An itch formed behind her solar plexus, urging her to ask. "Do you have any other leads?"

"We're working a missing child alert from Southern Utah. Some of the details match, but we haven't verified prints." His mouth drawn down, he scraped a hand across his chin. "Remind me what your link is to Josh."

Norah's gaze slid sideways as she scrambled for a response. She wrenched her focus back to his face and volunteered a thin slice of the truth. "He appeared to be in an abusive situation, but after the man pushed me, I was so stunned, I froze."

His eyebrows arched, and he tipped his chin slightly. "Your cheek doing better?"

She caught herself rubbing the spot and gave him a sharp nod.

"Ever get his last name?"

Fidgeting, Norah winced at the gruffness in his tone. "The boy's name is Joshua Kwail." She pointed at the artist's sketch she'd helped with and a fuzzy security photo. "That man is dangerous."

Jackson studied the drawing. "Mouth's tight. Mean."

"Yes, but the police artist didn't quite capture the predatory coldness in his eyes."

"Something lost in translation?"

"Exactly. The rattlesnake quality." The urgent itch in the center of her chest expanded.

"The boys," Grandfather chewed at her.

She couldn't delay any longer. Still feeling like a dung beetle pinned in a display case, she slipped on her heels and rose. She needed to return for Josh immediately, so she'd have to explain herself to this pushy cop. "I left a message for Nate a few minutes ago. I found Josh at the Shelter this morning. His mom died over the weekend. I'm on my way to see him."

A smile ghosted across his lips. "I'll drive." He grabbed her raincoat, helped her into it and opened the door.

Surprised, she murmured, "Thanks," while she zipped her briefcase.

His hand dropped to the small of her back, spreading tingles. She pulled away, hurrying toward the elevator.

He trailed her without comment, but once outside, he herded her toward his car.

Norah hesitated. "I'll follow you." She pointed to the hybrid in a nearby space. "I have to pick up Amber at 3:30 for soccer."

"Nope," he said, giving his head a decisive shake. "You're coming with me. I'll have you back here by 3:00." He opened the door and handed her into the passenger seat before loping around to the driver's side.

Frowning, she yanked her seat belt into place. At least he hadn't handcuffed her and stuck her in the back seat.

He slid in and closed his door, studying her as he started the car. "County Children's Shelter?"

She gave him a quick nod.

After a few minutes, he broke the strained silence. "So you coach?"

"Yes. For Amber's team."

"She's your daughter?"

"Amber? No, I'm single. I mean she's not…" Babbling again. She fisted her hands in her lap. What was it about this guy? Tonight, she'd take a long, hard run and work him out of her system. "Amber's my niece. She came to live with me a year ago August, after my sister died."

****

A giant lump strangled his throat. Where was it? Josh tossed the black plastic bag on his bunk and dug through his stuff. He pulled out his shirts and jeans and threw them on the floor. His comb. His toothbrush. Where was his Hacky Sack?

He blinked away the tears. Had to be here. He dumped everything on the floor and searched the whole pile again. There, mixed with his dirty underwear.

Joy blazed through him. Grabbing the multicolored toy close to his chest, he sucked in air despite the pain squeezing his throat.

Mom.

Calming memories flowed along his fingers and soothed all the nerves in his body.

Mom. On the couch. A pile of bright yarn on her lap. Her crochet hook weaving, she radiated love.

Josh shoved the toy into his pocket and walked back toward the playroom. Touching it would help him fight the visions that battered him.

He climbed into his window seat, careful to sit on the right side. Too much pain had soaked into the other corner. He couldn't stop the despair from leaking out the bright blue cushions and into his mind.

He leaned his cheek against the cold glass. Would Ms. Redfox really come back? He gazed through the window toward the street. The rain had stopped. The sun peeked between the clouds, and sunlight glared off the wet sidewalk.

A blonde woman charged across the parking lot. Josh sat up straighter and studied the way she walked. His heart dropped into his belly. Aunt Gina? Why was she wearing that stupid frizzy blonde wig?

She stopped outside the door and rubbed a tissue under her nose. His heartbeat thudded in his ears and chills spread to his toes. He stood on the bench and searched for Uncle Kenny's white truck. Not in the parking lot. Or out on the street. He double-checked and heaved a sigh. She'd come alone.

She hurried across the lobby toward the counter. He ducked behind a palm tree and spied on her through the glass wall between the playroom and the lobby. With the door propped open, he'd be able to hear them.

Aunt Gina plunked a plastic grocery bag on the counter and sniffed into the tissue. "I came for my nephew, Joshua."

The receptionist looked puzzled and pushed her big round glasses up her nose. "Who are you?"

"Gina Swank, Stacy Kwail's sister. Josh was brought in yesterday." She sniffed loudly again.

"Oh, yes, you're his next of kin from Arizona. Dr. Milligan has been trying to contact you."

"I was out of town." Aunt Gina turned and shot a quick glance outside.

Josh followed her gaze. A big black camper van had parked near the entrance, but he still didn't see the white truck.

"I didn't know Stacy was…" with a muffled sob, Aunt Gina dug out another tissue and blew her nose.

The receptionist pulled some papers from a file drawer and hurried around her desk. She patted Aunt Gina's shoulder. "You sit here. Dr. Milligan will return from lunch in a few minutes. He'll need to speak with you, but you can start filling out these forms."

"Please, I'm so upset. Can't I take Josh home and worry about that later?"

Josh crossed his fingers and prayed the receptionist wouldn't give in.

"It'll only take a few minutes. Didn't Dr. Milligan say your phone was disconnected?"

"Yes, I moved to be near Stacy." Aunt Gina blew her nose again, sounding like a warped kazoo.

"With the judge's okay, the Doctor can sign Joshua out to you overnight and schedule a hearing in the next few days. I'll need your ID."

Aunt Gina grabbed something out of her purse. "That's my old address. I haven't had time to change anything."

The woman studied the card through her glasses, her eyebrows squeezed down and her lips pressed together. For a moment he had hope.

Aunt Gina scribbled on a paper and held it out. "My new place. Can't you please hurry? I want to go back to Stacy's apartment and lie down. The shock…"

After glancing at the clock, the receptionist stood. "Let me take you to see Josh while we wait."

He charged across the room and climbed into the corner window seat, holding his breath while the receptionist approached. The room was nearly empty except for two big kids stretched out on the couch, watching Nickelodeon reruns.

Aunt Gina hurried over to him with her high heels

clicking on the tile. "Oh, you poor baby."

He cringed, but she grabbed and nuzzled him anyway. She didn't smell like Mom, and the hollow place in his chest ached. He squirmed out of her hands and stared at her. His eyes felt gritty.

Sniffing loudly, she patted his cheek. "I got here as soon as I could, Josh. We can go home right now."

The receptionist laid a hand on her arm. "I'm sorry, Mrs. Swank. We need to wait for Dr. Milligan. There has to be an official release."

"Why?" She yanked Josh against her side, squeezing the air out of him. "I'm his only relative. Aren't I, baby?"

He clamped his mouth shut and tried to shrink away. Her touch felt jagged. Painful. Not calming like his mother's.

"Just wait here while I see if Dr. Milligan has returned. We should have everything cleared up very quickly." Frowning, she gave Gina a long stare and left the room.

Aunt Gina grabbed his arm. "Come on, kid. We're outta here."

Chills raced over him, and he looked around nervously. His pulse thundered in his ears. "But she said to—"

"I don't care what she said. Come on! Now's our chance." She jerked him to his feet and hustled him across the playroom, her nails digging into his arm.

Panic clutched at his throat. He fought her grip and dragged his feet to stall for time. "I need to wait for—"

Her face pinched like she had a mouthful of lemons. "Who? Some social worker? You want to be stuck in this hell hole forever?"

"No, but I'm scared of Uncle Kenny."

"I'm divorcing that creep. I left him in Las Vegas. But no judge will ever let me raise you. You'll be trapped here for the rest of your life."

Afraid he'd barf all over the floor, he stared at his shoes. He hated this place. But Ms. Redfox had said she'd come back, said she'd help him, said he had to stay here and wait for her. "I mean…I need to pack my stuff. My new jacket—"

"Forget your stuff." She reached into the grocery bag and pulled out his mother's quilt. "Look, I brought this for you."

Josh buried his face in its folds, and his eyes swam with tears. Oh, God. It smelled like Mom.

Gina lifted her fake blonde bangs off her forehead and showed him a big purple bruise and goose egg. "I'm scared of Kenny, too. But I'm the only family you've got, Josh. I'll stay here and take care of you. You can take care of me."

Yes. Family. Protective warmth welled inside his chest, and he met her gaze. And if he stayed here, maybe he could see Ms. Redfox and get her help with his gift. "Can we keep the apartment?"

She smiled at him, and her dark brown eyes seemed kind. "Sure. I need you Josh." She grabbed his arm and hurried him across the lobby.

He didn't struggle, but he searched the entry hall for the security guard and forced down the bitter taste in his mouth, clutching the quilt closer.

She punched the button behind the guard's station, and the door opened. Grinning, she tugged at him. "Come on. We're going to Disneyland. I've never been there."

As they rushed outside, he glanced at her. Maybe everything would be okay. She'd brought him the quilt.

When he hesitated, she snatched the quilt from his hands and opened the door to the big black truck.

Josh's heart raced so fast he couldn't breathe. His hands clenched into fists.

Uncle Kenny grabbed him and heaved him inside.

"Let me go, you liar!" he yelled and kicked out.

But Uncle Kenny just laughed and backhanded him across the face.

Josh crumpled into a heap, pain searing his cheek. He tasted blood.

Uncle Kenny started the motor. "What took ya so long?"

"Stupid receptionist."

"Sit on the floor, runt." Kenny yelled at him and gunned the engine. They bolted from the lot almost hitting another car.

Aunt Gina pulled the blonde wig off and ruffled her dark hair into place, chuckling. "The bitch wanted to check with a judge."

Uncle Kenny snorted. "Fat chance."

Sticking a cigarette in her mouth, Aunt Gina lit it and blew out puffs of smoke.

Josh wrapped his mother's old patchwork quilt around his shoulders and huddled on the floor. "Where are we going?"

"Shut up, runt. I got driving to do."

****

A camper van squealed out of the parking lot in front of the car. Adrenaline spiked Jackson's pulse rate. Swearing, he stomped on the brake and waited for the rig to finish a left turn. Big. Black. Shiny. No plates?

Probably missed the paper tags.

He glanced at Norah's shocked expression and her white knuckles gripping the chicken bar. Then he whipped into the last empty space in the Shelter parking lot.

"Niece?" he repeated, lips twitching upward.

"Yes." Norah stared at her hands.

Some of the tension in his shoulders eased. The lady wasn't married. But there was a kid in the picture. Could he deal with that? He yanked the parking brake harder than necessary.

When he opened her door, she stepped out and bent to collect her briefcase from the floor. Oh, yeah. She had one very nice, lithe, female body. Toned, but curvy. Almost lush. A world-class ass and her legs. Man! Long and tan and leading directly to heaven.

When she straightened, his gaze dodged away, but he couldn't suppress the grin. Yeah, he'd figure out how to deal. Once she finally decided to tell him the truth, he'd let her know he was interested.

Jackson slanted a glance at her. "Nate didn't say if Josh was your case." His palm drifted to the small of her back again, guiding her along the landscaped walkway to the modern building. Sunlight glinted off the wide, rain spotted windows. A hint of warmth from her skin seeped through the thin raincoat, and the gentle sway of her hips promised magic.

She walked briskly, but this time she allowed him to escort her. "Josh is my responsibility."

"Why?" His brows folded into a frown.

She stepped back and studied him carefully. "Trust me, he's in trouble, and I can help."

He watched her from under hooded eyes, and his

mouth firmed. She'd sure dodged that question. But she twitched like a perp on the verge of confessing. Her eyes blinked and shifted, her hands jittered. The pulse at her temples jumped. Standing next to her, he caught the faint scent of fear. No need for a polygraph machine. She was lying her ass off.

She glanced at the ground, at the building, back at the car, anywhere she wouldn't have to meet his gaze and swiped moisture from her forehead.

His blood pressure soared. More lies. Shit. What was she hiding?

A middle-aged woman wearing a beige suit that matched her cropped hair slammed out the front door, blinking through her oversized, round glasses. "Did you see a boy?"

Jackson stared at the frantic woman and shook his head.

Norah stood silent beside him, suddenly absolutely still. "No," she moaned and covered her mouth with her hand.

The woman craned her neck, scanning the parking area. "Oh, dear. Oh, dear. I left for just a minute to go get Dr. Milligan. Gina Swank must have snatched him."

****

"Joshua Kwail is gone," Norah spat into her cell phone, studying Jackson's unreadable face as he drove. She inhaled a deep breath and quieted her tone. "I saw him this morning, and now he's gone."

"Who took him?" Nate Kapulani asked over the crackling connection.

"His aunt."

"Not much we can do if she has legal custody."

"But she doesn't, officially. She sneaked him out,

right past the idiot receptionist. I warned Milligan not to let the uncle near Josh, but she didn't read the memo." Norah clamped her jaw, glaring at the cop behind the wheel. "I missed Josh by two minutes because your sergeant camped out in my office and grilled me."

Jackson's shoulders lifted in a how-the-hell-was-I-supposed-to-know shrug.

Rubbing her temples, she leaned against the headrest. Her head pounded, and her hands shook with fear. At least she didn't have to drive. She probably couldn't, with the spirit voices clamoring. "The judge refused to step in. She blamed their actions on grief and scheduled a hearing for Thursday."

"Nothing official we can do till then."

"Josh can't wait until Thursday," she said, more certain than ever she had to act quickly. "The situation stinks. All Josh's clothes were left behind, even his sketch book full of drawings."

"Hmm," Nate mumbled.

She hung on to the panic bar while Jackson made a quick right and then left. "At least Dr. Milligan assigned me his case officially. Detective Marino's taking me over to the mother's address on South Fourth. Maybe we can still catch the Swanks."

"Keep me posted." Nate broke the connection.

Norah flipped her phone shut. She hated feeling vulnerable, without a guide or road map.

"Go after him." Grandfather shouted.

"I know, I know," she mumbled, her voice terse.

"Wanna tell me what you know?" Jackson parked at the curb across from a tan stucco four-plex straight out of the seventies. He looked sideways, and she felt the cool sweep of his gray eyes.

Heat rose on her neck. "What? No. Nothing."

"Uh huh." He trailed her silently to Stacy Kwail's front door.

Norah peeked through the frosted glass sidelight but couldn't see much in the unlit interior. "The apartment wasn't sealed?"

"Death ruled natural causes." Jackson pounded on the door again, rattling the aluminum-framed windows. He shrugged and leaned on the buzzer. "No one's home. Let's try next door."

They wove through a thicket of potted plants, and he knocked loudly on the thin door.

A short, elderly woman in a bright pink and purple housedress peered out.

He flashed his shield. "Detective Marino. This is Norah Redfox, Joshua Kwail's custody advocate. And you are?"

"Gloria Rittenberg." Her hands fluttered to her cheeks and then smoothed her salt and pepper hair. "I'm so relieved someone official has come. That poor boy. Those swindlers cleaned out dear Stacy's things this morning. Trashed the apartment. I just called the landlord about the damage."

Norah's knees weakened, and she grabbed Jackson's arm for support.

Mrs. Rittenberg shook her head, searching their faces. "What's wrong? Is Joshua okay? They didn't steal him, too, did they?"

"Mrs. Swank left before signing Joshua out officially. She needs to bring him back until the custody hearing on Thursday," Jackson explained.

"We were hoping to speak with them." Norah stepped forward.

The woman gave a loud snort and crossed her chubby arms. "Fat chance. They haven't been back. I'd lay odds those thieving rats won't return."

"Do you have any idea where they might have gone?" Norah asked.

"They talked about Las Vegas." Mrs. Rittenberg tapped a nail on her lip. "But Gina said they went there last weekend for their anniversary."

The woman's brows knitted. "Wait a minute. Joshua told me once they used to live in Arizona. Give me a sec, and maybe I'll remember the town."

Norah closed her eyes briefly. Grandfather's nagging had grown to a roar.

"Can we see the apartment?" Jackson folded his notebook.

"No problem, but I can't stand to go in there again with you." The woman rummaged in one pocket, coming up with a wadded tissue and the key. "Just drop this back before you leave." Shaking her head, she closed the door.

Norah followed Jackson into the Kwail's apartment and stood stock-still, her heart in free fall. Trash and torn papers covered the worn shag carpet. Every cupboard in the tiny kitchen had been ransacked. The phone dangled from wires ripped out of the wall. A glacial wave of fetid odors crashed over her and she shivered. "What a disaster."

Seeming unaware of the cold, Jackson snapped on latex gloves. He crossed the room, grabbed the cord, and held the headset up to his ear. "I'll see if I can put this puppy back together. Might be a message. Have a look around, see if something strikes you."

She reached for a coffee mug full of old cigarette

butts.

"But be careful," he added, pulling a second pair of gloves from his pocket. "We'll send the crime scene detail over for a look."

She nodded and snapped on the gloves. Rubbing her arms to ward off the goose bumps, she stopped by the gold and brown flowered couch and wrinkled her nose. "What's that smell?"

Jackson laid a hand across her shoulders and sniffed. Then he froze for a second, blinking like she'd blindsided him. He cleared his throat. "Uh, sex."

Her face flamed. "Oh." She pivoted and escaped toward the bedrooms.

As she walked down the hall, the violent residue lurking in the air buffeted her senses. Tension coiled inside her. She fought to keep her tenuous composure by concentrating on Jackson's solid presence in the kitchen.

She sucked in a breath and staggered backward. The destruction in the first bedroom made her flesh crawl. The vile emanations were concentrated in there. Unwilling to face the evil yet, she crossed the dingy hall.

Josh's bedroom was even worse than the living room. Clothing dumped in heaps. Books shredded. Video games smashed. Vicious anger permeated the room. Even though it had been hours since Kenny Swank had been there, his stench clung to everything.

She kicked aside a pile of clothes and picked up a torn paper. Unfolding the drawing, she recognized the ancient, Sinagua symbol for the sun she had seen on the website.

Kneeling, she dug through dirty socks and

schoolbooks and searched for other drawings. Only one. A small picture of a saber-toothed cat lay crumpled at the bottom of the heap. She smoothed it against her leg and rose.

By now Josh could be anywhere. Her stomach pitched and plummeted. She rubbed the bridge of her nose. If only that damn, stubborn detective had let her do her job, she'd have been at the shelter in time to prevent the kidnapping.

She hesitated in the doorway of the larger bedroom. Nausea raced through her body. A rancid taste rose in her throat. But she had to confront the evil leaking from Stacy Kwail's room and find out what happened.

Icy fear flooded every pore, but Norah stepped over the threshold and saw an otherworldly flash. A ghostly female form convulsed on the bed. Then love and concern flared from her despite the vicious reek.

Norah stumbled and fell to her knees, transported to the spirit sweat lodge. Waves of heat rose from the bright fire and coarse sand sifted through her fingers.

Grandfather towered over her, scowling. He wore an odd robe and that creepy staff squirmed in his hand again.

She bunched her shaky muscles and stood, struggling to bank down rising hysteria. What had shifted her world on its axis?

Grandfather's black eyes and long white braids were familiar, but he spoke with an odd voice and in an unfamiliar tongue.

Norah gasped. Across the fire pit, a young woman with dark hair sat cross-legged in the shadows. She wore a patterned tunic and shawl over high buckskin boots. Tears coursed down the woman's cheeks as she begged for help with sherry-colored eyes. Josh's eyes.

Grandfather waved a hand, and a great cat spirit screamed. The top of his staff congealed into a serpent's head with glittering obsidian eyes, and Norah suddenly understood his words.

"You must follow the boy to his ancestral lands, child. To the Sinagua. But you cannot complete your task alone. Your destiny—"

"Norah!"

Her eyes snapped open. Why was she huddled on the floor?

Jackson shook her once more. "You fainted. What's wrong?"

"I need to go after Josh. His mother was murdered."

"What do you mean?" He helped her stand, but she collapsed against him, trembling.

"He's in danger." Her fingers curled around his jacket lapels, and she gazed up at him.

Something hot, primal flashed in his eyes. He tilted her chin. "Tell me what's going on."

Her heart rioted like cherry blossom petals in a spring wind. She dropped her lashes and buried her face against his chest.

After a moment, she peeked up at him, her face aflame and pushed away. "I'm sorry, Jackson, but I can't explain. I have to pick up Amber now. Then I'm going to Arizona."

Chapter Four

Jackson ignored the shift change chaos in the bullpen and hustled into the captain's office.

A pile of reports spilled from Nate's in-basket, and he pounded furiously on his keyboard.

"Have any luck with Tyrell's ID?" Jackson asked.

Kapulani loosened his tie and looked up. "Fingerprints match the kid in Utah. Name's Tyrell Parker."

"Thought I might go over to the hospital. Drew said the boy was doing better." He caught the pained look on the captain's face. "What?"

Kapulani leaned back, tapping steepled fingers against his mouth. "Dr. Peterson called a few minutes ago. Tyrell didn't survive."

"Damn. Poor kid." Jackson needed to punch something, but he gritted his teeth and squashed his temper.

Kapulani gave him a moment and then said, "If it helps, he never regained consciousness."

Jackson slumped into a chair and stared at the floor until he could speak. He cleared his throat. "I had a thought. Remember the truck Norah Redfox spotted?"

"The uncle's rig?"

"Description was close to the pickup at the hospital, so I checked. Norah's partial matches that plate, and she confirmed the ID."

Nate straightened. "I see where you're headed. With the truck ID, we could pull Swank in and hold him."

"The aunt, too."

"I'll get the warrants started."

"Only one problem." Jackson puffed out a breath. "When we brought the key back, the landlady said Swank was driving a different truck. Black camper van with Nevada plates. Coulda been the same rig that nearly hit us at the Shelter, but there weren't any tags on that one."

"Probably pulled 'em off." Kapulani shrugged and rubbed a hand over his square jaw. "Shame we can't connect Josh to Tyrell directly, but the white pick-up could tie the Swanks to both boys."

Jackson stood, blood pressure hitching, and cracked his knuckles. He prowled over to the window and stared out into the night. "The neighbor swore the Swanks were up to no good. Norah agreed, even insisted we check out the mother's death."

"Stacy Kwail's death was stamped through as natural causes, but I'll alert the coroner, send out a CSI unit."

Jackson chewed over possible connections. "I need to head back over there tonight. If the landlady can ID the hospital security photo, that'd hogtie Gina Swank to Tyrell."

The captain tapped a pencil on his desk, looking thoughtful. "The shelter receptionist said the aunt was a blonde, but that doesn't mean much. See if we can dredge up enough for an APB on both vehicles."

Jackson shifted his weight from foot to foot.

"Norah's headed for Arizona tomorrow morning.

She insists Josh is in great danger."

"Say what?" Kapulani barked, his thick brows lowered.

"Tried to talk her out of it, but she's one stubborn lady."

"Arizona law enforcement's informed. What more does she think she'll accomplish?"

"Hell if I know." Jackson ran his hand through his hair and perched on the arm of a chair. Norah's evasions still bugged him. She wasn't telling him the whole story. "I'd like to bring her in for questioning."

"Hold on, Marino. One thing I know for sure, Norah's absolutely straight. No need to drag her in. Something's going on here. If you want to know more, go ask her."

His gut plummeted. Jackson raised his palms to object. He didn't need this garbage. "What the hell's that supposed to mean? I did ask her, and she danced around the truth like a ballerina. You think I can't smell a lie?"

The captain wove his pencil back and forth between his fingers. After a minute, he stopped and leveled his gaze, looking resolved. "You know, I think you look a little tired, buddy."

"Huh?"

"Yeah. Long time since you took a vacation. I think you could use a few days off."

He cringed at the gleam in the captain's eyes. "Now?"

"Desert air might be just what you need."

Adrenaline sprinted through his veins. He scowled and jumped to his feet. "Hold on, Captain. Last thing I want to do is traipse around Arizona with a looney."

Kapulani gave a stubborn half smile. "Tough. That's an order."

****

Booted out of the downstairs coffee shop when it closed, Norah stood shivering in the cold starlight. *"I don't need help, don't want help. I can find Josh on my own."*

"The hunter must accompany you. You cannot succeed without him," Grandfather repeated.

She paced the walkway fronting the converted cannery and checked the address twice against the number Jana had given her..

The lights were on in Detective Marino's loft, but she still couldn't work up the courage to ring the bell. Even a double chocolate mocha hadn't inspired her, but somehow she had to convince him to come with her to Arizona, even though he didn't trust her. He hadn't believed her lies from the beginning, and after her performance in Stacy's bedroom, he must have thought she was nuts.

Pausing under a lamppost, she stuffed her hands into her jacket pockets and jiggled to keep warm. Face facts. He wouldn't have believed her even if she'd been truthful. An everything-by-the-manual cop, no matter how charming, would never have swallowed her story of spirit guides and time twisting.

Grandfather had demanded Jackson make the trip, but the reason stymied her. She snorted. What reason? Grandfather had never given her an explanation, although his commands were clear enough.

She gritted her teeth and demanded, *"Why won't you explain?"*

Silence.

"You know, this sucks." Norah shook her head in disgust. She'd helped fifteen people change the past, but this time nothing seemed right. Weird spirits had invaded Grandfather's sweat lodge, and she suspected she'd seen a ghost. A very unhappy ghost.

She rubbed her arms against the chill. How could a cop help her send Josh back in time? *"If I'm not convinced, how can I sell Jackson Marino on the idea?"*

Silence.

She twisted her mouth in a grimace. Most women would flutter their eyelashes at a hot guy like Jackson and trail after him with their tongues hanging out. Apparently she needed him, too, but not to warm her bed. Even that brief embrace in the apartment demonstrated she should avoid him or risk losing her gifts.

A man walked by and gave her a long appreciative whistle. She sniffed and headed for the entrance.

The freezing wind gusted past. *"Trust the cop,"* Grandfather finally murmured in her brain.

Her stomach twisted in a knot. She hitched her bag higher on her shoulder and trudged up the steps. *"Easy for you to say, old man. You're not panting every time he looks your way."*

****

With a frustrated sigh, Jackson glanced at the growing case file on his dresser. He hadn't saved Tyrell, but he'd make the bastard who tortured him pay.

Jackson put on his favorite Ella Fitzgerald CD and turned up the volume. Mellow horns backed her throaty voice singing "God Bless the Child." He jammed a pair of running shorts along with a stack of CDs into his overnight bag. Some kids didn't get much blessing.

Jackson speared his fingers through his hair and sank onto the edge of the bed. What had the captain been thinking? Sure, he saw the need to keep an eye on Norah. God knew he wanted to help Josh escape Tyrell's fate. But hunting was a solitary job. He didn't need a spooky lady around, especially one he couldn't trust. She set his radar pinging every time she spoke. Lies slid out of her mouth like butter off a hot ear of corn.

He grabbed his boarding pass off the printer. There'd been no problem finding the flight Norah had booked. By pulling a few strings, he'd put himself on the same flight and moved both seats to the front of the plane. He tucked the ticket into his jacket pocket, dumped an extra box of ammo on top of the shorts, and zipped the bag shut.

Now he had to figure out how to break the news so the beautiful Norah Redfox, Esq., wouldn't run screaming in the opposite direction. Or knee him in the family jewels.

Suddenly thirsty, he paced through his living room toward the kitchen. He could call her tonight, but it might be better to just show up at the airport tomorrow. What would she do if he waltzed onto the plane and sat beside her? He imagined her pissed-off look and smiled briefly. Nah. He'd better get there early, before she discovered the seat change.

Jackson dug a cold beer out of the fridge. Might be worth the aggravation to see her reaction. With a chuckle, he kicked back on the couch and hiked his feet onto the coffee table. Ella sure had a fine voice.

Closing his eyes, he pictured Norah's exquisite

face. What was it about her that mesmerized him? Hair as soft as silk? Dark, expressive eyes, killer cheekbones, or her long, sexy legs?

He downed another draw, enjoying the cold slide of liquid on his throat. Every time he got within ten yards of the lady, his dick jumped to half-mast. But damn it, she didn't fit any of his rules.

"Why'd she have to be a lawyer?" he grumbled. He'd had one lawyer in his life, and the former Mrs. Alicia Marino had brought him nothing but pain.

Norah was raising a kid, too. He didn't play with women on the mommy track. He rolled the cold bottle across his brow. "Forget her, buddy. Too many complications." Women like her wanted more than he could offer. It wasn't fair to a child to move in and out of a single mother's life. And he always moved on.

But she was beautiful. His smile broadened, remembering her silky skin. He itched to get his hands on her and lose himself in her softness.

He swirled the last of his beer. Yep, the razor sharp attraction was there, but her skittishness still puzzled him. What had made her pull back? No way she didn't want him. He'd watched her eyes. He could always tell.

Tipping his head back, he stared at the high ceiling. Maybe this trip to Arizona was a Godsend. A few steamy nights together, and he'd get her out of his system. They could keep the affair brief and more importantly, separate from her niece's life. Laughter rose in his chest. They'd both come back smiling.

His phone buzzed across the coffee table. "Yo."

"Everything set?" Nate asked.

"Yeah, we're on the first plane out."

"Jana's keeping Amber."

"Captain—"

"I hear you. But trust me on this, Marino." He clicked off.

"Sure." He hung up and let out a long, very noisy raspberry. "Easy for you to say, buddy. You're not rock hard from thinking about her."

The doorbell echoed through the loft. Jackson crushed the empty aluminum can and loped toward the door. He opened it to the lady in question and managed to keep his jaw from sagging. A trickle of suspicion stirred in his gut. "Norah. Kinda late. What do you want?"

"I-I need a favor, a big one," she stammered. A faint blush teased her cheekbones. Under her jacket, her soft gold sweater and black jeans clung in all the right places. The top revealed a shadow of cleavage, and the pulse at her throat throbbed double-time. She was nervous.

He smiled. Good. Didn't feel like she was trying to trick him.

"Come on in, have a seat, and tell me what's going on." He wanted to reach over and trace the little line creasing her forehead, but just sat next to her on the couch. Not too close, but near enough to catch her scent. Any minute she'd have him howling at the moon. He pulled himself together and repeated, "Tell me."

Her gaze darted around the room from the high-end sound system to his vintage Fender Stratocaster electric guitar. Okay, she was stalling. He eased back to wait her out, draping one arm over the cushions.

She licked her lips twice and then blurted, "Can you come with me to Arizona? Help me find Josh?"

He managed to cover his grin. Barely. This was too

easy. But it might be enlightening to string her along for a bit. Maybe he'd even wrangle the truth out of her. He pulled on a worried face and hesitated. "Well…"

"I really need your help." She leaned forward and peered up at him through her lashes.

She sounded so desperate he didn't have the heart to continue the farce. Besides, there wasn't much blood left in his brain for strategizing. He snickered on the inside and scooted closer. "Matter of fact, Captain gave me the rest of the week off."

"Nate did that?" Up popped that little frown line again.

Pulse hammering, Jackson nodded and reached for her nape, twirling a stray lock of soft hair around his fingertip. He couldn't take his eyes off her mouth. "It'll be my pleasure, Norah, every step of the way."

Her eyes widened, dark brown and huge. "Whoa!" She snatched his hand away and dropped it like she'd grabbed a snake.

Stunned, he stared at his fingers, unsure how to react to another rebuff.

She hitched over one place and glared. "You've misunderstood, Detective. I need your help to find Josh and put things right, but let's keep this relationship professional."

Gritting his teeth, Jackson rose and switched off the music. Sultry jazz was the last thing he wanted to listen to now. He turned up the lights and sat on the arm of the chair next to the couch, leaning one elbow on his leg.

What would an honest reaction from her look like? "We confirmed Tyrell's ID and located his folks."

A wide smile lit her mouth and eyes, her whole

expression.

But before she could speak, he added, "We told them he died this afternoon."

Genuine pain seemed to ripple across her face. "Oh. I'm so sorry," she said softly and heaved a deep sigh.

That was real enough. He rubbed his knuckles against his jeans. "Make you a deal. Tell me what's going on with Josh. Level with me, and I'll go to Arizona."

Hands twisting together, Norah studied him for a full minute before she spoke. "Okay. I know this sounds weird, but I have these feelings about people."

"Like a hunch?"

She nodded, her gaze serious and intense. "You're a cop. You know about strong intuition."

"Sure, from details you don't realize you noticed."

"Sometimes, but sometimes it's more complicated." She hesitated. "Anyway, I know Josh is in danger."

He held back his response.

She snorted. "Crazy woman, right?"

"Didn't say that."

"You didn't have to." Her beautiful mouth twisted into a frown. "Your face said it for you."

Waiting for her to continue, he narrowed his eyes, more curious than spooked.

She hesitated and then took in another long gulp of air. "I'm a shaman, trained in the Lakota tradition."

When her eyes shifted a fraction of an inch to the right his radar started pinging. Another evasion. He straightened, jaw muscles clenched.

"Never mind about that." Her hands fluttered at

him. She swallowed hard and then reengaged. "What I feel is stronger than intuition. There are times I, uh, meditate and know someone's in trouble. I guess some people would call me psychic."

"Bullshit." He hissed under his breath. "That kinda garbage is for kooks and scam artists." Grabbing her arms, he leaned close, face-to-face and nose-to-nose. "Give me the real reason."

"That's it."

Releasing her, he scrubbed a hand over his chin. She remained very still, no eye dodge, no nervous self-touch. Man, she was good. He frowned. Better push harder.

He held out his palms. "Bear with me for a minute. Somehow you feel Josh is in trouble?" He restrained the air quotes, but added, "Not only because you saw the uncle knocking him around, but because of these intuitions?"

She chewed on her lip a moment and then nodded. "I'm sure."

"Does the captain know about this psychic, uh, talent?"

Her chin raised a fraction, and she paused as if to consider her next admission. "Yes, Nate believes me. I helped Jana once, a long time ago."

A frigid shiver shot up his backbone, and the skin on his shoulders crawled. Now he was spooked. He let out a long, low whistle and rose to patrol the room.

The captain and Jana bought this hocus-pocus? How had she sucked them in? Didn't make sense. He couldn't jostle the facts into place.

He stared out the window for a moment. If this was a con, she was very, very good, but his gut said she hadn't told him everything. Fists on his hips, he doubled back and loomed over her, watching carefully. "Exactly what do you know about Josh?" Ah, there went the eye twitch.

She shifted her feet. "It's hard to explain, but one thing I know for sure. Without you, he won't survive."

****

Kenny yanked down the bill of his cap to block the desert sun glaring over the horizon. He shouldered the door open and strutted into the motel room. Gina sprawled flat out on the gold bedspread, still in yesterday's ratty jeans, with her limp hair dragged back into a ponytail. She'd smashed half a dozen cigarette butts into a water glass on the side table.

Josh sat on the floor watching some stupid game show. He turned his head and grinned. "Breakfast!" He jumped up to grab the greasy bag.

Didn't seem to be any need to starve the runt. He got visions at the drop of a hat. Kenny shrugged. He'd bring Josh chow as long as it didn't cost too much to feed him, and he could drum up an act for the marks.

Gina stirred, rolling onto her side. "Say thank you to your uncle."

"Thanks, Uncle Kenny."

"No problem. Here's your shake. Go watch TV."

Josh glanced hesitantly in Gina's direction and returned to the floor. "Are we still going to Disneyland?"

"Sure. Soon as I finish my business here." Kenny pulled Gina to her feet. "Come on. I wanna sit outside."

She followed behind in her noisy flip-flops.

The air had cooled overnight but still stank from the layer of smog hanging over Vegas. Neon lights flashed from the titty bar across the street, and the highway roared in the background. Kenny grabbed a couple plastic deck chairs and dragged them over near their door.

Gina sipped on her coffee and dug into the hash browns. "Want some?"

He shook his head and lit a cigarette with shaky hands. He was stuffed. He'd polished off steak and eggs at the casino while he waited for his money.

"Did you get in to see Charlie?"

"He'll be back in a couple hours, but I got cash for the TV. After I fence the rest, we'll head south."

Gina leaned over and dropped her voice. "Good. We shouldn't use the credit cards anymore. Even in a dump like this, the cops can track us."

His fingers tightened on the cigarette. There she went again. Giving orders. But he tapped his ash onto the cement and pretended to agree. "Yeah, yeah. Who knows? Maybe the old bitch finally did report it."

"Great. I'd feel much safer."

He chuckled to himself. Gina only thought she knew what was going on. "Sure. We'll take off soon as I see Charlie."

She pursed her lips. "Are you high?"

"Nah," he lied, taking a deep draw on his smoke. He leaned back in the chair and let the buzz take him. He'd used the last of his cash on gas fifty miles from Vegas, but pawning Stacy's junk had given him enough for a couple lines and a blowjob. Took the edge off for a while, but the coke made his cock ache for some ass.

Gina smacked her lips and waved her half-eaten breakfast sandwich at him. "I don't see why we're in such a hurry. I mean I didn't even have a funeral for

Stacy. I can't just leave my only sister in some morgue."

His jaw clenched at the grating tone of her voice. She was always harping on him. "Worry about that later." Grinding his cigarette out, he stomped over to the door and peeked in.

The runt was out cold. He picked up the shake off the floor. Tempting to give Gina the rest and shut her up, but the high he was riding had made him horny. He tossed the cup.

Gina appeared in the doorway in time to see him pick up the kid and drop him on the rollaway.

"My God, is Josh all right?"

"He's fine. A little extra sleepy so he won't bother us now."

She touched the kid's forehead and tucked that ratty old quilt around him.

Just the frumpy little mother these days. Why the fuck had she stopped taking care of herself? He deserved a hot piece of ass.

"I don't like it, Kenny," she whined. "Hell, some of those scams I helped you with were a kick, but this is serious. We just snuck Josh out."

"He's your flesh and blood. Nothing they can do."

"That makes it even worse." She twisted her hands. "Kenny, baby, Josh isn't some throw-away punk, some random kid like Tyrell. He's family."

The deep lines around her mouth made her look worn out, and he was sick to death of her bitching. Yeah, he deserved better. Soon. The new girl at the casino had taken rough stuff from him and begged for more.

"And what about the meeting with the judge?"

"Huh?"

"The judge," she harped. "It'd be better if we got legal custody of Josh and didn't…"

"Kidnap him?" He leaned close, towering over her and flexed. "I know what I'm doing. I lined us up another job, a sweet one. Charlie's hooking me up with a guy who'll pay big for talent like the kid's. No more fake séances. No more living over the tattoo parlor."

She glanced away but didn't respond.

He jerked the curtains shut and glared at her. "Take care of him. Keep him happy until we find the diary."

"But he doesn't know where the damn thing is," she said, drawing out the last word until his teeth ached. She angled both hands on her hips. When her chin jutted forward, he clenched his fist to keep from punching her.

"Don't push me, bitch," he growled. "Stacy must have told him something."

"I asked him again while you were gone. He doesn't know. Stacy never showed him the journal."

He cocked his head toward the rollaway. "Maybe. Or maybe he's lying, and I'll beat the answers out of him."

"No!" Gina grabbed his arm. She showed him her teeth, pretending to flirt. "You said he's really good. We'll make a killing." She traced the barbed wire tattoo on his biceps. "Mmm, Kenny, you know your muscles make me so hot. Please, Kenny. Please don't hurt Josh."

Chapter Five

Hunting always went best in the early morning. But Phoenix would be bustling before he got a shot at the Swanks' trail. Jackson shifted in the leather seat. At least he'd splurged for first class and snagged the bulkhead so his knees weren't wedged against his tray table. He glanced down the narrow aisle. Good thing, too, because the plane was full.

Even before take-off, Norah had conked out in the window seat. Yawning, he stretched his arms and legs. Man, he needed some more shut-eye. He'd spent the night staring at the inside of his eyeballs. He'd drifted off a few times, but crazy dreams kept jerking him awake.

Norah muttered in her sleep, her thick lashes silhouetted against her beautiful, smooth cheeks. Should he shift her back onto her own headrest, or draw her closer and run his fingertip over her soft skin? Asleep, she might look innocent as all get out, but the fairytale she'd spun last night still gave him the heebie-jeebies.

He couldn't wrap his wits around her wild story, or the fact she'd duped the captain. Jackson sneered. The world he lived in had three dimensions. Anything real could be seen and touched and tasted.

Psychic claims were bunk. Time went one direction, and dead was dead.

Leaning back, he closed his eyes. His grandmother's wake flashed in his head. An icy shiver gripped his spine and shook hard.

Eight years old and frightened, he'd sat alone in the back pew and refused to look at his favorite grandmother's body in her casket. Arms crossed, head down, he'd sulked while the rest of his family recited an endless Rosary.

Then a light touch had brushed his face. He'd turned, his eyes wide, and his heart thumping madly in his chest, to see a much younger Nonna beside him. Her hair still black, her face unlined, she'd smiled at him and swept her hand over his hair. Then she'd offered her cheek for a kiss, like she always did. When his lips touched her face, he'd smelled the light vanilla fragrance she wore, like the sugar cookies she'd baked just for him.

With a shudder, he rubbed a hand over his jaw. He'd had a crazy imagination as a kid, but now he knew better than to believe in ghosts.

A blonde flight attendant in her early twenties entered the cabin with a tray of snacks. His gaze slipped down to check her out. Shapely legs in sexy heels and a gymnast's body with supple curves. He wasn't sure when the airline had gone back to short skirts, but he was all in favor.

She returned his perusal, smiling, leaned against his seat and gave her head a provocative toss. "Well, good morning and welcome to the free and easy skies. Snack?"

Not bad for an L.A. film-star-wannabe, but she didn't spark his interest today. "No thanks," he said softly and waved her off with his free hand.

The plane lurched, and she almost landed in his lap. "Sorry." She balanced one hand against his shoulder and purred, "You will let me know if there's anything you want, right?" The playful scrape of her nail along his arm promised him that anything could include as much heat as he wanted.

He inclined his head toward Norah. "Thanks, but I'm kind of busy."

"Shame." She shrugged and wiggled down the aisle.

His lips quirked. Another time he might have played. At least sniffed around.

The plane hit another patch of turbulence, and Norah turned into his shoulder. His arm swept around her, two ticks ahead of his brain. His back stiffened. Now why the hell did he do that? He flexed his fingers to release some tension and looked over at her. He drew in a breath, and her scent filled his nostrils: a clean mix of shampoo, soap and warm, compelling woman. By her delicate fragrance alone, he could find her in a crowded room with his eyes shut.

He fiddled with his ear lobe. Last night she'd thrown him a curve, one he probably deserved. When she landed on his doorstep, need punched him in the gut. With every moment he spent with her, the craving intensified, but when he made a move, she'd shut him down.

This morning when he picked her up, she was as jumpy as a barefoot kid on hot asphalt, fidgeting and talking non-stop. He'd touched her a couple of times, casual, gentlemanly touches on her elbow or back, but each time she shied away. Was he contagious? He frowned. Or threatening?

He brushed his fingers gently up and down her arm, watching goose bumps wash over her smooth skin. A warm sense of pleasure curved his lips into a smile.

She snuggled closer and splayed one hand out on his chest. Wonder what she'd do if she woke up right now? His smile widened. Probably hiss and spit at him, after she bounced off the far side of the cabin.

He smoothed a lock of hair away from her face, savoring the silkiness. No question the lady was high maintenance. Maybe he couldn't trust her yet, but he could damn well enjoy her. All he had to do was keep her contained and away from the hunt.

He had an itchy feeling about Gina Swank's address in Phoenix. Probably a fake. But maybe the captain would trace the white pick-up by the time the plane landed and give him a second option.

Jackson relaxed his arm. Norah's eyelids twitched as she dreamt. Hopefully, the Swanks had left some tracks. They seemed clever enough, but not too careful.

****

Norah sat on the cool dirt floor, her hands folded in her lap. Firelight flickered through her closed eyelids.

Grandfather poured water on the heated stones and steam billowed around her. Ritual herbs crackled in the embers, overlaying the heat with an acrid tang.

Sweat tricked down her brow. She opened her eyes. The ethereal woman she'd seen before stared across the flames at her with sad, golden-brown eyes.

"A ghost?" Norah whispered.

Rattles shook, and she pulled the rough wool blanket closer. Even though the sweat lodge was stifling, she shivered. "I can't do it, Grandfather. I can't see the way forward."

"It is never easy to forge a new path," Grandfather coaxed. "Sometimes you must falter first. Trust and the vision will come."

Breathing deeply, she focused her thoughts again, feeling the packed earth under her. She slowed her pulse to match the cadence of the drums. White light and shadows danced, and the drumbeat faded until all she heard was her own heartbeat.

Then she was transported to a new place, a round, Southwestern kiva, tucked inside a limestone cliff. A narrow shaft of sunlight penetrated the fissured rock, highlighting dust motes in the hot, parched air.

A sun-browned man stood before her, armed with a flint knife and holding a staff that coiled and twisted in his hand.

They were alone, but she wasn't afraid.

In the dimness, she recognized his pale brown, gold-flecked eyes. The elder she'd seen before. A beautiful turquoise amulet shaped like a jaguar's head hung on his bare chest. His long, black hair, crested with silver, had been braided with leather thongs and an eagle feather. Shaman.

She lowered her eyes and sensed his radiating strength. A very ancient, but very powerful spirit.

Setting down his staff, he folded his legs and sat before the smoldering fire. He lifted a water pot with a black and white snake design and drank deeply. Then he opened a closely woven basket and sifted through the grain inside, pulling out a small, bone flute that fit in his palm.

She frowned, but she held out her hand. "Shall I take it?"

Smiling gently, he shook his head. "It's not my place to play this for you, daughter."

"Then what do you wish of me?"

The light folded in on itself until she saw nothing but a pinpoint. "Come to me, and you will know."

Something shifted under Norah's head, and she bolted upright. The roar of the airplane engines startled her after the peace of the vision. Her face flamed. How had she wound up with her head on Jackson's shoulder? Flustered, she sat up and stared out the window.

"Are you okay? You were having quite a dream." He turned her chin and inspected her closely, brows knit as if with concern.

She nodded and licked her lips, ferociously thirsty.

"Here." He handed her a water bottle.

She drank deeply. "Better," she said with a nod. "Thanks."

"Were you dreaming about Josh?"

She shook her head and rubbed her forehead with her fingers. "Not exactly." A shiver started at her nape and coursed through her whole frame.

He settled back in his seat, and his deep gray eyes studied her intently. "You mumbled something about a ghost."

Heat rose on her cheeks again, and she glanced around the cabin. "I don't believe in ghosts."

"Something we agree on. Course I thought I saw a ghost once, when I was a kid." He chuckled wryly. "My imagination ran away with me, but I got over it pretty quick after Pop soaped my mouth for telling lies."

Norah frowned at him and considered saying more, but the plane took a sudden dip, and her stomach launched into her throat. Her gasp became a muffled shriek, and she clutched the armrest. The walls of the cabin seemed to close in around her and cold sweat broke out on her brow. "I hate flying."

"Just updrafts near the mountains."

She glanced out the window at the roiling clouds below them and swallowed convulsively.

"Lean back and close your eyes." He glanced over with a satisfied smile . "Enjoy the ride."

She felt a tug in her belly and searched his face, insanely tempted to accept the forbidden comfort he offered. She wove her fingers together in her lap.

The plane slammed into more turbulence, and the seat belt sign flashed.

****

Outside the rent-by-the-hour South Phoenix motel, Norah stood in the scanty shade of a Palo Verde tree, shielding her eyes with one hand. Tumbleweeds bounced past on sand-filled wind, and dirty white rocks reflected the midday sun's glare.

She glanced at her watch and rubbed the back of her hot sticky neck. Almost 1:00 p.m. Pompous jerk had made her wait outside in the heat so she wouldn't interfere with his precious interrogation. "Shit, shit, shit. He's been inside that run-down dump way too long."

Her chin came up. "And now the damn cop has me talking to myself." She headed for the entrance. With each step, the blistering heat from the asphalt seeped through her soles.

The motel door slammed open, and Jackson stomped toward her. He looked bigger than ever. His brows were drawn in a deep vee. His back and shoulders, and fists were rigid.

"Did you find the Swanks?"

"No. Nothing," he said, an acid edge to his gravelly voice and herded her into their rented SUV.

He slid in, touched the steering wheel, and jerked back his hand with a hiss. "Damn. It's almost October. When does this freaking place cool off?"

"You should have parked in the shade."

With a shoot-to-kill glare, he cranked the ignition.

The air conditioning blasted stale hot air in her face, and Norah rolled down her window to let the heat escape. "Ouch. You need oven gloves to handle this seat belt buckle."

Jackson accelerated out of the lot.

"You didn't learn anything at all from the manager?"

He shook his head and fiddled with the earpiece to his phone.

"What about local law enforcement? That's why you tagged along, right?"

The muscles in his jaw flexed. "Tagged along?" Gray eyes glittering, he made a derisive half-snort. "Right. I need to report in."

She ignored the twist in her stomach. "But what about…?"

"Relax!" He held up a silencing finger. "After I talk to Nate."

Norah glared at him, her hands clenched. Why had Grandfather demanded she work with this pushy jerk of an if-I-can't-touch-it-it-ain't-real cop?

Jackson eased back in his seat. "Hey, Captain. Got zilch on the Phoenix address. Manager never saw the Swanks. Never heard of them. But that guy makes a religion out of never noticing nothing."

"Joshua needs help," Grandfather nagged in her mind.

"I know." Folding her arms, she stared out the open window at the bleak, bare mountains to the north. Something was out of whack, but she couldn't quite focus in on it. She felt hounded by the spirits, but not obsessed like she usually did when she prepared to twist history.

"Course I pushed him hard. He wasn't covering," Jackson said into the phone.

She glanced at him and frowned. Was Jackson interfering with her gift? He'd admitted seeing a ghost as a child. Maybe he'd blocked his own sight for so many years he'd also inadvertently jammed hers.

She blew damp bangs off her forehead. Whatever. She still had to find Josh and send him back in time. If she had to, she'd dump this control freak cop and strike out alone.

"Well, that's something. We'll leave shortly." Jackson clicked off, geared down and maneuvered the car onto the crowded four-lane boulevard.

"So where to?"

"Jerome. Arizona DMV finally came through with an address for the white pickup."

Grandfather went silent.

She angled toward Jackson, leaning forward in her seat. "Great! Let's go. I'll help drive."

"Nope. I know a place we can score a late lunch. Best Mexican food in the world."

"Why waste time in a restaurant? We can grab some fast food and eat in the car on the way."

"Been a long day, and I need real fuel."

"What about Josh?"

"Relax. We can make Jerome in a couple hours." Jackson flipped a turn signal and drove the SUV into a jammed parking lot.

Her hands curled into fists. She eyed the car keys.

Jackson switched off the ignition. As if he'd read her mind, he flashed a smug grin and pocketed the keys. "Wait here, or come in and eat. Up to you."

She jiggled one foot. No, too damn hot out here to make a statement.

Grumbling under her breath, she trailed him into the cinderblock restaurant. She frowned at the name. Why call a greasy taco joint the Teepee? She shuddered and rummaged in her purse for antacids. Had to be lousy food.

The hostess led them into the dining room. Blaring noise assaulted her ears. Spanish warred with English, metal clanged from the open kitchen, bouncing off the terra cotta walls and floor. Crude, faded prints of native children with outsized, flash bulb eyes must have hung on the wall for half a century.

Folding her arms, Norah slumped into a dull orange booth across from Jackson. Closing her lids, she took several deep slow breaths. She felt more grounded, more patient again. Her stomach rumbled. "The food smells good."

"Okay if I order? Can't go wrong." Jackson shouted over his plastic menu. At her shrug, he raised an eyebrow. "You like some heat?"

She leveled her gaze. "I can handle whatever you can."

"Deal." He winked and motioned for the waitress.

A round-faced, dark-haired woman sauntered up with a dimple-framed smile. She slid iced tea and a basket of tortilla chips onto the table and took their order.

"Best salsa in the world." Jackson grabbed a chip and shoveled in a mouthful.

Norah took one and dipped a corner into the chunky, greenish mixture. But when she bit, pain seared her mouth, threatening to close her throat. Choking, she grabbed a drink and gulped. The cold tea cut the burn, so she chugged the rest.

"Too hot?" Chuckling, he handed her his glass.

She cleared her throat, finally able to breathe. "No. Just went down the wrong way."

"You might like this one better." He pulled on a devilish grin and handed her a second bowl from the basket before shoveling in another mouthful of that radioactive waste he called salsa.

Norah drank more tea and slanted him a skeptical look. This time she tasted something besides hot. Jackson flagged the waitress.

"I'll order a pitcher. But wait till you try the green beef enchiladas."

"Green?" Visions of long forgotten leftovers in the bottom of the fridge made her shudder. Was he trying to poison her?

"Green chilies." Jackson grinned and waggled his eyebrows. "Trust me."

She lifted her napkin, blotting the beads of sweat from her upper lip.

Finally, their lunch arrived, the aroma hypnotic. Fragrant cheese still bubbled around the edges. Norah's eyes widened. Half a dozen different dishes crowded the platter. "I'll never finish."

Jackson leaned toward her. "That's okay. I will."

His dimples deepened and a blissful smile crossed his luscious, full lips and crinkled the corners of his half-shut eyes.

She couldn't help but smile. "Are you in heaven, Sergeant?"

"Close. Last time I came here there were twelve of us in that corner booth. Captain brought the unit down here for SWAT training."

She dragged her gaze away from his mouth and tossed her hair over her shoulder. "I'll bet you got plenty of attention."

"Yeah." He gave her a long look, and his face lit up. "'Bout caused the hostess a heart attack when we came clumping in wearing fatigues and combat boots. We'd secured our weapons but hadn't wiped off the camo paint."

Norah finished the beans and rice and enjoyed the chili rellenos, although she avoided the incendiary red peppers. "I guess I was hungry."

He surveyed the rest of her lunch. She rolled her eyes but shoved the plate toward him.

"Wouldn't want to waste food." He smiled contentedly and finished her lunch, peppers and all.

When the waitress delivered the check, Jackson grunted his thanks and dropped a couple bills on the black tray. He pushed back from the table, studying Norah.

She blushed under his scrutiny and dropped her lashes. Guilt for her boldfaced lies and evasions clawed at her. But why was her heart turning handsprings? "Thanks for lunch. The food was an adventure."

He reached out and spread his hands on the battered Formica table, palms up. "Now fill me in.

What's really going on?"

Norah looked through the wide window behind him, toward a jagged horizon line. Thunderheads topped the distant mountains. "My job is to recover Josh before his custody hearing."

His smoky eyes narrowed, but his gaze never left hers. "What aren't you telling me? Nothing I hate worse than working with someone I can't trust."

She chewed her lip thoughtfully. No way was he ready for the truth, and this wasn't the time or place. "What do you mean?"

"I've logged too many hours in the interrogation room for you to fake me out with that innocent smile." His eyes flashed a stark, stony gray. "Something's wrong. First you fainted in the Kwails' apartment and then had a nightmare on the plane. Both times you spouted gibberish."

"I told you, I took a motion sickness pill. That's why I had trouble waking up on the plane. Besides, that bedroom reeked." She wrinkled her nose and waved a hand in front of her face, meeting his intense gaze. "The smell was enough to knock anyone out."

Toying with the condensation on her glass, she sucked in a couple quiet breaths to slow her heart rate. She looked up, and her eyes widened to the size of Olympic swimming pools. Shivers crawled over her skin.

Jackson sat back against the booth, head cocked slightly to one side. Next to him sat a middle-aged woman with short, permed hair and strong, Italian features. Dressed in a pink shirtwaist and pearls, she passed prayer beads between her gloved fingers.

Norah caught a faint wisp of old-fashioned

perfume and stared down at her hands. Her knuckles had turned white, and she flexed them to release the blood. She peeked up, blinking rapidly.

The woman was still there, smiling. She reached over and patted Jackson's hand.

Frowning, he shifted sideways, looking uncomfortable. He rubbed one finger over his mouth.

Between blinks, the woman vanished. Simply vanished. Norah went cold all over, her skin clammy and rippling with gooseflesh. Her stomach dropped like she'd eaten a three-ton hailstone. "J-Jackson, there was a woman sitting right next to you."

He cradled his fingers, rubbing the back of his hand. "What?"

"Didn't you see her? The little old Italian lady in the pillbox hat? She looked like someone's grandmother. You flinched when she touched you." She sniffed the air. "I can still smell her scent. Vanilla."

His face paled and deep ridges appeared on his brow. He rose to his full height. "Bullshit."

Chapter Six

Thunk.

Norah's right foot stomped an imaginary brake pedal, and the floorboard shuddered. Her fingers clutched the hard plastic armrest, knuckles white and stiff and aching.

The SUV swung around another hairpin curve. Her stomach lurched. She clamped her lips together to contain a hiss. A line of cold sweat popped out along her hairline.

Outside her open window, a sheer thousand-foot drop-off bordered the steep, narrow road. The sight twisted something inside her, but she couldn't close her eyes or she'd be sick.

No looking down.

No guardrails.

No protection from the breathtaking drop.

Shivering, she huddled in her sweatshirt and focused straight ahead. The outside temperature now hovered in the mid-forties, while Phoenix had sweltered at a hundred and five.

The road made a hard left, and the tires skewed sideways on loose gravel.

Whomp. Her foot slammed down again, as if an evil imp had seized control of her leg.

Jackson pulled out of the skid almost immediately, downshifted and glanced her way.

"Nervous?"

Her cheeks flamed. "No. Just a little queasy." She repressed a shudder and shot him a weak grin that didn't quite cover the lie.

"Uh-huh." He grinned, but didn't look at her this time. "Almost there. We'll make it before the storm strikes."

She pressed her shoulders into the seat and breathed in deeply through her nose. She hated mountain roads. Hated memories of childhood bus trips over the Rockies she'd spent huddled on the floor hugging Mama's legs. Hated the taste of bile brewing at the back of her throat.

They screeched around another ninety degree turn, and the road doubled back on itself. She gritted her teeth, glancing out over the broad vista several thousand feet below the tall, cone-shaped mountain. Craggy, flat-topped mesas glowed red or golden where light shafts from the setting sun pierced the slate-gray thunderclouds shadowing the desert floor.

Her stomach clenched and rolled in warning, so she jerked her gaze back to the roadway. In the distance, the skeletal remains of a small town huddled on the bare mountainside. A few buildings had lost their grip, tumbled down the steep slopes and lay in ruins like tinker toys abandoned on a mound of dirt. But a few structures still perched atop steel girders sunk deep into the exposed rock.

The SUV groaned around a corner onto a one-way track and slowed.

"Welcome to Jerome." Jackson flexed one hand before curling his long, tanned fingers back around the steering wheel. "This your first ghost town?"

The eerie vision of the ghostly woman in the restaurant flickered into her mind and all the warmth drained from her face. She laughed, a high, tight sound wrenched from her throat. "I told you, I don't believe in ghosts."

"That's a good one. After what you said at the Teepee?" He flashed his engaging grin and mumbled, "Understandable a man might be confused."

Heat crawled up her neck and frustration scraped her already raw nerves. Grandfather's new toss-her-in-a-cauldron-of-strange-spirits-and-see-if-she-drowns approach had hit a new level of inscrutability even for him.

Privacy. That's what she needed. When would she have some time alone to figure out what had happened to her gifts?

The SUV wound slowly through narrow, crowded lanes. Jackson broke the silence. "Here's the street."

Light from a restored gallery glowed into the dusk. She spotted the address numbers and pointed uphill. "That's it. On the left between the liquor stores. But it's past five o'clock. Do you think the Swanks might still be here?"

"Could get lucky."

After Jackson parallel parked on the narrow, cobbled street and set the emergency brake, she zipped her sweatshirt and scrambled out onto the uneven pavement. Planting her feet, she let the grounding power of the earth seep through her body. Enduring. Elemental. Healing.

The chill wind beat against her face and whipped her hair while she drew deep breaths of fresh air tinged with ozone from the coming storm. Gradually her heart slowed to a healthier rhythm, and the nausea drained away.

She scanned the downhill side of the street and noticed a brightly painted Victorian storefront. A sign shaped like rounded, feminine legs in fishnet stockings and high heels creaked with each gust.

"The House of Joy." Jackson gave a low, rumbling chuckle, and his dark gray eyes glinted with humor. "Picture doesn't leave much question about what kind of joy that place used to sell. Want to check out their merchandise?"

Blushing, she turned and climbed onto the two-foot-high wooden sidewalk, focusing on the fliers stuck inside the darkened window. "Tattoos, séances, palm readings. And aura photographs, whatever they are." How could anyone possibly film something so ephemeral?

"Quite a repertoire." Jackson stepped behind her, and his solid form reflected in the grimy window, framing her smaller body and blocking the bitter wind.

She widened her perceptions and looked closer at his image. In the fading sunlight, his aura seemed similar to Nate's, but a warm, orange glow grounded the blue-green corona. The brown slivers meant many life changes.

Puzzled, she tilted her head, concentrated and pushed deeper. No, the glow held more blue than green. He cared deeply, had a strong code of ethics and fought for what was right. But his aura had unfinished edges, and his emotions were in turmoil.

She jerked back and blinked away the sight. Whatever. Jackson's feelings were none of her business.

He stepped around her and rattled the doorknob, then cupped a hand and peered through the glass again, frowning. "Nobody's here."

"We could hang out for a while and see if they show."

He tapped the window. "Christmas lights are still up. Probably been closed for months."

Pain rose in her chest, and her heart thudded dully. She leaned against the doorjamb. "Won't we ever find that poor kid?"

"Don't give up yet."

Shoulders sagging, she turned for the car and glanced across the landscape. The clouds massed over the desert had darkened and converged around the mountain. She could no longer see the red mesas scattered over the desert floor. In the distance, lightning flashed, sending a shudder down her back. She pulled up the hood of her sweatshirt and tucked her unruly hair inside.

Jackson placed a big, warm hand behind her waist and inclined his head toward the SUV. "Starting to rain. What say we check in with the sheriff? Hear what he knows?"

She hesitated. "I wonder if there's another entrance to this building. See the windows up there? It could be an apartment."

"Good thought." He jumped off the curb and backpedaled to the middle of the deserted street, lifting one hand to shade his eyes while his gaze followed the long block of two-story buildings. He nodded sharply and jogged toward her. "No side streets along here. Bet the sheriff will know how to find the back door if there is one. Hop in."

Norah chafed her hands together and slid into the passenger seat. At least it was warmer inside.

As Jackson started the SUV and edged away from the curb, she cupped her fingers over the heater vent and glanced back at the tattoo parlor.

A curtain twitched in the window above the store. Her pulse surged, and she reached for the door handle. "Wait. Let me out. There's someone upstairs."

He slammed on the brakes. "You sure?"

"No, but I have to check." Norah opened her car door and hurried back to the tattoo parlor. Shivering in the drizzle, she peered up at the window.

Nothing.

The curtains remained still and the windows blank.

No lights on anywhere.

She hugged her arms around her chest, bouncing to keep warm.

Still nothing.

She heaved out a breath that billowed fog into the cold air and trudged back to the car.

Jackson raised his brows, but kept silent.

She wiped the moisture from her face. "It was probably my imagination. This whole mountain gives off creepy vibrations."

****

Jackson guided Norah up the stairs to the stone building crowning the mountain. She was climbing just fine, but he liked holding his hand splayed across the small of her back, where he could feel her muscles bunch and shift.

Lord, he wanted to turn her into his arms and kiss her lush mouth. Wanted to entice her into his bed. Wanted to make love until she could barely think or walk or do anything but respond.

His fingers slipped lower on her slacks and molded the sexy upper curve of her hip.

She kept climbing, didn't turn and snap and growl.

Blood pulsed heavy in his body and pooled in his groin. Yeah. Once they found Josh and locked up the Swanks, he'd do exactly that. Find some quiet place where he could turn up the romance. Maybe not come up for air for a couple days.

That'd get her out of his system.

A faint scrape of shoe against concrete caught his attention.

Across the street, an elderly priest sat on the steps of an old stucco church. He wore a long, black cassock, shiny with age. Fifties-style horn-rimmed glasses perched on his pale, bulbous nose.

Jackson waved. "Afternoon, Padre."

Forehead wrinkled, Norah smiled tentatively at the stocky, balding man. "Father."

The priest nodded, tracing the sign of the cross in the air. "Good afternoon, children."

A shiver skipped up Jackson's backbone, one vertebra at a time. He frowned and zipped his jacket. Had to be the nasty weather system closing in.

He opened the scarred door for her, and their footsteps echoed through the musty building. The pressed-tin ceiling was intact, but paint flaked from the ornate wood moldings in thin, metallic strips. Must have been a nice place. Once.

The sheriff's office took up one corner of the large, half-empty ground floor. Inside the dimly lit room, a tall man with an old-fashioned star pinned to his khaki uniform shifted his size fifteens off his desk and stood.

Six four or five, maybe one eighty. With that thin face, he'd have passed for a young Clint Eastwood, except for his rusty hair and unruly mustache.

The sheriff adjusted his duty belt and extended a hand. "Travis Wood."

Jackson returned the smile and met Wood's strong grip, introducing himself and Norah.

"My pleasure, ma'am." Sheriff Wood cocked an eyebrow and checked Jackson's shield. "Long way from home."

"We're searching for a missing boy," Norah explained. "We'd appreciate anything you could tell us. His name is Joshua Kwail."

The lawman twisted his mouth and scratched a cheek with his long fingers. "Kwail? Heard of the family. Used to live down in Verde Valley. How old is the kid?"

"Twelve. He might be with his aunt or uncle, Gina or Kenny Swank."

"Son of a bitch." He blushed, fiery color filling in the blotches between his freckles. "Sorry, ma'am."

A smile tweaked Norah's lips. "No problem. Sounds like you know them."

Wood grinned. "Sorry to say I do. Kenny Swank might look like a movie star, but he's a slippery sidewinder who'd steal his own grandma blind." The lawman's gaze swept her and settled on her chest.

Jackson frowned, and his shoulders stiffened. He angled between Norah and the leering sheriff and handed Wood a stack of photos. "Mind taking a quick look through these?"

With sharp, purposeful movements, the sheriff returned to his chair and fanned the pictures, tapping the first shot. "Yep. That's our local sexpot, Gina. Looks even wilder in the blonde wig. Seen this truck before, but not in a couple months."

"Then where are they?" Norah asked in a forced voice, like an over-cranked guitar string .

Jackson studied her expression. Lined brow, pinched lips. She looked strained. Maybe a little desperate.

Leaning back in his chair, Wood stroked his moustache. "Last night the bartender at the pool hall reported seeing a light on in their shop, but the place looked deserted when I drove by."

Jackson hooked a finger under his belt loop. Damn. "Norah thought she saw a curtain move upstairs. Any idea how we can get behind the building?"

"Alley's not marked, so it's kinda tricky." Wood found a tourist map of Jerome and traced the convoluted route with a marker.

"Thanks." Jackson tucked the page in his pocket.

The sheriff scrubbed a hand over his ruddy face. "My deputy can watch the place. Got a fistful of warrants for Kenny Swank. Swindles, credit card fraud, grand theft, drug dealing."

Norah's shoulders slumped, and her face paled like fear and exhaustion had washed over her.

"We'll let you know if we see anything." Jackson held out his hand to Wood.

"Not likely they'll show up 'round here. Best bet might be talking to George Kwail at the trading post in Verde Valley. Gotta be a relation." Wood glanced at the big, round industrial clock on the wall and stood. "Getting late, but George should be there tomorrow."

"Then we might as well head to Sedona for the

night," Norah said with a quick sigh. "I'm ready for a hot bath."

And some privacy, Jackson thought, wrapping his hand around her waist. When she edged away, he tipped Wood a quick salute and turned toward the exit. "We'll check in tomorrow."

The sheriff followed them outside and shaded his eyes, gazing east. "Can't drive down the mountain tonight. Might have gotten down half an hour ago, but once the roads ice over, they get real slick, real fast. If you slide off the pavement, it's all over."

Jackson glanced down the street at the elegant hotel built along the cliff face and pulled Norah closer. "Thanks for the tip. We can find something up here."

Wood shook his head. "Big biker do in town this week. Harleys everywhere. Lousy weather for it, but the new hotel's booked solid. You could try the Connor, over on the other side of the park." He gave them a wink. "But some say its haunted."

****

Norah braced against the glacial wind. The gusts blew stinging darts of rain against her face, but the itchy sensation between her shoulder blades made her anxious and uneasy. She pursed her lips together and tucked her hands inside her sweatshirt. "We need to check out the back of the tattoo parlor."

"Now?" Jackson beeped the lock and opened the car door. "You heard what Wood said. We should find a spot to ride out the storm. That drizzle will turn to sleet any time."

"It'll only take a few minutes. Then we'll know."

He grunted something unintelligible but shoved the SUV into gear.

Three turns later, Norah straightened in her seat and squinted at a dark gap between two buildings. "There, that's the alley the sheriff drew on the map. We go left and drive along the foot of the hill."

He maneuvered behind a warren of buildings and snaked along the rutted, weed-choked, dirt road, dodging the rusted machinery and crumbling chunks of cement.

The SUV rocked over canyon-like potholes and edged along the cliff. Boulders, splintered lumber, and twisted metal pilings lay scattered on the steep slope like they were poised to slide down on top of the car if anyone breathed too hard. She leaned away from her door and clenched her teeth. No point in complaining. This was her brilliant idea.

An eternal half mile later, he nosed the SUV into the cliff face behind the double flight of wooden stairs marked on the map.

Norah stepped out of the car, and the wind howled around her. The alley was choked with garbage and stank, even in the bitter cold. As she trudged forward, she breathed through her mouth to avoid the foul odors.

Behind her, Jackson's footsteps suddenly stopped.

She turned and saw him bend over a muddy rut. "What?"

"These tracks are fresh." He squatted and measured the print with his hand. "Gotta be a truck or van."

A push of adrenaline doubled her pulse rate. "The Swanks?"

He stood and surveyed the fold-up door set under the stairs. "No way to know when, but the garage was opened recently. The leaves and trash are pushed to one side."

With his hands fisted on his hips, his chest and shoulders looked amazingly broad and strong, his legs long and powerful. Strange, liquid warmth spread deep inside her. Norah squeezed her mental shields shut and turned toward the building. "Let's look upstairs."

"You really want to climb those?"

"Yes." Shivering from the cold, she clung to the railing and picked her way up the damp, rickety wooden steps. With fewer buildings in the way, the wind blew even stronger at the top, unimpeded along the dead end alley.

Jackson followed her. His weight swayed the staircase, and she grabbed for the top railing. The steps creaked, and vertigo robbed her lungs of air. She closed her eyes, waiting until he stood beside her.

He grabbed a yellowed newspaper from the landing and rubbed it over the old wooden-framed window, smearing the dirt into an opaque mess. "Can't see much."

"Maybe we could break in?"

He snorted. "Want the sheriff after us, too?"

"But we need to know if Josh was here."

"Face it. No one's here."

She sighed.

"Come on. I'm starved. Let's find a room and get some dinner." When he started down, the staircase groaned and swayed with each step.

"Try the door," Grandfather, silent for most of the day, shouted in her mind. *"You must go in."*

"Okay, I will. But I'm sure it's locked."

Jackson stopped and glanced up at her. "Say something?"

Rather than answer his question, she turned the

rusted doorknob. When it opened, her mouth dropped, and she blinked rapidly.

"Norah, wait. We don't have a warrant."

She could hear him bounding back up the stairs, but she stepped inside. The air was surprisingly fresh and smelled of brewed coffee. Her hands twisted together, and she gritted her teeth. "They were here. Damn. They were right here, probably laughing at me while I stood in the rain and gaped up at the window."

Jackson studied the litter of fast food wrappers scattered on the battered table. He flicked aside a crust of half-eaten hamburger bun. "Probably this morning. But they left in a hurry."

She stomped over to the window and lifted one corner of the filthy curtain. "I knew it. See? This looks out over the street."

"Nothing we can do now. If the Swanks were here, they're long gone."

"If?" She dropped the fabric, glanced around the darkened room again, and walked to the unmade bed crowded into one corner. A sudden chill skated over her, but the feeling had nothing to do with the wind whistling through the open door. If Josh was gone, why had Grandfather ordered her inside? She studied the room, focusing on rags piled on the rough plank floor.

"Come on, Norah." Jackson waved at her from the entry. "Don't want to piss off Wood."

She kicked the pile over, and her heart leaped in her chest. Gasping in a quick breath, she grabbed the old quilt and held it up. "Josh was here. This must be the quilt he wanted me to bring him. See? The cat matches his drawing."

Jackson crossed the room and fingered the cloth.

"Now do you believe me?"

He made a quick sucking sound and knelt near the wall. Rubbing his fingers together, he sniffed and looked up at her. "Had to be within the hour."

Her grin froze, and her stomach dropped like it had tumbled to the bottom of that damn cliff. She shook her head slowly. "Why?"

He held up his hand, now smeared with rusty red. "Fresh blood."

Chapter Seven

"The runt almost got us busted." Kenny growled under his breath.

Gina drew on her cigarette and flicked the ashes out the window. "How did that woman find us so fast? And who the hell was the guy with her?"

"Even from fifty yards, he smelled like a cop."

"Yeah, he walked like he had a badge stuck up his ass, didn't he, lover?" She curled her fingers around his thigh and squeezed closer to his side. "But we got away clean. You're too smart for us to get caught."

"Got that right." Kenny ground his teeth together. Good damn thing he had a brain the size of a planet, 'cause the universe was stacked against him. Even looked like they were in for thunderstorms tonight. "Never get a fucking break."

He took the Verde Valley exit under the interstate, pulling onto Main Street. He glanced in the mirror. Sweat broke out on his neck. A black and white three cars back. He slowed the truck to a crawl and inched through the dumpy, sun-baked town squatting by a riverbed.

As far as he knew, his rig wasn't hot, but the newly minted ID he'd snagged in Vegas wasn't primo quality. And his prints were on file. Fucking speeding ticket could broadcast his location and the rig's description like a neon sign to every cop with a warrant.

He drove through the Trading Post lot and parked around back.

"George is still here." Gina unbuckled her seat belt and slid toward the door.

"Good thing."

She moistened her lips and batted her eyelashes at him like she always did. "Want me to stay with Josh?"

He smacked the steering wheel instead of her ass. "No. George will talk to you before he'll give me the day of the week."

She nodded and fussed with her hair, putting glossy red gel on her pouty lips.

"Ain't got all day."

"Right. Okay." She slipped on her heels and swayed toward the front door of the trading post.

Kenny rolled down the window and shouted. "Five minutes. Get the crap and get out."

Gina winked and wiggled her sweet ass through the entrance.

That bitch loved taunting him, loved the thrill of pushing his control to the edge. A grin arched his lips. Yeah, mothering the runt might have distracted her, but he had her hooked. She needed a real man, and he'd give her what she craved. Kenny curled his hand into a fist and flexed a powerful bicep. His smile widened. Crossing his arms, he sat back to wait.

The runt, sprawled on the bench seat in the back, moaned in his sleep.

Cold anger ripped through Kenny's chest. His jaw clenched and the veins on his neck pulsed. Damn kid had cost them a sweet hidey-hole by sticking his nose out the curtains. Now they'd have to find another place to hang out till he finished his deal with the hotshot at the casino.

Kenny dug out a smoke, lit it, and took a long draw. The buzz calmed him. What if he hid in plain sight? The casino had secured parking. He could stow the rig until Vince had time for him.

He rubbed his fingers over his mouth and chuckled. When he wasn't fucking Gina blind, he'd distract her with room service and the Westhaven broad's credit cards. If he kept the kid out cold, he could stash him in a room. Maybe he'd even let Gina mother the runt. Punish her later.

Now if only she could sweet-talk her idiot cousin out of the journal, they'd have the treasure by tomorrow. This weekend tops. He smiled and drummed along to the music on the radio.

Kenny twitched and checked the clock. Seven minutes already. Damn, how long did it take to ask a couple questions and grab an old book? He flicked his ash out the window. Stupid bitch better not be flirting. He wanted to be socked in at the casino before the storm hit.

Glancing between the seats, he checked the kid. Still snoring his brains out. Turning, he leaned back and touched Josh's arm with the cigarette. A hot rush of pleasure swirled in his groin. The hiss and stink of burning hair, and the kid's sleepy half-moan pulled his mouth into a broad grin.

Okay. Runt wasn't going nowhere.

Kenny locked the truck and headed for the store. Remembering his father's sly grin while Kenny watched him abuse that neighbor's kid put an extra strut in his steps.

When he slammed through the front door, Gina

stood near the back of the store across a glass counter from her cousin. She turned, and her face went white, but she winked. He swallowed his jealousy, for now. Hopefully she'd been smart enough to charm the diary out of that son-of-a-stupid-squaw.

Kenny glanced over the crap in the front of the store. Nothing but tourist shit. Kiddy cowboy hats. Rubber bow and arrow sets imported from China. He snorted through his nose. Shit. And the cops called *him* a con man. He sauntered over, adjusting the look in his eyes.

Frowning, Cousin George straightened and made a show of locking the display case. Pushing sixty, he carried an extra forty pounds, and his heavy jowls sagged when he frowned. With those long black braids, his face looked like he belonged in a cartoon. "Haven't seen you in a while, Swank."

Gina glanced up at him with a sappy smile, and a blush climbed her neck.

His fists clenched, but he smiled and draped a hand over her shoulder. Bitch had been flirting. "What ya doing sweetheart?" he asked in a real syrupy tone. When his thumb dug into her neck, she winced and tried to shrug off his hand, but he tightened his vice-like grip.

"Kenny. We were catching up. I was just about to tell George the news." She shot the old coot a sideways glance and crossed her arms under her boobs, pushing the luscious tanned globes higher. The low scoop of her T-shirt almost exposed her bare, rose brown nipples. His hand itched to slip inside and squeeze while he peeled down her jeans.

"What do you really want, Gina?" George asked

with a bored sigh, even though his gaze was fixed on her tits.

Kenny set an arm on the counter and flexed his biceps. Forget it, Geezer. You're too fat and too old to get it up. Too ugly to ever get a chance.

"We're moving back to Arizona." Gina pointed at the cat eyes glittering from a turquoise face in the glass case. "We came for the necklace."

George grunted. "You stole enough to get it out of pawn?"

Sucking in a harsh breath, Kenny thrust out his chin. He dragged a wad of cash from his front pocket and fanned it between his fingers. "Nobody disses my woman. How much did Stacy owe you?"

George gave a low whistle,but didn't unlock the case, just eyed the bankroll.

With a pouty little huff, Gina tapped a fingernail against the glass and held out her palm. "George? The necklace. How much?"

"It's not yours, it's Josh's. Albert wanted Stacy to keep it for their son."

"Stacy died last weekend," Gina blurted.

"She what? No." George stared at the floor and swallowed slowly. His eyes squeezed shut, and his mouth puckered like he was damming up the waterworks.

Kenny held in his snicker at the priceless look on the old coot's face, but Gina patted George's shoulder like a fucking little mother. "We're raising Josh now. Before she died, Stacy told me to get the necklace back for him."

The old man's dark eyes narrowed, and his frown deepened. "I just got a letter from her last week."

"Yeah, well. She was diabetic. Went just like that." Kenny snapped his fingers.

Gina stared at him for a long moment and then cleared her throat and faced George. "And I took care of her didn't I? For weeks."

"Yep, you did. Good care." Kenny yanked her hard against his side and kissed her forehead.

Gina's lip quivered. "Jesus, George. She was my only sister."

George rubbed a weathered hand over his mouth. His expression hardened, and his dark brown eyes glittered. He knocked Gina's hand away. "Keep your dirty money. When Josh is old enough, he can come get it himself."

"Give me the damn necklace, and I'll take care of it for Josh." Gina shoved the bills forward.

With a sigh, George scooped up the cash and unlocked the display case.

Kenny stuck out his hand, but George made a point of giving the turquoise and silver necklace to Gina.

She snatched up the piece, stowed it in her purse, and slid around the counter. Fingering a tray of rings that had been left out, she flashed him a look.

Kenny shifted closer to cover her moves and asked nonchalantly, "Think I could try on that hat? I could use one in this weather." He grabbed a mirror from the counter and angled it at Gina while George silently turned and then handed him the white hat.

George's gaze tracked Kenny's movements as he strutted over and preened in front of the full-length mirror, admiring the Stetson.

"I'll take it." In a much better mood, Kenny peeled off a couple more bills while Gina pocketed a handful of jewelry. "Did Stacy leave anything else with you? Maybe a little book?"

George shook his head, and Kenny's stomach lurched in disappointment. Where the fuck was that book?

Then George's black eyes narrowed and bored into his. "You mean the pioneer journal?"

Kenny smiled his suck-em-in smile. "Stacy didn't have it with her when she died. Said she'd pawned just about everything before she left for California."

Gina snuggled up next to him. "We wanted to keep the diary for Josh, so he can read the family stories. Come on, George. She must have brought the thing to you."

George looked down at her, his frown deepening the crevices of his face. "Yeah, but now it's in the museum, safe under lock and key."

****

Thunder crashed overhead and huge drops of freezing rain splattered on Norah's coat. Two seconds. Much closer than the last strike.

A red neon sign flashed through the downpour. She sprinted toward it and ducked under the awning of the Victorian hotel.

Jackson squeezed in beside her and pointed at the vacancy sign. "Looks like we're in luck."

When he pushed the door latch, an old fashioned bell tinkled overhead. "You grab us a couple rooms. I'll go get the SUV, maybe figure out dinner." At her nod, he bent his head low and galloped back into the storm.

She shook the rain off her coat, folded it over her arm, and walked through the crowded lobby-cum-handcrafts-and-souvenir shop to the antique counter.

"Do you have two rooms for tonight?"

The blonde waif behind the counter beamed a bright, attractive smile, although her lips were coated with whitish gloss. A kilo of black liner and mascara framed her sparkling hazel eyes. "We have one. We had a cancellation a couple minutes ago—somebody who didn't want to drive up the mountain in this storm."

A quick twist in Norah's belly propelled waves of heat up her neck. "One room? That's all?"

The clerk shrugged. "Room six has two beds and space enough for some privacy. I don't think there's anything else left in Jerome tonight. There's a big—"

"A big motorcycle convention in town." Norah rubbed her cold hands together. Could she trust him? Trust herself? A shiver of foresight gripped her. Asleep and vulnerable beside an enticing, virile, charm-your-panties-off, gorgeous male? Impossible.

"That room is my favorite. It's gi-normous, with a huge claw foot tub plus the stall shower," the clerk added with a coaxing lilt. "I can't wait to go home tonight and warm up in a bubble bath."

Norah blew out softly. Sharing a room looked like her only choice tonight. At least there were two beds. No, she wouldn't succumb to any forbidden impulses. She could rely on her strength and training.

"I'll take the room. The thought of a long hot soak sold me." A package of lavender scented bath products and lotions caught her eye. Norah nodded at the clerk and handed over her credit card. "Would you ring up this bath set, too?"

"You bet."

Norah accepted the room keys and tossed them up and down in her hand, staring at them. The weird, squirmy sensation heating the pit of her stomach had to be fear.

Outside at the curb, Jackson beeped the horn.

The clerk followed her glance. "Oops. That must be your boyfriend. Can I take your bath goodies up to your room?"

"Thanks!" She dashed outside and closed the car door just before a flurry of hail ricocheted off the windshield. Pea-sized balls pinged onto the hood and roof and icy sludge pooled at the base of the windshield wipers. "The sheriff was right. The weather's turned nasty."

"How'd you do at the hotel?"

"We got their last room."

A grab-her-by-the-hormones light flashed in his eyes, and he let out a low, rumbling hum. "Great."

"It's a very large room with *two* queen beds," Norah said, lacing her voice with a chilly edge. She worried her lower lip again and wiped her damp face with her hands.

He stared at her for a long moment while the windshield wipers squeaked and then gunned the engine. "I Googled Jerome. There's supposed to be a couple good places for dinner. Gourmet." He put the car in gear and headed uphill.

"Really?" She shook the water from her hair and started pulling out bobby pins.

"Yep. You up for an adventure? The Asylum has a table, but the décor is unique." He grinned.

Tempting warmth radiated through her, like his grin had plugged into her nervous system. "The Asylum. Good place for crazy people."

"Or a spooky woman."

****

Jackson zipped his jacket closed against the driving sleet and dashed up the switchback from the parking lot to the restaurant entrance.

"I better go now, Amber," Norah shouted into her phone over the roar of the wind. "I'll call tomorrow. Love you." She turned off her phone and flashed him a half-hearted smile as he mounted the steps.

"Your niece?" He held the door for her. "She okay?"

"Blissful. She thinks this is a great big slumber party."

"Staying with the Kapulanis?"

"Yes. Amber and Molly play soccer together." Norah brushed a strand of hair behind the delicate curve of her ear.

His fingers tingled and warmed. "We could head home tomorrow."

She shook her head. "Not unless we find Josh. I'd never hear the end of it."

"From whom?"

"My…uh…supervisor."

She'd dropped her eyes a little too fast, and his radar pinged again, tweaked his guts. Damn. Would she ever come clean?

The hostess, dressed in a sleek and very sexy devil costume, seated them in a quiet corner of the crowded, upscale restaurant. The place looked like Halloween on a drug soaked rampage. Outside the window, the storm blustered, but he could barely make out the steep drop to the next level of mountainside below. The rain and churning clouds obscured any lights from the town.

He ordered a good bottle of cabernet and a

vampire-cloaked sommelier with a dribble of fake blood below one fang poured their wine into large crystal glasses, and left the bottle.

Jackson studied Norah openly across the candlelit table. The cold wind had heightened the color in her cheeks, and her eyes sparkled.

Slow heat swirled through him, bumped his pulse a notch. Maybe he should thank his lucky stars the ice storm struck when it did. Her niece was out of the picture tonight, and with nothing to do until the weather broke, he could concentrate on the beautiful woman facing him. He leaned toward her and raised an eyebrow. "Quite a place."

"I suppose that coffin fits the season, but do they really need those?" She gestured at the row of wax zombie and monster heads lining the shelf behind her

"Place is decorated this way all year."

She glanced sideways and shuddered at the life-sized rats with glowing red eyes. "Don't the creepy crawlies ruin your appetite?"

"Not tonight. Besides, it's all in fun." Holding the menu, he scooted closer and pointed at an entrée for two. "I'm starving. Want to share their special rack of lamb?"

A brief smile flickered over her lush mouth, and she lifted her menu. "Maybe."

She looked exotic in the candlelight, with her smooth, tanned skin and big mahogany eyes. He wanted to taste her full lips, capture her mouth and warm the softness of her skin. One step at a time. He squeezed her hand.

The prospect of spending the night in the same room with her had his heart dancing a mean hip-hop.

But what did she think of the idea? Was she happy? Maybe not. She'd grimaced and chewed on her lip when she relayed the news, refused to meet his gaze. Could be she was just embarrassed.

He watched her across the table while she studied the parchment menu. Usually she wore her hair slicked back and twisted up. No nonsense. Professional. Almost severe. The style accented her broad cheekbones and huge eyes, but made her seem unapproachable.

Tonight, the storm had created havoc, and she'd left the thick mass loose in a glossy black riot around her face. He wanted to comb his fingers through it and nuzzle the rain-scented tangle.

He thought of holding her, and anticipation zinged through his veins. Once they were alone, he'd kiss her, nibble on her long neck and inch her onto the bed. He ached to unbutton that proper blouse and smooth her beautiful skin, test the weight of her full breasts, the narrow span of her waist and the feminine curve of her hips.

Then he frowned again and cupped the bowl of his wine glass in his hands, inhaling the spicy aroma. Even if she agreed, they only had one room tonight. With every woman, no matter how alluring, he'd always left before morning. Always. He'd left his lovers satisfied, but he'd always left.

He always operated under the engraved-in-cold-granite rule, and it kept everyone happy. No way would he ever land in the same kind of mess he'd blundered into blind when he was young and stupid.

He twisted the stem of his glass and then lifted it, searching her profile. Determined chin. Strong nose. Her moist, wet-dream-of-a-mouth hooked his gaze and drove hot pulses south. Would one night be enough?

She turned to him. "What are you staring at? Do I have mud on my face?"

"No. You're beautiful." He touched his glass to hers, watching a slow blush flame her cheekbones. To hell with the rules.

****

With a guilty twinge of heat, the last sip of Norah's second glass of wine slid down her throat half an hour later. Her muscles had relaxed into the warmth and quiet of the evening, while Grandfather's nagging voice had been surprisingly silent. She chewed a savory bite of roasted potato.

From her seat in the corner, she watched Jackson through her lashes. He ate with gusto, seeming to enjoy every bite of the lamb special in between his intriguing stories of cop-on-a-mission exploits, and close calls capturing bad guys.

He shot a glance her way and caught her peeking, then smiled. "Interested in coffee?"

"I'd love an espresso and maybe some dessert."

He pursed his lips and then called the waiter over. "We'd like two espressos and a chunk of that chocolate cake I just saw go by."

"Ah, a fellow chocoholic?"

"You too?" He bumped the fist she offered, his long, strong fingers brushing against the back of her hand. "Nothing like it, especially the double dark stuff."

"Nothing?" Norah raised a single brow.

"Well, almost nothing." He angled toward her and cupped her hand with his.

Her fingers tingled at his touch, and heat raced up her arm straight to her chest. Staring at the tablecloth, she cleared her throat, and reached for her water glass, gulping a quick mouthful. Damn. She'd done it again. Goaded him into making one of those suggestive, eyebrow waggling, you-know-exactly-what-I-mean comments.

She thumped down her glass. But the problem was she didn't know, not exactly. Well sure, she understood the mechanics of sex. Tab A into slot B. Health class had taught her what went where and why. But the feelings and emotions coursing around in her body and in her head were new and terrifying territory. Territory she was forbidden to enter. Ever.

She plopped her napkin next to her plate and started to rise.

"Wait."

"I need—"

"No. Just listen. I'm sorry. My comment was out of line." He didn't touch her again, but put out his hand, palm toward her.

She settled back into her chair.

"Look…" Like he was struggling for words, he stabbed a hand through his hair until it stood an inch higher.

She had to smile, couldn't help herself. "It's okay, Jackson."

"I'm not really sure how to talk to you. You're not like most women, I uh…"

"Sleep with?"

"No. Date."

She raised the other brow and tilted her chin.

"Okay." He lowered his voice, "Sleep with."

Face burning, Norah played with her napkin. Shit. Her stupid hormones had taken over her mouth, and she'd teased him again.

At that moment, the waiter interrupted with their coffee, dessert, and the check.

Jackson signed the credit card receipt and returned it to the waiter. "Let's talk about something else. Tell me about you."

"Me?"

"Yeah. I want to know more, spooky lady." With his elbow on the table, he rested his chin on his fist. "You keep giving off mysterious little clues, like you know a lot more than you're letting on."

Her gaze dropped instantly, and her arms crossed over her chest before she could stop them.

He smiled knowingly.

She gritted her teeth. Caught off guard again. It took every dram of self-control to refocus and steady her gaze. "Like what?"

"Nate said you have special talents."

"He did?" Norah ignored the pulse pounding in her throat and took a bite of chocolate cake.

The nod was almost imperceptible. "I'm assuming he didn't just mean playing a mean boogie-woogie on the piano."

"No." How could she distract him? Her gaze darted around the room until it was caught by the silent howl carved on a ghoul mask. She focused back on her fork. "M-m-m, this cake is heavenly."

He clinked his spoon against the side of his cup. "It has something to do with helping people. You said you helped Nate and Jana. How?"

"It's complicated, hard to explain," she said, her voice trailing off. She shoveled in another bite of cake and closed her mouth. Now what? This guy was not ready for tales of twisting time and spirit guides.

"Try."

She met his focused stare. He wouldn't give up until she revealed something, but what? She cleared her throat and took a moment until her heart rate steadied. "Okay. Do you remember when we were at the tattoo parlor? There was a sign in the front window about photographing auras."

"Sure."

"Well, I don't need a camera."

His eyebrows sprang at least an inch above his eyes, but the humor in his expression told her he wasn't buying it. This time he tapped his spoon on the table. "O-kaaay. So what do you see in mine?"

She didn't need to unblock her senses. In the candlelight, his aura had glowed around him all evening. Practical. Focused. Sexual.

She blew on her coffee before she sipped. "Next to your head, there are warm, clear reds topped by a blue corona a hand span wide. You have strong powers of persuasion and observation, a keen intellect, but you're also earthy and grounded. You're a guardian, a hunter."

She glossed her hand over the aurora writhing about him, so real, and alive, and powerful.

A quick shiver snatched at his shoulders, but his expression remained very still. He caught her hand and folded it into his warm, strong fingers. "And?"

"The brown streaks here and here"—she slipped free and pointed—"mean a life change, something big…"

A smile played on his face, but his raised, skeptical brows gave him away. "No way to prove it, is there?"

Her heart jittered, but liquid warmth coursed

through her. Staring at her smaller hand captured by his large one, she lifted one shoulder. "I guess we could buy one of those photographs."

His laugh filled the space around her. He squeezed her fingers. "So who are you always talking to?"

She twisted her mouth into a derisive smile and leaned back so her shoulders rested on the chair cushion. "The last few days? Mostly you."

"No. When you think I'm not listening."

"No one."

He shook his head and waggled four fingers toward her in a 'fess-up gesture. Candlelight played across his face.

"You won't believe me."

He leaned back, too and waited. His dark gray eyes were serious, his face somber, but every muscle in his body was rigid, as if already rejecting her response.

"I tried to tell you before." Memories of years of visions and almost inconceivable experiences chased through her memory. Letting loose an unproductive sigh, she glanced around the mostly empty restaurant and summoned what little courage hadn't already ducked out the back door without paying.

"Who?"

She met his gaze straight on and laid her hands on the table, palms up. "My grandfather."

"See, now that wasn't so tough. Problem is. I don't see any little old man trailing us."

She let one shoulder rise and fall. "He's been dead for ten years."

Jackson rubbed his chin for a minute. "That puts a different spin on it."

"If you didn't want to know, why did you insist?"

With a quick shake of her head, she stood. "I'm ready to go."

Silently she let him escort her past the macabre decorations and outside under the starlit sky. The storm had broken, but black ice covered the mountain road and glowed in the frigid moonlight.

He closed the restaurant door behind them. "I'll go get the car."

"I don't mind walking with you. I should work off some of that heavenly chocolate torte."

He shrugged and offered her his hand. Good thing. The worn wooden stairs were slick, and the wine she'd drunk had her head spinning. She hitched in a long breath of cold air.

They crunched across the gravel drive in silence, and she smiled to herself. Washed clean, the air smelled of damp desert, and the sky sparked with stars. A wonderful dinner. A handsome, every-woman's-dream-man holding her hand. Even if he did think she was a total nutcase.

He stopped suddenly, turning her toward him.

A little surprised, she glanced up, frowning.

His tense mouth looked like an overwound spring and a muscle twitched on his left cheek. "What if I told you I believe you?" he asked, his voice low and rumbling.

"Why?"

"Because I have talents, too."

She blinked twice and cocked her head.

"I'm very good at ferreting out facts." His arms folded around her, and his warm lips brushed her cheek. "Crazy as the whole story sounds, you're telling the truth."

She drew her palm across his jaw, and the rough sensation ignited a throb that started at her center and made her toes curl.

His eyes held shadows, but she could see his smile in the moonlight. He lowered his head, and she closed her eyes. His lips touched hers briefly, and he brushed her hair back from her cheek.

His second kiss was firm, tasting like spring, like life.

She breathed in his heady male scent, and his slick, velvet tongue traced her mouth. She twined her arms around his neck, absorbing his warmth.

His hands played in her hair for a moment, then smoothed down her back and caressed her hips, waking a hunger she'd never expected to feel.

When he dragged her closer, every nerve in her body pulsed. Her breasts formed tight, aching points, pressing against his hard chest. She moaned softly and opened her lips to him.

He deepened the kiss, and she shuddered at the feel of his tongue inside her. His mouth was gentle but hungry. Heat bloomed in a chain reaction, radiating through her veins.

The magic stirred a craving to move even nearer, and she felt him, shockingly hard against her belly. Liquid heat coiled inside her, tearing a low cry from her lips. Jolted by her treacherous response, she broke the kiss and buried her face against his chest, listening to his heart race as his warm breath stirred her hair.

This was what her sisters had sighed about in the dark, giggling and teasing. She'd never understood before why they whispered to each other about overwhelming need. She'd always held herself apart, feeling superior, too spiritual to be blindsided by lust.

"I…" Her mind was blank. The multitude of words she used as armor deserted her.

He smiled and eased his hold, pressing a kiss on her forehead, his mouth tender and moist on her skin.

Her stomach fluttered, but the gentle kiss struck her conscience like lightning.

Shit.

She wanted to shrink to the size of a dust mote and fall to the center of the earth.

She squeezed her eyes shut and fisted her hands. She could never be intimate with a man. Any man. Besides, her response wasn't fair to Jackson. With every fiber of her being she yearned to go back in time and erase these moments.

He grinned and touched her wrist.

A shiver tickled up her arm.

He raised an eyebrow. "Come on. You're cold. We have a nice, warm room waiting."

Chapter Eight

A tread squeaked under Jackson's foot. His pulse jumped. Norah's quiet steps whispered behind him on the steep, carpeted back stairwell of the gay nineties hotel. A seductive cord of awareness and arousal surged through him, triggering a grin. Easy to imagine this entrance used to be the open-air access to a bordello upstairs.

Windows edged the stairs on both sides. He glanced left into the darkened-for-the-night lobby. Through the watery glass on the right, he could see the bar next door. Two scarred pool tables. Beer on tap. A couple denim-and-rodeo-buckle locals and a clump of leather jacketed motorcycle toughs.

Deep-pitched laughter rolled through the walls. Jackson shifted the weight of his overnight case and swiped a palm across his neck. Shooting some pool might be a smarter choice than spending the night breaking all his rules with a spooky lady.

He caught a hint of her tantalizing scent, and his blood throbbed heavy and strong, like the ice storm had melted into a muggy, half-naked, tropical smolder. He hadn't been this horny in a long time.

Pausing on the landing, he checked out the long hallway flanked by glass-knobbed doors and grinned at Norah. "I feel like a teenager sneaking up the back way. Gives the night a sexy edge."

She glanced up at him with a guilty look and a shrug.

"Not that I ever snuck around." He let his wicked grin morph into an eye roll and a chuckle.

Her expressive brows rose. She shouldered past him with a delicate snort. "Yeah, right. I can tell when someone's lying too, Detective." She thumped down her suitcase on the old fashioned green carpet patterned with fat pink roses and examined a small brass sign.

When she turned toward him, a rosy flush glowed on her cheeks, and her gaze fixed on his chin. "Um, room six is to the right."

He hefted her bag along with his own. "Lead the way."

At the last door on the long hall, she fumbled with the oversized metal keys.

"Can I help?"

She handed them to him. The door creaked open. When she stepped inside, her shoulders relaxed, and she heaved a sigh.

Puzzled, he poked his face around the jamb. The queen-sized beds were at least twenty feet apart and facing different directions in the huge, high-ceilinged room. Bumping the door closed behind him, he planted a kiss on the tip of her nose. "Which one you want?"

She scrambled back and sank onto the closest gold plush bedspread with her hands twisting together in her lap. "This one's fine."

"Sure you don't want me guarding the door?" At her curt headshake, he added, "You want to shower first?"

She shook her head mutely.

Could she really be that nervous about staying here

with him? He dropped their bags onto a nearby table. Weird, given the blatant hunger in her kisses.

Crouching until his eyes were level with hers, he tipped up her chin to capture her gaze. His hand tingled, and the warmth from her soft skin raced through him like wildfire and nestled in his groin. But her color was off, pale beneath the fire on her cheeks. Her pupils were tiny, with too much white showing around her big, brown irises.

He dragged his thumb over her lower lip, and heat bubbled in his veins. "You okay? You look like you saw another ghost." He angled his face toward hers, wanting to kiss her again. Taste her.

But she shoved his hand away. "No! No. I, um, I'm exhausted and frightened to death for Josh."

"Nothing more we can do tonight. Might as well relax."

She jumped to her feet on the far side of the bed and grabbed her purse, holding it in front of her chest. "Sorry, I guess I can't help worrying. Go ahead and use the facilities." She waved her hand in the direction of the bathroom.

A frown bunched the skin between his eyebrows. Her panicked expression and hunched over, defensive body language didn't make sense. No reason she should be this skittish. Juggling the room keys, he gave her a quick smile and tilted his head to the side. "Listen, it's a little early for me to hit the sack. Why don't I go downstairs, hang out for a bit, and give you a chance to get settled?"

Relief flashed across her face. Damn. Norah was scared of him. He scratched a spot behind his ear. Or maybe playing some female chase-me game. Either way, he'd opt for being smart.

"But the lobby's closed. Where can you go in this cold?"

He kept his easy smile in place. "There's a bar next door. Not much to look at, but I saw some pool tables."

"I didn't mean—"

"Norah. It's no problem. If I play a couple games, it might give me a chance to talk to the locals casually, see if there's any gossip about the Swanks or even about local law enforcement."

She hitched her purse onto her shoulder. "Then I'll come with you."

"No need. Relax and have that bubble bath you talked about. Be back in an hour." He gave her a quick salute and closed the door before she could insist.

****

Jackson shrugged off his jacket and surveyed the bar. The bricks and plaster gave off haze and a faint aroma from a century of cigars and roll-your-own smokes. Three locals nursed a pitcher of suds at the long, mahogany bar, but the motorcycle crowd had vanished.

One of the pool tables stood empty. Travis Wood and a hefty, bald guy with tattoos all over his arms and neck had 'em racked up at the other.

Sheriff Wood broke, sinking one in the corner. After missing his next shot, he straightened and turned. "Evening, Marino. Didn't expect to see you here tonight. Not alone, anyway."

The bald guy stepped up behind Wood, grinding a cube of light blue chalk on the tip of his cue and eyeing Jackson silently.

Jackson returned the appraisal. Guy had a belly the

size of a Smart car. "Scored the last room at the Connor. Thanks for the tip, Wood."

"Yeah? The last room? What about Norah?" That freaking gleam resurfaced in the sheriff's eyes.

Tension coiled in Jackson's chest, grabbed his gut, and squeezed. Prickly, urgent and unexpectedly territorial tension. Hell. Throwing back his shoulders, he widened his stance, broadcasting his claim. "She wanted a long soak before bed. Saw you from the stairs and thought I'd come down and give you an update."

Wood's mouth and sandy eyebrows quirked. "Update?"

"Yeah. We stopped by the tattoo parlor. Fresh tire tracks led into the garage."

Wood's eyes narrowed into a focused glare. "What aren't you telling me, Marino?"

"Upstairs door was open, so Norah barged in." When the sheriff groaned, Jackson held up a palm. "I know, I know. Couldn't stop her. But she found some of Josh's stuff. And some fresh blood stains."

"Hell. That poor kid." Shaking his head slowly, Wood rubbed the back of his neck. "I talked to the sheriff in Verde Valley. Turns out Josh's dad was an army buddy of his. Earned a bundle of medals, but didn't make it home from Afghanistan."

Jackson winced. "Damn shame. Any new leads on the Swanks?"

Frowning, the bald guy lumbered up beside Wood, tucked his pool cue in the crook of one elbow, and crossed his brawny arms over his chest. "You know Gina?"

"Settle down." Wood bumped the guy's shoulder. "Rocky Hummel, Sergeant Jackson Marino. He trailed

Kenny Swank from Northern California, looking for a missing kid. Rocky owns this place. Leads the volunteer fire squad."

Veins popped out on Hummel's temples and neck, but he offered Jackson a paw. "Lemme know if you catch that lying crook. Took me for a bundle."

Jackson met the guy's firm grip without a flinch. "Kidnapping warrant's for Gina. Swiped another boy before Josh."

"Hold on just a minute. Had to be Kenny," Rocky growled. "Gina mighta been a wild child, mighta caused some trouble here and there. But until she met Swank, there was no meanness in her."

With his pulse thundering in his ears, Jackson didn't try to keep the sarcasm from his tone. "Then she's learned some nasty new tricks."

Red flushed the big guy's neck and mottled his face. His arms straightened at his sides. His hands fisted. "Watch your mouth, buddy."

Thrusting out his jaw, Jackson closed the distance between them. "Yeah? Caught her on camera dumping a kid at the hospital. He died anyway. Abuse and starvation."

Letting loose a grunt, Rocky backed off, rubbing the bridge of his nose. "Man that sucks. You know, I thought she'd finally settled down. Then Swank showed up. The snake roared into town one weekend, married her the next, and took over her business."

Grimacing, Wood thumped him on the back. "Old news, Hummel. Now we gotta find the Kwail boy. Marino, I'll have the Swanks' place searched. Already set up a watch."

"Norah has a sixth sense when it comes to kids."

Jackson scraped a hand over his stubbly chin. "We can make a run down the mountain in the morning."

Wood scribbled on a scrap of paper and held it out. "Here's Kwail's address on the Rez."

"Got time for a game of nine ball before you go up to your lady, Marino?" Rocky heaved a sigh. "I'd like to buy you a beer."

****

Now that her hands had defrosted, she'd tackle the snarls in her hair. Peeling off her shower cap, Norah cinched the belt on her flannel robe around her waist. She sat at the dressing table and wiped the fog off the mirror with a hand towel. What a mess. The wind and the moisture had worked together, twisting her hair into knots. Her brush snagged, and pain shot through her scalp.

The old building creaked in the wind. A shiver ghosted across the nape of her neck, and she scanned the dark corners of the room. Her body had finally warmed, but this place still gave her the creepy crawlies.

She clamped down her mental shields and brushed. Sometimes her sensitivity was a pain in the ass, but she'd been given unique gifts that made the world a better place. At least sixteen people, counting Nate Kapulani, were alive today because she'd twisted time. Sixteen decent, honorable people each had fulfilling lives. Each had a positive impact on dozens, if not hundreds of lives, thanks to her abilities.

Her stomach tied itself into more tangles than her hair. She tapped the back of her brush against her hand. What if she had sex with Jackson tonight, was fool enough to jettison her gifts for a few moments of oh-my

God-take-me passion?

When he kissed her, she'd actually been tempted for a moment. She glared at her weak, selfish face in the mirror. Who would stay dead if she acted like a brainless lump of hormones? What chunk of history would stay polluted and distorted?

When the brush snagged on another knot, she jerked harder. Tears stung her eyes. Beguiling grin or not, gorgeous body or not, she should be ashamed of having so much trouble resisting him.

She dropped the brush in her lap and rested her chin on her upturned hands. He'd liquefied her spine and turned her will power to gummy oatmeal. But allowing herself to be overwhelmed even by a metric ton of lust was embarrassing. Appalling. Indefensible.

She frowned at the mirror again and touched her lips. Her cheeks flamed. Maybe she'd given him the wrong impression when he'd kissed her. Maybe? She snorted in disgust. Like maybe the sun is gonna rise in the east tomorrow? She'd screwed up, and she had to apologize.

With her hair finally tamed into a long braid, she felt calmer, more centered. She zapped a cup of water in the little microwave and stirred in a packet of instant cocoa. She took a sip of the hot chocolate and headed for bed with her book.

The room still gave her the creeps, but she'd ignore that and keep her *mea culpa* with Jackson on an entirely professional basis.

She plumped her pillows and squirmed back against them, but couldn't get comfortable. The air carried an eerie chill and the hint of decay made the skin between her shoulder blades itch.

Something poked and pressed at her mind again. She closed her eyes. Not Grandfather. Not the Sinagua Magician or his snake spirit. Not an ancient presence, but powerful and determined. Curious, she let her shields slip a fraction.

Her heart crashed against her ribs.

A presence with chromium yellow and muddy vermillion tentacles. Shudders rocked her. She slammed her defenses back into place, but the spirit clawed and tore at her mind.

Sweat trickled down her neck, and she trembled with effort while she fought to patch each tear and rebuild her mental shields.

By the time she'd finally shut out the unnatural thing, every muscle ached. She drew in a dozen slow, shaky breaths and sipped her cocoa.

A soft knock at the door echoed through the room. She squared her shoulders.

Jackson entered, smiling, and his gaze swept her face. "Feeling better?"

"Yes, thanks. Exhausted, but I'm finally warm." She gave an exaggerated yawn. "I think I'll fall asleep fast."

He bent to kiss her forehead, brushing his warm mouth over hers. His beard rasped against her cheek, and he smelled of beer and cigars.

"See you in the morning." Jackson grabbed his toiletry bag and closed the bathroom door behind him. The shower started, and he whistled a melody she recognized from somewhere.

Coward. She hadn't found the strength to apologize, and she'd completely forgotten to ask him if he'd found out anything. She massaged her temples.

Maybe that wasn't a bad thing. Their little talk would go more smoothly in the morning with her clothes on, her hair up and the breakfast table between them.

With a sigh, she re-opened the latest book club selection. After a few pages, her attention started to drift. When the water in the bathroom shut off, she reached for the light switch and snuggled against her pillows. Her mind raced, but she squeezed her eyes shut and counted the pulse beats thudding in her head.

A few minutes later, Jackson emerged and moved around the room almost silently.

Norah couldn't resist. She opened her eyes a slit and peeked. Languid warmth swirled inside her. The soft, knit boxers clung lovingly to his amazing backside. She licked her lips, watching his shoulder muscles bunch as he pulled down the blankets. When he turned and slid beneath, she caught a glimpse of his magnificent chest and taut abdomen and an enticing bulge below. Her breath caught.

"Sleep well," he rumbled, with the hint of a chuckle in his deep voice.

She flipped onto her side with her back toward him and cupped her burning cheeks with her cold hands. Why had she even looked? Now she'd never go to sleep.

Eventually, she dreamed of ghosts.

Hordes and armies of ghosts.

Sinagua and Yavapai, Italian and American, male and female ghosts.

Kindly, smiling ghosts and grasping, greedy ghosts, all pushed at her mind.

A sudden gust of freezing air blasted under the door near her bed and shocked Norah awake, gripping her in a swirling cloud of fear and pain and rage.

Her skin electrified. Every hair stood on end and swarms of bees buzzed inside her ears. She screamed and bolted from the bed, backing away from the spirits that streamed under the door. Her heart hammered against her breastbone. She pushed her hands in front of her to ward them off. But one ghost shivered through her, melted into her body and froze her limbs.

Cold. So deadly cold.

Fighting to escape its clutches, she caught a quick flash of a woman dressed in a corset and black, red and violet ruffles. Fishnet stockings and button ankle boots. Flaming orange hair in a loose topknot. Curls trailed over her bare neck and arms.

Glaciers froze inside her bones. Spasms shook her muscles. From inside her body, the woman, Mary, groped for Norah's voice and opened her mouth in a scream.

A specter in black loomed over her, shook her by shoulders, and coiled his strong fingers around her throat.

Clawing at his hands, she gasped for air but couldn't escape his grip. Her lungs burned, and spots danced before her eyes.

Then her back hit a warm, solid mass, and the miasma evaporated.

Disoriented, Norah could only stutter and stare at the fine trembling of her fingers. Her knees weakened and threatened to collapse.

Jackson scooped her up in his arms. "You're okay. I've got you."

She buried her face against his neck, sobbing her thanks, while gulping in huge gasps of air.

He carried her to his bed and sat back against the headboard. Tucking her head underneath his chin, he flipped the blankets over both of them.

Her body ached and shook. So very cold.

When the tremors finally subsided, he ran a hand along her cheek and turned her face toward his. "What happened? A nightmare?"

"No. S-sorry I woke you. I g-g-guess I have to ch-change my answer," Norah sobbed.

He looked down at her silently "Which answer?"

"G-ghosts. They c-can hurt you."

"You saw a ghost?"

"Two. The woman hijacked me for a moment." Norah shivered. "Her name was Mary. She was very young, but not so innocent. The man strangled her."

"A woman was murdered in this room?" He sat up straighter and encircled her in his arms.

"No, out in the hall near the landing. A long time ago, otherwise I couldn't stay in here." Meeting his gaze, she ran her arms over his shoulders and around his neck. "Thanks for holding me. You broke their grip. She demanded my help, but I can't do anything for her. I was terrified he'd kill me, too, in his rage."

Jackson's forehead furrowed. "How could a ghost kill you?" His arm curled around her, and the heat in his gaze reached deep inside her, touching off hungry pangs of need.

Her focus drifted to his lips, lush, warm and ever so talented, before being drawn back to his gaze. She relaxed against him, almost as if something in his eyes was connected to the most secret and defended parts of her, making them soften and moisten. The beguiling notes of a flute melody, no, the song he'd played on his oboe, threaded through her mind.

She blinked and gave her head a little shake. "I…I don't know, either. Nothing like this has ever happened to me before."

His warm hand stroked her arm, her back. "You're safe now. But how did you know her story?"

"She invaded my mind." With a shudder, Norah snuggled closer, feeling the deep rumble of his words through his chest. Her blood pulsed under her skin, warm and liquid and soft. "I can't talk about it any more tonight, not with them out in the hall, clawing at me. Maybe tomorrow, if you want."

"Weird. I think my hair's standing on end from just the abridged version." He kissed her forehead.

She dropped her gaze, unable to meet his penetrating, deep gray eyes any longer. Before she could move away, he tilted her chin up and covered her mouth. His heat felt so clean and right. Her heart fluttered, and her sensitive lips opened under his coaxing. When he sucked her tongue, a shuddering moan erupted from deep inside, and she pressed herself against his chest.

He shifted her sideways onto the pillow and buried his nose in her hair. One hand cupped her nape, while the other traced a flaming path along her collarbone.

Her mind went fuzzy and hunger gripped her. She melted inside. Her hands fumbled against his chest. They fluttered down and stroked his bare muscled back while he reclaimed her mouth. He nipped her lip and soothed it with his slick tongue. Kissing her deeply, he caressed her face and shoulders with gentle hands.

She wondered fleetingly if she should stop him, but just for a moment she gave herself up to his warm hands and consuming mouth. After the sensation of death engulfing her very bones, he made her feel so alive. He chased away the numbness, made her aware of the blood surging through her veins with every heartbeat.

When he eased her satin pajama top off a shoulder, one button fell open. His hand cupped her breast and tested its weight. "Beautiful," he murmured. His fingers closed over her, stroking the nipple. He tugged and squeezed gently and it furled into a sensitive peak. Sweet, wonderful sensations chased through her body.

His palm slid over and did homage to the other breast, stroking and teasing, raising blissful flickers of need.

She whimpered and moved her thighs together, feeling feverish. The slick fabric of her pajama pants was damp and felt so good rubbing against her skin. She needed to be closer to him, so very much closer.

As if he heard her thoughts, he released the last two buttons and slid her top aside. His warm, bare chest covered hers. The coarse hair rasped over her sensitive nipples, sent bolts of electricity crashing against her center.

Under his boxers, his rigid length nestled against her and felt so right. Hissing out a breath that was half moan, she shifted her legs apart, allowing him to settle a leg between hers and move closer to her emptiness.

He broke the kiss with a shudder. "Norah, sweetheart?"

"Hmm?" Her fingers slipped through his thick, wavy hair and caressed an ear. Her eyes opened slowly, and she smiled shyly up at him. She gently touched his lips.

"I want you, you know that. You sure you want this, too? You had a rough day."

"Want this? Want—oh, my God!" Her face blazed, and her whole body tensed with a sick sense of guilt. She was half naked and in his bed. His weight pressed her into the mattress. He was ready and hard and pulsed against her thigh. Worse, he had every reason to think she was willing. Her hands flew to her cheeks. "I can't do this! I'm so sorry, Jackson. I can't take the risk!"

"That's okay, if that's what's worrying you." He kissed her fast and hard. "I can protect you, sweetheart." He reached sideways and opened a drawer.

When his weight shifted, she scooted away and jerked her top back over her shoulders. Her fingers groped for the buttons. She could just die. A merciful God would reach right down and fry her to a crisp. Just sprinkle on some salt. No need for ketchup.

Her cheeks burned so hot, they were probably crimson with shame. He'd been the one to call a halt. She'd almost sacrificed her gifts, her responsibilities and for what? A few moments of bliss.

She scooted off the bed. "No. You don't understand. This is just physical pleasure. Just lust. I can't—"

He closed his eyes and blew out a frustrated breath. "Right. Glad I asked." He shoved one hand into his hair and leaned against the headboard. "Wouldn't want you doing something for the simple pleasure."

"You don't understand. I have so much more at stake than you possibly could. I can't give in to…to urges." She folded her arms across her chest, hiding her breasts.

He gave a stiff nod, his jaw rigid and his eyes hard

and cold. "Yeah. I understand. Don't think another thing about it, Norah. I should never have expected an uptight lawyer to…" He looked away and let the sentence drop.

She recoiled as if he'd slapped her. For an instant, she only wanted to retaliate. "To what? To give herself to a horny cop?"

"Right. That's enough." He stood and stomped toward the bathroom. "I should have known. You're just like my ex-wife. Too good for a mere cop."

Her stomach clenched when she recognized his pain. "Jackson. That's not what I meant. Please. Let me explain."

"Go ahead and use the bed. I'll sleep by the door. Right now, I need another shower."

Chapter Nine

"Are we close to Disneyland?" Josh ground the heels of his hands against his eyes and peered out the rear window of the camper. His pulse bumped, and he sucked in a breath. Under tall metal lampposts, trailers and motor homes were scattered around the huge parking lot.

Dropping her gaze, Aunt Gina ground out her cigarette. "We're still outside Vegas. The guy who owns this place owes Kenny some money." She pointed through the bug-spattered windshield toward a Casino with neon lights flashing into the darkness.

His throat scraped like sandpaper, and his tongue stuck to the roof of his mouth. "Did I sleep a long time? I'm really thirsty."

"Yeah, you were wiped out. Here. Want a drink?"

He guzzled half a bottle. The warm water splashed into his empty stomach, and a wave of nausea rolled through him. But he sloshed some more liquid around to rinse away the nasty taste in his mouth.

"Do you see Kenny?" she asked with a funny trembling in her voice.

Josh peered out the tiny window over the sink and shook his head. His stomach rolled and growled painfully.

"Watch for him, okay?" She pulled something from her big lumpy purse. Light glinted off silver.

Even from across the camper, electricity lifted the hairs on his arms. Drawn by the shiny beadwork, he slipped between the front seats and stood next to his aunt.

She put the necklace over her head and smiled at the rearview mirror.

Josh squinted at her reflection. The old jewelry looked funny on her. Too big and too powerful for her to wear.

He leaned closer. An animal carved from a lump of turquoise the size of his fist hung at the center of the necklace. A ferocious wildcat with glittering black eyes and sharp, ivory teeth glared at him.

His heart raced like he'd dribbled the soccer ball all the way down the field and scored a goal. Power swelled from the necklace and tendrils of magic licked at him. He tried to swallow, but his mouth had gone dry again.

"You have the strength," a voice murmured in his head.

His chest swelled, and he straightened his shoulders.

"Claim your property," the voice urged. *"Take it. The woman is of our blood, but unworthy. Weak."*

Unable to resist the impulse, Josh reached out. "The necklace belongs to me. It was my mother's."

But Aunt Gina slapped his hand away. "Not anymore."

His jaw stiffened. Tension bubbled inside his chest, as the craving to touch the carved turquoise grew. "The cat is mine."

"Someday it will be, when you're old enough."

Frowning, he jutted out his chin. "Why not now?"

She only chuckled and patted his cheek. "You're still a kid. This necklace has been in our family for a long time. Grandma used to hide it in an old coffee can under her bed. Sometimes when we were little she let Stacy and me look, but never touch."

"Take what is yours. Consume the ancient magic and grow powerful."

He wanted to grab the necklace and run into the desert. Instead, he squeezed his hands into fists. The nails made painful dents in his palms.

Aunt Gina patted him again. "Chill out. Stacy and I thought we'd never grow up either."

"Take the necklace. She cannot stop you."

Josh scowled, but didn't react.

Her lower lip quivered, and she blinked a few times. "I'm sorry about your mom, Josh."

The ice around his heart cracked, and fiery cold poured into his veins. A loud rushing noise, like the crash of waves drowned out the voice in his mind. His knees went wobbly, and he grabbed the back of the driver's seat.

"Before we came to visit you, I hadn't seen my sister for almost five years. But I missed her." Gina whimpered and gave a big, gloppy sniff. "She left the Rez after your dad was killed, but I always wished—"

"I can't think about her now."

"But you and me," Aunt Gina continued in a voice that had thickened and lost some of the whine, "We take care of each other because we're kin." She weighted the last word, like it was really important. Really true.

He eyed her. "That's a lie. You tricked me."

"I need you Josh. I'm sorry I lied. Kenny made me

say that. How can I make it up to you?" She scraped a tear away with her hand. Then she unhooked the necklace and held it out to him. "Here. This is yours."

The cold spot in his chest melted around the edges. "Maybe we should help each other. But that means always telling the truth."

Her eyes opened wider. Then she smiled and pulled gently on his ear lobe. "You bet, kiddo."

Footsteps crunched across the gravel. "Fuck, fuck, fuck," Uncle Kenny growled.

Cruel shivers crawled over Josh again. The burn marks on his arm stung, and he covered them.

"Gina. God damn it. Open the fucking door. This shit is hot."

She tossed him the necklace. "Don't let Kenny see you have it." She winked and scrambled out her door.

The necklace seared his hands, and he swallowed hard, resisting an army of visions. He shrank back, dropping the carved turquoise onto the carpet between his knees. He gulped a few shaky breaths and rubbed his palms on his legs.

"Did you get the money?" Aunt Gina asked in a syrupy voice.

The driver's side door slammed shut, and the smell of tacos wafted back, but nausea rose in Josh's throat.

Kenny tossed him a package wrapped in greasy yellow paper and shoved a shake into his hands. "Drink up, kid."

"I'm not hungry."

Kenny whipped around, fisting one powerful hand. His pupils were huge, and his face had turned red and blotchy. "I said drink the fucking shake, runt, or I'll pour it down your throat."

Josh's pulse throbbed in his ears. "Yes, sir." He took a long, noisy slurp through the straw. The chocolate didn't quite disguise a funny aftertaste, and he wrinkled his nose. But Kenny leaned over the seat glaring at him, so he took a second drink. And another.

The engine roared, and the truck lurched forward.

"Kenny?" Aunt Gina whined.

"Stop nagging me, bitch," Uncle Kenny thundered.

His voice sounded scary. Dragging the necklace with him, Josh scooted further back and hunched as small as he could.

"Time to go get the journal."

Josh frowned. Suddenly Uncle Kenny didn't sound so mean. He almost sounded excited. Happy.

"How?" she asked. "The museum's closed for the night."

"When I checked the place out this afternoon, I flipped a window latch in the john. I'll lift you up. You sneak in and grab your book."

A wave of dizziness grabbed Josh. He felt sick to his stomach and a little tired. He rubbed his head with the cool, wet cup. How could he be sleepy again so soon?

Away from the Casino's huge flashing signs, the night was dark. No moon, or maybe it was hidden behind the clouds.

The movement of the truck lulled him. His lids drifted closed, but he jerked them open and gritted his teeth. He couldn't see the necklace in the dim light of passing headlights. But when he picked it up, the power built.

"Joshua," the eerie voice called to him. *"Come to me."*

142

The necklace hummed in his shaky hands, but he felt no pain. He gritted his teeth and stuck it inside his shirt. Fear clogged his chest, but he couldn't resist opening his senses just a little. Many times in the past his mother had touched the carved stone.

He crossed his legs and centered his mind, holding the necklace close to his heart. For a moment, he saw her face, then swirling patches of color filtered behind his eyes, and he heard strange music.

Drums pounded from far away. Firelight crackled in an open pit. The smoke smelled like Christmas, but made Josh's eyes water and burn.

Warming his hands, an elder sat beside a huge rock covered in ancient designs. His braids were long and streaked with gray, his face weathered. He wore the necklace on his bare chest, and it looked right on his strong body.

Josh gasped. The man's eyes were the same golden color as his mother's. The same color as his. The man was kin. There was no reason to fear him. He opened his mind fully.

The sun beat down on his face, and Josh shielded his eyes, taking in the scene. Nearby, another man danced in the dust, kicking up small puffs with each toe-heel step. A gourd rattle shook to the beat, and the dancer chanted.

Josh yawned and shut his eyes. His head lolled to the side, and he slid to the ground.

"Wake up!" the Magician shouted.

But Josh did not move.

****

Why did women always want to rehash disasters? Jackson broke into a half trot, striding ahead of Norah toward the trading post in Verde Valley. With each step, the greasy lump from his breakfast sandwich hardened. Norah had the tenacity of a defense lawyer, so he probably should get the discussion over with. But right now he couldn't face a play-by-play.

He sucked on his teeth and frowned. Why had her rejection stung so hard? Get real, Marino. She'd triggered all the shit he'd taken off of Alicia before he finally realized that their travesty-of-a-marriage was dead.

Another lawyer? He knew better. Why hadn't he run away screaming when he found out? His gonads had triumphed over brainpower again.

He gritted his teeth and faced her. "Drop the subject, Norah. Now."

"But I respect you, Jackson. What you do is vitally important. Please let me help you understand," she said in a slightly breathless voice, taking two steps for each of his strides.

He swiveled around and waited for her, glaring, with his jaw set and eyes narrowed. She still wanted something, so this should be entertaining.

When she reached out to touch his arm, he jerked away and fisted his hands on his hips. He felt raw. Exposed. Why the hell did she keep poking him where he already hurt? "Look. No need to explain. No harm done. I forgive you."

"But—"

"Can we please focus on business? I still want to find Josh. Do you?"

She blinked up at him and averted her gaze. Bright spots of color lit her tanned cheekbones. "Yes. He's first priority."

Good. Right answer.

He shaded his eyes with one hand and stared through plate glass into the darkened shop. Tourist stuff, some cheap toys. Man, who knew they still made rubber bow and arrow sets?

A long, three-tiered shelf of books and brochures. Flat-topped display cases of jewelry and artifacts lined two walls, what looked like an office at the back on the left. No tourists. No staff. "The Ancient Sorcerer. Cute name to draw the New Age crowd. But no signs of life inside."

Norah jarred the locked door and a string of bells jingled. "I don't see anyone either."

"According to Wood, the guy who owns this place is related to Josh. But he's some kind of shaman. Not on a modern time clock."

Norah smiled wistfully and gave a soft sigh. "I know people like that. Strong gifts can make strong demands."

His stomach clenched, and an absurd strand of jealousy curled through him. Who'd brought that compelling smile to her face?

"We could come back later this afternoon. Is there anybody else we should talk to now?" she asked, inching closer.

He caught a wisp of her scent, lavender, soap and woman, but held his hands rigid at his sides despite the mixed signals. Touchy-feely moves from a beautiful woman had always felt like foreplay, but this seemed more like a bait and switch scam after last night. "Wood gave me a couple names from the Tribal Council. But the local museum is right across the street. Wait here if you want. I'm gonna check it out."

With Norah trailing him, he zigzagged between a car full of tourists and a decades-old Jeep covered in dust. In front of the squat adobe structure, the desert sun glinted off the light bar on a squad car. An uneasy trickle of sweat inched down his spine, and his brow puckered. No, three squad cars were parked at odd angles on the grass. "What the hell?"

"I wonder if there's a problem?"

Norah's warm, rich voice hummed over his senses and sent his damned hormones jumping again. He shoved away thoughts of her soft, lush mouth. Memories of how she'd kissed. Fantasies of what her moist, rough tongue might do.

Scraping both hands through his hair, he rounded a corner and stepped inside the museum bookstore. Cool, low light, ringed with big, glass covered photos. A knot of uniformed cops bunched in front of the cashier.

"Morning," he said and introduced himself to a stocky, dark haired, dark eyed cop wearing sergeant's stripes.

The guy shook his hand. "Doug Fredericks. Verde Valley PD."

Jackson offered his shield. "Pleasure. Can you tell me what happened?"

Fredericks eyed the badge and passed it back. "Break in last night. Someone came in through the bathroom window. Docent found a case smashed when she opened up around eleven this morning."

"Anything missing?"

"Cash box was pried open and emptied. Got a few bucks." He inclined his head at the crime scene tape. But the guy's thick eyebrows scrunched together, and he scratched his bullet shaped head. "They took an old book, too. Pioneer era journal George Kwail loaned the museum."

Jackson's pulse bumped faster. "The guy from the trading post?"

"Yeah." The local cop's dark, slightly almond shaped eyes narrowed. "You're a long way from home. What's your interest, Marino?"

"Locating Kwail. Following a lead on a kidnapping." At Fredericks' jerk of interest, Jackson held up a palm. "Kwail's not a suspect. Kid's his nephew."

"Okay," drawing out the syllables, Fredericks nodded. "Now I remember. Watch Commander said something during morning briefing. But you're not going to find George here this afternoon. Closes up shop and heads out into the desert for a couple days every year around this time."

Drawn by a cluster of photographed ruins, Norah wandered away from Jackson and the local cops. She grinned. That much testosterone in one small, low-ceilinged room ought to be illegal.

Passing through an oak-framed doorway, she took a deep breath of the stale, slightly musty air and stopped to look at a collection of pottery. The pair of tortoises on one black and white shard mirrored the petroglyph image in the photo displayed above.

She massaged her neck with both hands, but couldn't ease the tension. A dull ache throbbed behind her temples, despite the aspirin she'd taken with breakfast. Was she suffering from the wine she'd had with dinner last night? More likely from guilt.

Stammering with shame and embarrassment, she'd said precisely the wrong thing to Jackson. She'd never meant to hurt him, but it was her fault for misleading him. She glanced at his stern face and sighed. When they got back into the car, she'd make him listen.

He talked to the officers, but even in his jeans and faded polo shirt, he fit right in, his stance easy and relaxed, but still authoritative. Jackson was taller and leaner than the local cop who seemed to be in charge, and his shoulders were amazing. Something in his expression, maybe the glitter in his eyes and his slightly crooked smile, reminded her of the ghostly Italian grandmother.

Jackson chuckled, a deep, rolling, joyful noise that eased her headache and triggered a grin. Heat sparked and settled low in her body. Hidden spots loosened that had no business responding to a man.

No! Closing her eyes, Norah imagined a bone chilling frost that iced over all the private parts between her waist and knees. She knew the rules, and she'd follow them, despite the temptation.

She didn't need the man. Couldn't have him. Didn't even want him.

Liar.

She clicked to the next photograph. More animals and star people, complete with hands and feet, above a wildcat and a herd of deer or antelope. A long serpent looped around a solar spiral.

When she blinked, the reptile seemed to slither toward her.

Creepy shivers stung her neck, made all the tiny hairs bristle.

The snake's head rose off the photograph. Its dark eyes glittered with intelligence.

Coiling it seemed to gather strength and shot off

the picture toward her.

Her heart thundered in her chest like a dozen war drums. Cold, sick sweat beaded all over her body. She gave the spirit snake a stiff-armed push with her mind, but it flowed around the barrier she created like a mountain stream rushing around a twig.

Cold.

Unrelenting.

Powerful.

Through the choking thickness in her throat, she let out a strangled gasp.

Firelight.

Flames crackled and dancers' feet pounded out a rhythm that matched her pulse. The scent of burning juniper stung her nostrils.

The Magician faced her with his serpent staff raised. His golden eyes were wide, almost panicked and his posture rigid. But when he reached for her, a greedy expression overtook his features.

Tendrils of his powerful essence wound into her soul.

Nausea twisted her belly, and her lungs strained for air as she fought his domination.

He gave a gloating laugh, but through the horror of his violation, she sensed his anguish.

"You came to me in my desperation, daughter. You will serve me well."

Nausea rose in her throat, but Norah's only reply was to struggle harder.

"You will restore my tools to me and my power."

"No!"

"First find the boy and free him. I cannot reach his mind. Somehow he still breathes, but to me, he is

dead."

She jarred loose his control of her legs and backed away, but the Magician's power raced through her. His grip strengthened. Her bones, her muscles turned to unresponsive stone.

"The book is the key."

Before she could ask his meaning, someone moved to her side.

The hunter, clad in buckskin leggings.

She grabbed for him, touched his warm naked skin and crinkling hairs on his strong arms.

The spirit's grip dissolved.

With a shudder, she turned and buried her nose against Jackson's shoulder, inhaling deeply.

Soap, a clean safe scent that was his alone, but also the hot, bitter tang of anger.

Her cheeks flamed, but she looked up and met his gaze.

Fury lit Jackson's deep gray eyes and thinned his lips. His hands curled around her shoulders, strong, but not soft or gentle. His whole body stiffened, and he eased her away. "Make up your mind, lady," his voice rumbled.

She felt like a threadbare washcloth someone had wrung out and left to mildew. Every muscle ached with exhaustion and a gut-deep burn of shame thickened her tongue. "I-I'm s-so sorry. The Magician. His ghost—"

"Ghosts again? Great performance. Guess I'm officially your personal panic bar." Throwing her a grimace, he turned and marched out.

****

Jackson boiled with frustration. Nobody on the tiny Reservation knew a damn thing, and they'd checked every house. Either the Swanks hadn't been here, or they'd been real lucky and nearly invisible. Almost dark and the closest thing he had to a fresh lead was Doug Fredericks' suggestion he might find George out near Newspaper Rock on the Equinox.

Jackson glanced up at the last flickers of sunset. Tall banks of black clouds billowed on the horizon, and the still air crackled with electricity. Not the best time to explore unmarked dirt roads along creeks prone to flooding. Maybe tomorrow.

He glared sideways at Norah. Only part of the tension he felt was from the brewing thunderstorm. She wouldn't stop touching him, and every time she did, she refueled his ache for what she'd refused. He wasn't sure he'd survive another night in the same room with her and itched to head for Phoenix and his freedom. But that wasn't happening anytime soon. He had a job to finish, no matter how much his balls ached.

He picked up a rock and juggled it up and down, looking across the street at the closed trading post. "How the hell can Kwail run a business if he goes on walkabout without warning?"

Norah just shrugged, but she looked frustrated.

Got that right. Need swirled hot in his groin, and he hardened to a half-staff again. Give him half a chance, and he'd take her from frustrated to soft and yielding and satiated.

Oh, yeah. He'd grab her wrists and hold her arms over her head with all that soft tanned skin and those luscious curves stretched out on a bed, naked and vulnerable for his pleasure and for hers.

He could hold her captive and spend the night showing her exactly what pleasures she'd refused last night.

Shit. Scratch that image.

Time for a reality check, Marino.

He paced the wooden sidewalk. The familiar cold encased his heart. His ex had experienced all he had to give for three years, two months and eighteen days. But she'd happily thrown him on the dung heap for Wilfred Winfield Buttface the forty-seventh and his family billions. Jackson rotated his kinked up shoulders.

Norah Redfox, Esq., glanced up at him from the park bench. She looked worn out after their long, unproductive day. "Shall we try to find Newspaper Rock tonight?"

He hurled the stone into a gully. The limestone soil powdered on impact. "No, it's a long shot, but we can try tomorrow morning. We should head back to Jerome while the weather holds and see if Wood found anything at the tattoo parlor."

"I guess we can try this place again tomorrow, too."

He turned on his heel and stalked toward the SUV. Popping the locks, he held her door open out of habit.

"Thanks." She gave him a tentative smile.

He huffed around to the driver's side and slammed his butt down on the seat, his eyes straight ahead. Shit. He hated acting like a prize jerk, but couldn't help himself. He cranked the key and jammed the rental into gear.

After a few moments of silence, he reached for the CD player, but Norah cleared her throat and laid her fingers gently on his arm. "Jackson, I need a favor."

He jerked his hand away like he'd been singed. A favor had gotten him into trouble in the first place. Not true. He'd been sinking in hot, lusty quicksand long before she'd showed up on his porch. "What?"

"Two minutes."

Thunder rumbled, and the air inside the cab sizzled. He gripped the wheel harder. "What the hell does that mean? Two minutes of what?"

"Two minutes of your time before you start that lovely jazz blasting out the speakers." She shot him a knowing smile. "You can even clock me on your fancy watch."

"What? Why? You mean now?" He frowned at his left wrist.

"Park first."

"Fine. We need gas anyway." Signaling, he turned into a station. He nosed alongside a pump, turned off the engine, and got the fill-up started.

Shuffling his feet, he glanced at the hood. Could he get away with checking the oil first? Maybe she'd give up. He picked at a worn spot on his jeans. Those two minutes would turn into twenty and hurt like hell's worst torture.

He rubbed both hands along the outside of his thighs and climbed back in the cab. "Okay. Shoot."

"Nope. Set your watch first." Her eyes twinkled.

His heart did a flip-flop, and he ignored the surge in his dick. When had he turned into a masochist? But he fiddled with his watch and glanced over at her again, frowning. "Say your piece."

She held his gaze, her big brown eyes liquid with emotion. "I'm sorry. I truly respect your calling as a cop. I never meant to hurt you last night." She dropped her chin and let out a brief sigh. "No. That's not true. I guess I did want to strike back just for a moment. I felt hurt, but mostly half-dead with embarrassment."

One eyebrow shot up. "Okay." Admitting part of the problem had been her fault?

"I told you a little bit about my gifts. Choosing to give them up would represent a huge sacrifice for me. I have a unique calling to help people, too. I counted last night and sixteen people are alive today because I twisted time and reversed their deaths."

"Okay," Jackson repeated, his mind spinning. He closed his gaping mouth. "How…no, never mind. Details don't matter. I don't understand the connection to last night."

"What I haven't told you is that my gifts are dependent on me remaining a maiden, remaining untouched."

His frown had returned, and the muscles around his mouth screwed tighter than ever. "Not sure I follow, so do me a favor. Spell it out."

She took a deep breath. Her face glowed fiery red all the way up her neck to the tips of her ears. "I'm a virgin, Jackson." Her words rushed out in a torrent. "I'll lose my gifts if I lose my virginity."

His heart squeezed into his throat. He sat bolt upright. "You're a what?"

She gulped but kept her gaze firmly on his. "I'm a thirty-one year old virgin. I'm mortified you had to ask me if I was sure what I wanted before I put a stop to what—what happened last night. I feel like the worst sort of imbecile for leading you on."

"Oh, man." His head took a twisting roller coaster ride through space, and he looked away, grabbing the steering wheel for balance.

"You   had   every   right   to   believe   I

was…um…willing. I didn't mean to insult you. In fact…" She hesitated again, and he glanced in her direction.

With her fingers twisted together, she stared at her knees. "You're the only man who ever even tempted me, the only man"—she buried her face in her hands, and her words whispered through her fingers—"the only man who ever did more than kiss my cheek."

His jaw hung open. Completely blindsided, he blew out a loud breath and rubbed his hand over his mouth. His Adam's apple bobbed a couple times, but he couldn't come up with enough spit to swallow. He'd never imagined anything she might say could possibly make a difference, at least not in the plus column.

What a kick in the pants. His watch beeped, and he punched the off button. Then he reached over and stroked her hair, fighting to keep a stupid grin off his face. "I'm sorry, too. Sorry I wouldn't listen earlier."

"You couldn't know." She peeked up at him.

When their eyes met, all his protective instincts grabbed him by the throat, and his body reacted with fierce, possessive need. Primitive impulses roared through him, shaking him to his core. "If I'd listened, I would have."

"But—"

Spit it out, buddy. "Nope, my turn. You knew I was married before."

At her nod, he cleared the choke in his throat and continued. "My ex-wife Alicia was a lawyer, from a long, blue-blooded family line. She…I was fine as a boy toy in college. Married me to flip off her folks, I think. Even convinced me to take the law board exams. Top scores, but I went to the academy instead. Things between us got ugly, fast."

"And I said exactly the wrong things."

He tipped her chin up gently. "Think I hit you with some of my leftover baggage last night."

Her eyes were focused firmly on her hands. "I understand. There aren't many virgins my age."

"Not many as gorgeous as you, anyway."

Norah blushed again.

He clenched his own hands around the wheel to keep from reaching out and touching her. *Focus on the facts, buddy, and forget your aching dick.* "So what did you mean, you reversed a murder? That what happened with the captain?"

"Yes. Nate and another Sereno PD cop, Mike Gordon, would both have died many years ago without me. Actually they did die."

His eyes widened and a squadron of cold prickles marched down his spine. "Nope. No more. You just scared the snot out of me. Too much for my poor old just-the-facts-ma'am brain to handle."

He shifted in his seat to ease the pressure and clamped his mouth shut. As if imagining sex with a virgin didn't terrify him enough, he imagined it about every time he let his filthy mind wander.

But maybe they had some options. He understood virgin, but how technical were they talking about? Had she ever asked her grandfather the details? Jackson cranked the ignition. Exactly what did untouched mean?

Chapter Ten

"Why starve yourself?" Jackson's stomach growled like a grizzly at spring thaw. He swung the car around another hairpin turn and downshifted to climb the last grade into Jerome.

"I won't. I have an energy bar in my suitcase." Norah's eyes were squeezed shut, her fists curled around the armrest, her knuckles white. Her face looked pale, with a faint greenish twinge. She moaned. "Oh. I can't even think about food."

"Then keep me company." He turned the car onto a gravel road and followed the switchbacks through Jerome. On the downhill side, the sign for the House of Joy creaked in the wind. He ignored the odd twisting ache in his chest. No joy for him tonight. Didn't matter. One night with her would never be enough, not even close.

He cleared his throat. "No lights on in the tattoo parlor. Curtains upstairs are still drawn."

"That's our only concrete lead." She moaned again, but one eye opened a crack. "Can you see any signs of the stake-out?"

"Nope, but I wouldn't expect to. Deputy will be holed up around back so he doesn't scare off the Swanks."

She sat up straighter and peered out the window. "I'm worried. The Magician said Josh's mind was beyond reach, in a deep fog."

"Probably drugged."

"But why kidnap him and keep him dead to the world?"

"Self preservation?" He shrugged. "Might be why we haven't found any witnesses."

"But drugs are dangerous to kids." She rubbed little circles over her temples. "I can't stand feeling so helpless."

"The sheriff will have something for us tomorrow morning." Tonight he needed to blow off some steam, have a little fun with other people around. Normal people. Postpone the long, sleepless night alone with Norah and his aching dick.

He glanced at her again. Her shoulders had relaxed a little, and she had some pink in her cheeks. He wanted to pull her onto his lap and smooth the tiny creases between her brows with kisses. Move his hands all over her luscious body…

Nope. Down boy. Lust but don't touch.

No question. Tonight he needed a distraction. People and food, and maybe some music.

When he parked the car facing out over the cliff edge and stomped on the emergency brake, she gave a long sigh and shook the blood back into her hands.

"Want to walk around first? Get a little fresh air? Not sure you can handle food smells right now."

"I'll be okay once I get solid ground under my feet." She squinted to read the neon sign across the road. "The Haunted Hamburger?"

"Spooky. You'll fit right in." And maybe you're not the only one, he added silently, twisting his lips into a wry smile. Seeing ghosts explained a bunch of his weird early experiences.

"So far you've dragged me to a Teepee, an Asylum, and now a Haunting?"

His grin widened. "Live jazz tonight. Wood says all the local characters join in." He trotted around to help her out of the car. The barest touch of her strong, soft fingers ramped the pulse in his groin. He settled his palm on the back of her waist.

Gloppy weathered paint, decades thick, covered the wooden siding of the old frame structure. The building was square and squat, but a lighted, covered deck curled around one side and hung out over the steep slope. Laughter and the low roar of conversation filtered out the windows.

The brisk wind cooled his face and tossed her hair around. Guiding Norah up the steep incline, Jackson drew a deep breath of the chilly night air. Rich scents of grilled meat layered with caramelized onions and roasted garlic hit his nostrils and lit up his taste buds. Sharp, dark chocolate and the bite of jalapenos wafted out the wooden screen door.

They'd found a treasure.

Kitschy place. Clean but worn, from the bare floorboards to the rounded corners on the white appliances. Looked like nothing had changed since the fifties. Most of the gray and chrome Formica tables held people lingering over coffee or drinks or dessert.

Norah stopped in front of an enameled refrigerator case. "Ooh. Chocolate, chocolate everywhere and every bite for me."

He chuckled. "Bet that energy bar sounds kinda like cardboard now."

"Welcome to the Haunted Hamburger." A muscled

blond dude with a close-cropped moustache smiled brightly from behind the cash register. The waiter raised one eyebrow and stroked his chin as his gaze lingered on Jackson's zipper. "Outside okay, big guy? I have a table on the deck."

Resisting an urge to adjust the bulge from his half-staff, Jackson drew Norah closer. "Great. Just the two of us for dinner."

With one hand cocked on his hip and a pronounced swish in his step, the waiter led them to a small table and pointed out the specials. Jackson chose a double-decker with extra fries and coaxed Norah into ordering a grilled chicken salad before her dessert sampler.

After the waiter sauntered back toward the kitchen, Norah wrapped her jacket closer and wandered to the corner of the squeaky deck. She leaned over the banister long enough for him to admire the shape of her beautiful ass.

In a split second, he hardened painfully. Hunger pulsed through him. Hunger to claim her. Hunger to bury himself deep inside her moist, silken heat and feel her intimate muscles clench around him.

He'd start slow the first time. Gentle and patient. Kiss her, touch her, tease her until she came apart for him again and again, calling his name.

He swallowed hard. Face facts, Marino. Never would be a first time. Not unless technical virginity was good enough.

She scooted away from the rail and turned toward him, her brows puckered. "This whole place is built on stilts and gravel. It gives me the creeps."

"Relax. Arizona's not earthquake country." No need to mention the hollow, mined-out mountain beneath them. He eased back and wrenched his gaze away from the view of Norah's curvy shape. Beyond the twinkle lights on the deck, night had captured the desert. Moon wasn't quite full, but flickers of lightning, silent from this distance, flashed among the storm clouds that lay siege to the wide valley below.

Tipping back his chair, he grinned and crossed his legs at the ankle. He'd been careful not to spook her on the drive from Verde Valley. But like a kid who'd been warned away from the tall, frosted birthday cake on the kitchen counter, he craved another touch, however innocent. Just one little taste of that sweet icing, licked off her lush, moist lips.

He moved beside her and traced the curve of her throat with one finger. Soft. Warm. Smooth. "You have the most beautiful skin."

She squeezed her eyes shut, but smiled wistfully. "I can't tell you how much I wish things could be different between us."

He slipped one hand under her jacket and around her waist, but resisted nuzzling the top of her head. Tiny shivers coursed through her, and he smiled despite the throbbing ache in his groin.

Before Jackson could kiss her, the waiter swooshed toward them with a tray. "Order's up, you two."

As they returned to their table, Norah pointed to the five-piece band crowded into one corner inside. The bass player began tuning his instrument. "Looks like we get a serenade with dinner."

"Blues night. The best around," the waiter crowed. "We'll have this place jammed in an hour."

"What do you play?" Jackson asked.

"Just about every kind of game, big boy. Whatcha

offering?" The waiter gave him a salacious grin, and Norah chuckled.

"Uh, I…uh…" His cheeks burned despite the cool night air. Must have turned bright red.

Norah took his hand. "He's spoken for tonight."

With a quick, good-humored pout, the waiter served her a massive salad. "I'll check between sets to see if you need anything else." Untying his apron with a flourish meant for Broadway, the waiter presented his card.

She picked it up and giggled. "Thanks, but we're tourists."

"I can fix almost anything." With a wink, the man scooted behind the drum set and struck up a beat.

"You have to see this." Norah handed over a business card with a cartoon of their waiter wearing work boots and a tutu.

Jackson chuckled. "Even a Tinkerbell wand."

"But calling himself the Fixit Fairy?"

"Bet you'll remember him next time your faucet leaks." Jackson closed his eyes and absorbed the sounds. Mellow jazz floated out over the valley. He let the music flow through his body and soothe his nerves, ease the ache in his primed-to-shoot-fireworks dick.

****

The dessert sampler they'd shared was a killer. Norah sighed over the last bite of white chocolate mousse. She'd spend some tough hours on the elliptical to work off this meal. But she'd enjoyed the music and Jackson's quiet company almost as much as the food. Studying him, she took another bite of mocha cheesecake and savored the rich texture in her mouth.

After he'd finished dinner and about half of her

dessert, Jackson had focused on the band. He boogied in his seat and clapped vigorously at the end of each song. His full lips curved in a smile, and his dark gray eyes sparkled beneath thick lashes. He glanced at her and winked.

Her body hummed, and her cheeks burned. She reached for a homemade truffle and took a sip of rich ruby port.

But liquid heat pulsed under her skin and pooled deep and low in her body. She shifted in her chair. How could resisting him be so hard? She'd practiced her role for so many years, a totally oblivious, cold-as-the-arctic professional virgin.

He raised his thumb and finger to his mouth and whistled appreciatively. But all she could think about was his talented hands and his lips on her body last night. Her breasts hardened and ached . She closed her eyes and willed away the trembling little twinges between her thighs.

During a short break, she looked closely at him. A faint frown line had appeared between his eyebrows. "I've heard you on the oboe. And I saw an electric guitar at your apartment? What all do you play?"

Jackson shrugged. "Pretty much anything with strings or reeds."

"Several people have gone up and jammed with the band."

He glanced longingly toward the musicians.

"Go on. Can't hurt to ask." She waved with a challenging grin.

"You don't mind?"

"I'll listen."

He shrugged and walked to the front. After a quick

conversation, their waiter clapped Jackson on the back and handed him a sax.

Jackson tested the instrument with a quick scale. When the crowd cheered, he suggested a tune, and the drummer meted out the beat.

About sixty seconds into the first song, Norah had to pick her jaw up off the floor. Jackson had thrown himself into the music with a quick riff. One long low note vibrated down her spine and sent all her nerves tingling. Her breath caught. Slow heat swirled through her body and touched her soul, like he played just for her.

He was more than good. But why did that surprise her? He was amazing at everything he did. He was a damn good cop and last night—No. No. No.

She stared at her hands. No matter what her greedy body wanted, her gifts were more important. She needed to stand firm. Rely on her training. But why did her insides feel so hollow?

A long crescendo on the sax wailed toward her, just her, and her toes curled. Everything inside her trembled and arousal flared. A deep well of longing and recognition sent impossible fantasies whirling around her brain. She stifled the low, needy cry that rose in her throat.

The song concluded in a smash of cymbals. She looked up. Her gaze met his, and Jackson smiled at her. Her heart did an impossible triple twisting dive. Damn.

He took a quick bow to the appreciative crowd and, laughing, pulled her to her feet for a quick kiss.

Norah blushed at the catcalls. "That was incredible."

"You haven't seen anything yet."

****

Cold shower? No, her hands and feet were already frigid, but that didn't seem to faze the burning private parts in between. Norah clicked open the glass door and twisted the taps. A long hot shower would not only warm her numb toes, but might help lull her hormone-overloaded imagination.

She tested the water temperature. Good. Maybe tonight she could keep her dignity intact even though she'd be sleeping in the same room with that gorgeous man.

She sighed. Her self-control hung by a filament of spider silk. There'd been something mesmerizing about Jackson's mouth on the reeds of the saxophone, hearing him play his sultry, seductive music. A certain illogical, damp-and-pulsing part of her still wanted his mouth and hands all over her body, coaxing those sounds from her.

The wailing melody he'd played affected her like he'd played a love song for her alone, almost like the ancient courtship ritual. The sensations had captured her soul and awakened dangerous, hidden parts of her treacherous body.

Stories she'd heard told around an open fire flitted through her memory. A maiden hearing a hunter's flute echo in the night would recognize him as her own from the melody.

But her heritage wasn't Jackson's. He knew nothing of traditional Lakota courtship. To him, the sax just made beautiful soul-stirring music.

She tucked her hair into a shower cap, unwrapped a fresh bar of the fancy herb-scented soap and stepped into the steamy glass stall. The stinging droplets bounced off her shoulders and torso, drawing blood toward the chilly surface of her skin. She turned her back and stood on top of the drain, letting the spray flow over her body and puddle into warm pools around her icy toes.

After a few minutes, she braced her back against the wall, and massaged first one foot and then the other under the hot spray. Finally, she felt thoroughly warm.

She soaped a washcloth, lathering her legs and massaging as she went, dissolving the kinks in those muscles. She moved up her body, enjoying the gentle, invigorating rasp of the terrycloth when she scrubbed her hips and thighs. She spread suds between her fingers and up her arms to her shoulders before washing her neck and chin.

Turning her back on the hot spray again, she worked the rough cloth under and then across her breasts. Remembering Jackson's crisp, curly chest hairs brushing against her nipples, she shivered, despite the heat. Her hand stilled. His long warm fingers and hot moist mouth had teased them until they were stiff. She brushed one palm over the sensitive, aching peaks. Pleasure arrowed straight to the damp throb between her thighs, and she bit her lip.

A wave of heat rose on her cheeks. She scrubbed her belly, determined to stay all business. But when she moved the washcloth lower, her breath hitched. With a harsh gasp, she dropped the cloth.

Her sex felt tender, almost swollen. Norah touched herself gingerly with her fingers. Hot need seared through her. She jerked her hand away, and clenched her legs together with a shudder. No. This was all physical. Only her body wanted Jackson, but it craved him so desperately she ached.

She straightened her spine and stuck her face under the showerhead. She was a maiden, a seer. Wasn't her current discomfort appropriate punishment for what she'd almost done last night? She forced a chuckle. Good grief. Her actions had been completely wrong. She had no intention of repeating the same mistake tonight.

She set her teeth and imagined the shower flushing sexual needs, even sexual awareness right out of her. She cranked the hot water tap fully open and closed her eyes, visualizing a sweat lodge. The steam would purify her mind and body and give her the strength to resist Jackson.

No, the strength to resist herself.

She drew in a deep breath of the herbal steam and tried to separate out the various natural scents in the soap. Lavender. Tangy sage formed the top note, layered above new mown hay or some other sweet grass. But what else? Rosemary? Lobelia? Surely not natural tobacco.

Her eyes snapped open. The glassed in shower and the elegant, high ceiling bathroom had evaporated. Instead, the rough log walls and dirt floor of Grandfather's lodge contained fragrant steam.

But what did she have on? She'd never appeared this way before in a vision. She wore a pale, fringed and beaded buckskin dress. She ran her hands down her hips and thighs. The skirt was supple, and the beautiful leggings felt soft as butter.

She sank onto the ground before the round fire pit, relieved to see only Grandfather facing her. He raised his chin and watched her silently with his own piercing black-brown eyes, not the strange, topaz eyes of the

Magician.

Her cheeks heated. Could Grandfather see her lurid, inner thoughts? Read the forbidden desires that lingered despite her best efforts to banish them? Hoping to distract him, she broke the silence. "Why have you called me?"

He frowned, his bushy white brows bristling, and waved his hands in front of him. "You ask as if you did not know, child. Your old path has closed off. Vanished."

A hard, guilty knot formed in the pit of her stomach. "What? Grandfather, what do you mean? I haven't found Joshua yet, and he's in grave danger. Surely you can't want us to break off the search when we're so close."

He shook his head, his white braids swaying. "Of course not, but if you wish to rescue the boy, you and your hunter must walk the new path that has opened for you."

"My new path?"

He threw his head back and laughed. "Is this not always the manner of maidens? Your grandmother blushed and stammered in the same fashion when she finally realized her hour had come."

Norah's mouth gaped. Surely, he couldn't mean what she suspected.

Grandfather smiled indulgently. "Yes, child. You finally understood when he played again tonight. You felt his music. Your deepest senses recognized the hunter as your true mate."

She sat straighter, spreading her open hands palm up on her knees. "But...but I was born to remain a maiden, a shaman. Always." She heard the plea in her voice. "I was born to see the wrinkles in innocent lives. Born with the gift to warp time and heal those lives."

His grin broadened. "My child, you were also born to bear the next generation of gifts to the Buffalo People. Your children will carry talents that will heal our people and our land."

She sputtered. "Surely not. At least not yet."

"It was too late when you first heard him play outside the tent."

Her heart tripped in her chest. She stared at him, first with shock and then with growing wonder. She looked down at her clothing again and slapped her palm to her forehead. She was dressed as a bride. "Is that why I couldn't twist time?"

"Yes. Women have always sacrificed to bear children for our people, as you shall." Grandfather lifted his hand and disappeared.

The vision shattered, and Norah snapped back to the shower stall, shivering in the tepid stream of water.

She climbed out of the shower and dried herself carefully with the fluffy bath sheet. She quickly braided her hair. What if Grandfather was right? It would explain why she couldn't go back in time. Couldn't change what she had done when she'd first seen Josh and that creep, Swank. Couldn't chase Jackson from her mind.

She exhaled and froze, reaching for solid earth far below and the uncanny awareness deep inside her. Grandfather's words felt right. A part of her had recognized Jackson, even in the crazy disguise he'd worn. His warm smile had shone through and pierced her awareness. And his music had always stirred something hot and primitive no other man could ever touch.

Her cheeks flamed. With jerky movements, she hung her towel on the heated rack and reached for her ivory silk pajamas. For a moment, she held them between her trembling hands. Then she let the slippery fabric slide back onto the chair. No. She would go to him like White Buffalo Calf Woman who challenged the hunters, wearing only her own skin. And she'd face him now, before her courage deserted her.

With her pulse racing like a doe in flight, she reached for the door and opened it. She peered at Jackson, her heart in her throat.

He sat up in bed, leaning toward the small reading lamp, apparently engrossed in the latest thriller. "My turn yet? Or did you use up all the hot water?"

She stepped through the door, grinning. "Yes, you could say it's your turn."

When he looked up, his eyes bugged out. His book fell from limp fingers. With a deep groan that seemed to come from his soul, he jumped to his feet and grabbed the quilt off his bed, holding it in front of him. He draped it around her, wrapped her in its folds and hustled her back into the bathroom. "I know you're innocent, but you're not stupid. You're torturing me here, Norah."

She worked one arm free, stuck it out and held the door open, meeting his eyes. "I know exactly what I'm doing. I want to make love with you. Now."

He scrubbed his hands across his mouth and scanned her face. "Norah, sweetheart, maybe you think you do right now. God knows I want you so much I'm shaking. But less than six hours ago, you explained your gifts to me. I can't take that away from you. Away from the world."

How much of what Grandfather had said could she tell Jackson? Would he understand? Or recoil? She should probably keep it simple, but if she took the time to find the words to explain, she'd chicken out. "Don't worry. Everything will be fine." She leaned forward, dropping the quilt and kissed his chin. When her breasts brushed his shirt, a tendril of flame sprouted within her.

His breath whooshed out. He set his warm hands on her shoulders, holding her away from him and lifted his gaze to the ceiling. "No, Norah. You're thinking crazy. It must be the glass of port talking. Damn. Guess I have to save you from yourself again tonight." He gathered the quilt, lifted her, and carried her toward her bed.

She curled her arms around his neck, snuggling against his chest and was rewarded when his whole body shuddered. He smelled so good. Warm and manly with a hint of his own musk. Familiar. Hers.

When he placed her gently on top of the bed, she let the quilt fall away and drew his face toward hers. "At least kiss me goodnight. You can manage just one little kiss."

His mouth inched toward hers, but his neck muscles were taut as steel cables, resisting all the way. "I don't know if I can kiss you once and stop."

"Try, Jackson." She moistened her mouth, looking at him through half-closed lids. "Please."

He blinked three times and kissed her gently.

She snaked out her tongue and brushed his mouth, and he threaded his fingers into her hair, deepening the kiss. Holding her head still with his strong hands, he ravished her mouth.

Warmth spread from her lips through her body and pooled low in her abdomen.

With a deep groan, he moved, trapping her beneath him.

Her body softened and dampened, giving way under his indescribably exciting weight. She shifted so she cradled him between her legs, and his rigid length pressed against her. The warmth ignited into a raging storm. A heady sense of rightness and triumph filled her.

He kissed her cheeks, her eyelids, her jaw line. His tongue traced the rim of her ear.

She murmured his name. His mouth shifted to her neck, and his hands cupped her breasts. He touched her lightly, skimming his hands over her sensitive nipples.

She drew her fingers through his hair and over his broad shoulders, tracing his spine with her nails.

Suddenly, he stilled. Pulling the quilt back up, he pressed a finger to her lips. "Norah, sweetheart, I can't do this to you."

"With me."

"Okay, with you. I'm pretty sure hot and heavy sex wouldn't qualify for one of your time warping re-dos." He shushed her protest with another quick kiss. "After we have this case all wrapped up and Josh is safe, if you still want—"

"I will."

"If you still want sex in the stone cold sober light of day, I'll take you someplace where we don't have to put on our clothes for a month."

"Sounds like heaven. But can't we start tonight?" She wriggled and made a frustrated noise. "I'm kind of itchy and hot and wet in strange places. Aching. Empty.

I'm not sure what I need. Please, Jackson, teach me?"

He scrunched his eyes shut for a minute, motionless. Then he kissed her again and slowly peeled down the quilt.

Her pulse raced, and her skin heated. Norah felt exposed, like he saw her every flaw. Too much hip. The puckered scar on her side. The nest of curls between her thighs. Shyness battled her growing awareness and arousal. She crossed her legs and moved her arm over her breasts.

He caught her fingers in his and pressed a kiss to her palm.

"I-I'm past thirty. No one has ever seen me or touched me. I know—"

"You're beautiful. Now relax. I'm going to kiss you."

He did, paying homage to her neck and collarbones before settling on her breasts for long minutes.

Norah's head tipped back over his arm, arching toward his mouth. She felt antsy and squirmy inside. The warm emptiness between her thighs ached for him, and she lifted her hips. "Jackson, I want you inside me."

"Not yet." He smiled and traced her belly button with his tongue. His hand found the neediest spot and touched her gently.

Fire sliced through her, and she strained closer to his fingers with a gasp. "Please. Make love with me."

He scooted lower. Then he did magical, unthinkable things to her with his mouth and fingers.

Delicious tension coiled inside her. Instinctively, she sought something unknown with her whole body.

"Give in, Norah. Let yourself go." He slipped a

finger inside her while his mouth closed over her pulsing bud.

Wave after wave of white-hot pleasure burst through her. She screamed his name and reached down for him, desperate to draw him over her. Desperate to have him inside her. Desperate to discover more about this bliss.

But his mouth and fingers kept up the pressure. The tension rebuilt and intensified. Colors flashed and melted away. She couldn't find air, as the waves of pleasure broke over her again.

When he finally moved, he pulled the quilt up between them and held her close with her head tucked against his chest.

Chapter Eleven

Josh opened his eyes, and the bright fluorescent bulb over the sink seemed to bore a hole straight through his brain. His ears buzzed, and his head throbbed. He was alone in the camper, breathing stale, stuffy air, and his damp T-shirt stank from sweat.

He stretched his stiff muscles slowly. His joints ached like he'd spent days frozen in one position on the hard floor. And he was so thirsty. He closed his cracked lips and sucked on his tongue, but couldn't find any spit.

When he reached for the half bottle of water on the counter, his head swam, and his empty stomach convulsed in dry heaves. Groaning, he curled into a ball with his arms clenched around his aching belly and stared at the ceiling until his vision stopped swimming.

He rolled onto his knees and crawled toward the sink. Hanging on to the edge of the table, he pulled himself up and lurched for the water. A couple long gulps emptied the bottle, and his throat felt better.

He switched off the too-bright light and refilled the bottle from the tap. Leaning his elbows on the counter, he peered out the tiny kitchen window while he took another drink. Yeah, they were in that same stupid Casino parking lot.

A shiver rippled through him. Where was Aunt Gina? Had she lied again?

His heart stumbled. He groped under his shirt and pulled out the necklace, fingering the carved cat. At least she hadn't taken this away. Quiet warmth seeped back into his body. He sank onto the bench, curled up and rested his chin on his knees. His visions of the Magician seemed more like a dream, all jumbled and distorted.

His stomach growled, and the warm water sloshed around his empty insides. When did he eat last? Still queasy, he remembered drinking part of that crummy chocolate shake, but did he actually eat the tacos? He brushed his damp hair out of his eyes. Had that been a few hours ago? Or days? How long had he slept?

He'd already dug through most of the cupboards and eaten the last of the stale crackers. Even the crumbs. He scrambled over one of the boxes blocking the narrow walkway and peered out the back door. No sign of his uncle or of Aunt Gina. He rattled the knob. Still locked from the outside.

He scraped his fingers over his mouth. A crumpled fast food bag stuck out of the trashcan. His heart beat faster. If he hadn't finished his dinner, there might be leftovers.

With a grimace, he shoved aside the shake cup and pawed through the garbage. He found the squished end of a taco and a couple limp fries. A week ago he wouldn't have even touched them, but now, who cared? He stuffed the food in his mouth and tried to make even the soggy, wilted lettuce last as long as possible.

He licked the grease off the wax paper and dug deeper. Nothing else but gooey tissues in the bottom. The salt had made him thirsty again so he drank more water. But his stomach still gnawed on itself.

In his whole life, he'd never felt this hungry. His insides hurt. Chewing on his fingernail, he glanced around the camper. He hadn't looked in the drawer under the table yet. Maybe he'd find food hidden there. He got down on his knees under the table and dug around behind the empty beer bottles and soda cans. He licked his lips and grabbed a white take-out carton. Cookies?

The box rattled. His breath hitched, and he sat back on his heels. Biting his lip, he opened the lid and three used insulin syringes fell onto the floor. His heart tumbled, and horror gripped his stomach..

They looked exactly like his mom's, but she would never leave the needles attached. She always broke them off into the sharps container. Who'd hidden them in the camper? And why? Something was very wrong.

Carefully, he rolled a syringe back and forth across his palm. He closed his eyes and curled his fingers around the empty tube.

Evil impressions sucker-punched the breath from his body.

Uncle Kenny's face crystallized in his mind, polluted by a terrible blackness. The horrible image swamped his senses.

Josh shivered but let the vision focus.

Uncle Kenny had the syringe in one hand. He held Mom's wrists in the other. He planted his knee on her stomach. Duct tape covered her mouth.

She struggled against his grip. Her eyes were wide and showed white all around.

Josh's heart burned inside his chest, and he wanted to shout for help, but stuck in the vision, he couldn't speak. He could only watch like a spider on the movie screen at a real life horror film.

Mom clawed Kenny's hands. He cursed her.

She thrashed in her bed and fought his hold. But Kenny was so much bigger. And his muscles bulged.

He pushed one injection into her neck. Then a second.

Tears streamed down her face. Her back arched off the bed. Her whole body shuddered.

She went still, hardly breathing.

Her eyelids fluttered shut.

Kenny sat on the bed next to her. He waited, seemed to listen.

He ripped off the duct tape gag.

Her eyelids fluttered open.

She screamed a silent scream.

Kenny laughed and waved the third syringe. "One more in a minute, just to be sure. But first some entertainment from Miss Goody-Goody."

Pain ripped Josh. He needed to barf, but he swallowed the bitterness at the back on his throat.

Bastard.

He'd killed her.

Uncle Kenny had killed Mom.

Hatred poured through Josh. Cold, then hot. Acid burned his raw nerves.

He grabbed the edge on the table to keep his balance and bit his lip until he tasted blood. Somehow he'd make that bastard pay.

But before he could harness his rage and make a real plan, loud footsteps clomped across the parking lot gravel outside. Uncle Kenny's laugh rang out.

With his pulse racing, Josh shielded his mind. He hesitated for only a second before stuffing the empty insulin box and syringes under the bench.

Wrapping the quilt around him, he pretended to be asleep but grabbed the necklace on his chest. A burst of courage flowed into him.

Uncle Kenny flung the back door open, stomped inside and prodded Josh with the tip of his shoe. "Wake up, kid."

Josh smelled bourbon and cigars on the murderer's filthy breath. Rubbing his eyes, he sat up slowly. He could play dumb. "Hi. Where's Aunt Gina?"

"Inside."

"Can we eat soon?"

"Sure, kid. But we got a job to do first. Do it right, and I'll buy you a couple burgers." Uncle Kenny's eyes shifted from side to side.

Josh frowned and clenched his teeth. Liar. "What kind of job?"

Uncle Kenny sneered. "One that pays good."

****

"Man, I could use a smoke." Kenny yanked Josh through the Casino doors into a noisy lobby. He hurried past the banging and clanging slot machines.

"Would ya move your butt, runt? We're late. Vince isn't a dude you wanna keep waiting."

Josh kicked at his shins. "Stop hurting me! Help! Make him leave me alone!"

Heads turned.

"Help me!"

Kenny curled his hand around the runt's throat, picked him up, and glared at him. "Don't cause no trouble, or I'll bust your bony ass."

Gasping for breath, Josh nodded.

One skinny, white-haired woman ground out her

cigarette and prodded the geezer sitting next to her.

Josh's legs twisted in the breeze, and his face turned a darker red, but he narrowed his eyes and glared back.

"But first I'll bust your sweet Auntie Gina's face," Kenny added, his tone singsong and gloating. "One more trick, and I'll fuck both your asses."

When Josh cringed, Kenny laughed softly and dropped the runt on his feet, but kept a vice-like hold on his neck. Turning, he gave Ma and Pa Sucker an aw-shucks grin. "Sorry. My kid's acting up. Way past his bedtime."

Ma Sucker whispered loudly and poked at her husband, but he blew her off and turned back to his nickel machine.

"Come on Josh. Let's hit the sack." He gave the marks a friendly wave and headed for the elevators.

On the second floor, Kenny stopped outside the manager's office. "No more warnings. If you don't perform, you'll hurt so bad you'll wanna die." He banged on the door, and it opened.

A bodyguard in a too tight, too shiny sharkskin suit over a black polo and shoulder holster waved them inside. "Wait here."

As soon as the hulk disappeared through another door, Kenny lit a cigarette. His hands twitched, but he sucked hard and swallowed the nicotine, letting the smoke billow out his nostrils.

He peeked through the half-open door to the inner office and strengthened his hold on the runt. His heart beat faster, and he drew on the cigarette again. What a stash. Shelf after shelf of old Indian crap. Pots, jewelry. Big, mother fucking baskets. Jagged hunks of rock decorated with petroglyphs hung on the walls. How fucking much money could he make if he hawked old junk like that? Shit. Had to be pricey. Knowing Vince, very pricey.

He lit another smoke from the butt of the first. Dealing with whiny kids and spooky scams made him puke. A few nights in the desert with a pick ax, and he'd earn more than that skinny runt could make him in a month. And sweet, stupid Gina could show him the prime locations.

He crossed his arms and rested against a cabinet in the corner, staring across the room at the red headed bitch in the short skirt. Killer legs. Boob job. Collagen lips. But she looked like she could suck the gray off an elephant's prick and smile while she swallowed.

****

Josh shrank away from Uncle Kenny's painful grip. Bright lights, loud voices, noisy phones. The business office buzzed with activity, and the noise made his sore head pound harder.

The outer door was shut, and no one here would believe him if he asked for help. The stupid lady at the desk was making goo-goo eyes at Uncle Kenny. Josh turned around and stared at the wall with his hands in his pockets, rocking from heel to toe. He had to figure out how he'd make the bastard pay.

"Would ya sit down? You're making me nervous." Kenny squeezed the back of his neck again.

Ignoring the order, Josh glared up at him.

"Jesus. Stop staring at me, or I'll cream you right here."

The bodyguard leaned around the door. "Mr. Smith will see you now." He turned toward the receptionist.

"Natalie, why don't ya call it a night?"

After putting out his cigarette, Uncle Kenny shoved Josh into the quiet inner office. Puffing out his chest, he grinned. "Man, check this place out."

The bodyguard signaled them forward, toward a man with curly, reddish-blond hair. He stood behind a huge desk, twisting his diamond pinkie ring while his gaze tracked them across the room. "This the kid, Swank?"

Kenny gave an appreciative nod and glanced around. "You got some real nice stuff."

Vince Smith smiled proudly, showing bright white teeth. "Harvested those myself." He pointed toward the petroglyphs on the wall. "They can't guard all the sites all the time."

Kenny let out a low whistle. "Impressive." He cleared his throat. "Which piece you want Josh to touch?"

Vince took a key from his pocket and unlocked a safe in the wall. He crooked his head, and the bodyguard carefully took out a small basket and placed it on the desk.

Josh frowned. Why did they act like the piece was dangerous?

Stepping away from the desk, Vince drew a hand over his ear lobe. Sharp lines etched his tanned forehead and framed his mouth.

"Remember what I said," Kenny hissed and pushed him closer.

Vince shifted his weight from foot to foot, and Josh hesitated, his gaze fixed on his beat-up tennis shoes. Even from here he could feel the power radiating from the seed basket. The snakes woven around the rim seemed to slither.

"Go ahead, kid. That thing won't bite cha," Kenny growled and pinched his ear. "But I might."

Josh's empty stomach cramped.

Vince rubbed his chin and chuckled nervously. "That's one creepy basket. Ever since I bought the damn thing, I've had these dreams where someone's watching me. Someone with the weirdest colored eyes. That's why I wanted the kid to check it out."

Kenny's face split into a wide, self-satisfied grin. "Sure. Two grand, cash and the IOU you're holding."

Josh kept his focus on the thick, white carpet while the money changed hands. He'd only caught a glimpse of the blond man, but Vince was afraid. His pale, watery blue eyes were wide and looked weird with his dark, orangey skin. He kept jittering in place like he had to pee.

Next to Vince, the bodyguard waited with crossed arms. Buried in his wide face, his squinty black eyes never stopped moving.

Uncle Kenny shoved him again, and Josh stumbled closer to the basket. The room tilted. He grabbed for the edge of the desk. He closed his eyes and tried to swallow, but couldn't. Suddenly even being in the office suffocated him.

A haunting flute whispered in his head.

Stolen grave goods.

Magical tools.

Holy relics.

He hadn't touched anything, but despair and anger roared in his mind.

The fury washed over him and sucked him under. The room howled. Desecration.

Josh shook his head. One item didn't scream with anger, a small round water pot painted with turtles. The fake sat on the far side of Vince's desk.

Avoiding the seed basket and its creepy snakes, Josh leaned over and picked up the pot. Maybe he could fool these stupid men.

When he moaned and shuddered, everyone in the room sucked in a breath. Josh closed his eyes to slits and held the pot over his head, as if in prayer. "A shaman holds this in a sacred Kiva. Even in the darkness, I can see the silver surrounding him. And the gold."

"Gold!" shouted Vince. He leaned forward, his hands splayed on his desk.

Josh moaned again, louder. "Piles of gold. A Spanish treasure."

Vince's fingers shook as he wiped a hand across his sweaty forehead. "He said gold. Where?"

Uncle Kenny shrugged, but his face glistened with sweat, too.

The Magician howled through Josh's brain. *"Murderers. Thieves."*

Gritting his teeth, Josh clenched the water pot until his hands ached.

"Where's the damned kiva?" Vince screamed.

Josh glanced at the three men and squared his shoulders. Uncle Kenny had murdered his mother. Tricked him. Lied to him. And Vince was a thief. Josh gripped the pot and smashed it against the side of the desk. "I'll never tell."

Bellowing, Kenny grabbed for him, but Josh ducked away. He turned to run, hoping he had the speed to get out the door ahead of them. But Kenny tackled him half way across the office, and they both went down hard.

Pain seared his chest. For a minute he couldn't catch his breath. When he did, he squirmed and shouted, "Let me go. I hate you."

"Who cares, runt?" Kenny laughed and boxed his ears.

Agony speared through his head.

"I want that kid," Vince shouted. His face had turned purple, and spit flew from his mouth.

"No. I won't help you." Josh struggled against Kenny's strong grip. "He killed—"

"Shut. The. Fuck—"

"My—"

"Up." Kenny clamped a hand over his mouth dragging Josh back.

Rattlers hissed from inside the seed basket. Josh bit his fingers and shouted, "Mom! He murdered my Mom!"

"Ten grand and the fucking brat is yours." Kenny threw Josh onto a chair, yanked his arm back, and twisted.

Tears stung his eyes. "Stop! My arm!"

"Do as you're told, runt, or I swear I'll rip the fucking thing outta the socket."

Suddenly the snakes and the angry voice in his mind stilled. His pulse pounded against his ears, and his shoulder screamed with pain, but Josh gulped and nodded. "Yes, sir. Yes, sir."

Kenny grabbed the basket and shoved it into his hands. "Now."

Josh closed his fingers over the relic and shuddered. He felt no pain, only calming warmth.

Kenny dragged him forward until he faced Vince's desk, then stood behind him, breathing his foul breath.

Josh closed out everything, surrounding himself with the safety of the vision. His heartbeat returned to normal. The basket was tiny, but finely made. He fingered the woven grasses gingerly.

On the inside, a decorative rattlesnake coiled up the walls of the basket, guarding corn stalks. Josh closed his eyes, and waited to see the Magician.

Light golden eyes crinkled into a smile. "Courage, my son," the Magician said to him in a gentle voice.

With his arms to his sides and his stance wide, he kept his gaze on the basket. If he looked up, Vince would know he lied. "A woman made this, long ago. It's ceremonial, used in the snake dance."

"What else do you see?" Vince's voice squeaked, but he stepped forward.

Josh shrugged. "Firelight. People. I hear drums. Then darkness. The seed basket was buried for many years until raiders stole it, white men who desecrated a shaman's grave. Now whoever claims to own it is cursed." One corner of his mouth twitched. At least that part was true.

"Do you see the golden eyes?" Vince leaned forward and tipped up Josh's chin.

When Josh met his gaze, the man dropped his hand and jerked back. A deep frown creased his face. "I want him."

"Price went up."

"How much?"

"Fifty."

"Done."

"No. You can't do this. Murderer," Josh screamed.

"Swank, shut the fucking kid up while I go get your money."

****

What a stash. The crystal meth was hot shit. Kenny buzzed out of the men's room and hurried through the noisy maze of the late night casino crowd with a bounce in his steps. He patted the fat bundles of cash in his jacket and rubbed his hands together. He'd never seen so many C-notes before. Life was fucking amazing.

Now that the damn runt was Vince's problem, Gina would drop the little mother schtick. Maybe at first he'd promise her he'd get Josh back once she got her priorities straight. But it wouldn't take long before she remembered what a fucking stud she'd married. He grinned. Yeah. Then she'd just be grateful he hadn't offed the kid.

"What a phat fucking deal." He crossed the wide lobby and waited for the elevator. Better grab her and split.

While Vince had ducked out for the dough, he'd shoved enough dope down the kid's throat to keep Josh out cold for at least twelve hours. Maybe longer. Enough time to grab the treasure and bug out before Vince realized the runt was such a spooky little shit.

The elevator bonged on the top floor, and Kenny headed along the glitzy hall to the double doors at the end. After two nights sleeping in the camper, Gina had squealed like a tortured cat when he showed her the suite.

And the cash he'd given her to blow in the Casino shops had kept her busy while he'd done the deal with Vince. He chuckled and flicked his key card across the lock.

187

Sitting crossed legged on the round bed, Gina looked up and grinned when he entered the room. "Kenny, baby, I think I figured it out."

"About time." He grabbed the diary out of her hands and flipped a few pages. "Fucking book's full of weather reports and jam recipes."

"It's not the words, baby." She pointed to the pencil sketch in the corner of one page. "It's these little pictures. They're like a map."

His heart beat faster, and the red hot flush rode over his skin. "You know where?"

"I remember this one." She pointed to the picture of a long toothed cat that looked like some stupid kid's drawing. "See, baby? It's like the necklace. And I remember where to find the petroglyph that matches."

He grabbed her arm and dragged her close. "That's right. That's what a good woman does for her man."

"Yeah. Grandma showed us the cat lots of times."

He looked out the window over the dark valley. Shit. Storm clouds covered the moon. "We gotta wait for morning to head out in the desert."

"Maybe I can keep you busy." Backing away a step, she slipped off her bathrobe.

She was wearing something new, something sexy. Strips of black leather exposed more than they covered. Metal hooks and chains crisscrossed her body. She musta noticed his expression, because she smiled and did a slow turn.

"Man, you look just like a fucking porn star." He sauntered to the door and clicked the privacy locks shut.

Gina wriggled toward him and licked his ear. "I missed you. But where's Josh, sweetie?"

Red haze blurred his vision, and his hands fisted.

Always the fucking runt. He'd have to punish her. But he faced her with a crooked smile and a wink. "Vince took a real shine to the kid. Josh wanted to hang out downstairs with Vince's boys. Probably having a blast in the game room."

"But it's kinda late."

"This way we got some time alone."

Chapter Twelve

A faint sliver of light knifed between the drapes and the windowsill, glaring into Jackson's face.

Hell. He'd fallen asleep with his arms still full of Norah. Soft, sweet, sexy Norah.

The quilt had slipped away so her warm naked ass pressed against his boxers and the rock hard ridge of his morning erection. His nose nestled in her silky, braided hair, and he drew in her gentle fragrance.

One of his hands had snaked underneath her waist, holding her spooned against him, chest, legs and groin. His other hand was splayed across her lush breast, rolling the turgid nipple between his finger and thumb.

He shifted his hand off her breast and slid away. But she sighed and burrowed backward, sending aching bolts of pleasure through him.

His whole body felt electrified and focused on his sensitized penis. He'd never been this hard before. The temptation to ease the pulsing throb became almost irresistible.

When he shifted and pressed more firmly against her, he sucked a breath in between his teeth. His dick throbbed and a drop of moisture formed on the tip. One thrust, maybe two, that's all it would take.

What if he just slipped his penis between her legs? Slid along that moist, inviting cleft? What if he reached down and massaged her clit? No need to lodge himself inside. If he touched her, she'd moan and squirm and wake screaming with pleasure, still technically a virgin.

He shuddered and couldn't restrain another twitch of his dick. Stars burst behind his eyelids.

So good. But he had to stay in control.

Why not take what he needed? He could stay in control. Pleasure both of them, but not take her virginity.

Not steal her gifts from her.

God. Could he really resist pushing inside her moist heat? No flipping way.

Not if she begged him again. Hell, not even if she just asked. Or even smiled at him. Fuck.

So how could he get out of this tangle with his honor intact?

He'd managed to ignore his body last night. But she'd been so sweetly responsive to his touch that something instinctive had twisted his insides into knots. Something primitive, but God-awful strong.

He, Jackson Marino, was the only man who'd ever touched her. The only man who'd ever coaxed those sweet, joyful sounds from her. He swallowed despite the constriction in his throat and reached out to stroke her silky hair.

Good thing she'd fallen asleep quickly. If she'd asked him one more time, he'd have buried himself deep in her slick, welcoming warmth. Virgin or not, her gifts be damned.

Man-oh-man. In a few short days, this spooky lady had made him break almost every single one of his rules. Rules that had kept him sane all these years. But somehow he'd managed to make the right choice last night. Barely.

He brushed his hand across her hip and traced the gentle curve of her belly. An image of Norah ripe and round with their child flashed through his mind. Beautiful. His breath rushed out, stirring the curls on her nape.

Nope. Don't go there, buddy. That rule was unshakable and unbreakable. The rule with a capital "R". No way would he think about forever.

A long, long time ago, he'd vowed never even to imagine sharing his life with one woman again. He'd already survived the whole legal circus once. Divorce? A freaking piece of paper she'd bought and paid for. According to the church, he still had a wife, right?

Damn. So ease off the bed, hightail it to the bathroom and take care of business. He snaked his hand out from under her and shifted his weight.

Norah turned her head. Her big brown eyes smiled at him.

His heart twisted in his chest. "Good morning."

She touched his shoulder. "Where do you think you're going? Seems to me this is the stone cold sober light of day."

"Uh, figured I'd get that shower now." He scooted to the edge of the bed and sat up. "Time to head out after Josh."

She shifted onto her back and stretched. Her muscles rippled under all that beautiful soft skin, right there, where he could watch.

"Not yet." Gently, she drew him down with her strong, siren's arms. "It's barely dawn, and we have something to finish."

At the last second, he took hold of her wrists and tried to free himself. "Sweetheart, you're still a virgin, at least technically. We should wait until we wrap up the case. Then you can decide what you want. Never know when you're going to need to use your gifts."

Smiling, she drew her soft fingers over his cheeks and rubbed the stubble on his chin. "Grandfather spoke to me last night, but I was nervous and not sure quite how to explain. He said it doesn't matter." She grinned full on. "Apparently, 'technically' doesn't impress the tribal spirits."

He sucked in a guilty breath. "So last night…"

"No, absolutely not last night. According to Grandfather, my gifts changed when I first heard you play that oboe."

He framed her face with his fingertips. "My oboe? You mean at the Harvest Festival? Bullshit. I didn't touch you. We didn't even know each other. Hardly spoke."

"True. But your music touched me. Last night when you played for me again, I knew you, right down to your beautiful, chivalrous soul."

"My what? What are you talking about?" He shook his head slowly. "Norah, that's crazy."

"Maybe so. But last night you made me feel so good, Jackson. When you touched me and kissed me…" She gave a soft, moaning shudder. "I've never felt anything like that pleasure before."

His mouth went dry, and his lips flapped a couple of times, but nothing coherent came out.

"I can only imagine what an orgasm will feel like with you inside my body, sharing my pleasure." Closing her eyes, she drew one hand across her breast and made a blissful sound.

He groaned, his mind a blank. No surprise. Not

much blood left.

"Hmm. Don't you want to teach me how wonderful making love can feel?"

He stilled for a moment and then smiled. To hell with rules. "Norah, I want you more than I've ever wanted anything or anyone." His voice sounded gruff to his own ears, but she met his hungry lips with her own.

He felt her yield, reached between her legs and found her damp and swollen and hot.

She sucked in a breath and pressed against his hand. Then she bent her knees and spread her thighs, opening herself to him.

"God, you're beautiful." He lowered his mouth and tasted the swell of her breast, circling the nipple with the tip of his tongue.

She squirmed, and her fingers twisted in his hair. "Please. Please—touch me." Her heartbeat raced, and he realized she was holding her breath, waiting.

"Shhh. No need to hurry." He took the nipple into his mouth, sucked it deep and scraped lightly with his teeth while his fingers drew delicious circles between her legs.

She jerked and trembled, strained toward him, her movements clumsy, but so damn exciting.

He touched and teased until she moved her head from side to side, making soft, sexy noises.

Working first one finger and then another inside her, he stretched her warm passage, softening her, preparing her. His thumb skimmed her nub, circled, flicked.

Her nails sank into his shoulders, and she made a high keening sound, convulsing around his fingers.

A few moments later, she blinked up at him from

the pillow, her eyes wide and fixed on his. "Please Jackson, I ache for you."

Shaking with need, he grabbed a condom from the bedside table and rolled it on. He moved over her, pushed just the tip of his penis inside and paused, gritting his teeth. She felt incredibly, unbelievably good. His balls drew up, pulsing and ready to go off like a teenager with his first woman.

Think about Josh, or Uncle Swindler. Think about Tyrell hooked up to all those machines. Think about anything except the beautiful, welcoming woman beneath him. His spooky lady only had one first time.

"Let me inside, love." Holding on by willpower alone, he covered her mouth and slowly joined their bodies.

Her body stiffened in shock, and his very last rule shattered along with her innocence.

He stroked her hair, kissing the tears of pain from her cheeks and holding very, very still while she grew used to his invasion.

When she opened her eyes again, he kissed her softly and brushed his hand across her breast, tweaking her nipple. As he gentled her and stroked her body, her taut muscles slowly relaxed.

She twisted slightly under him and ran her hands down his back with a whimpered murmur. Her fingers glided innocently over his shoulders. Her nails scraped his back. She seemed to touch him everywhere at once and set his skin on fire. She slid her hands lower to palm his butt and squeezed gently.

Rising up on his elbows, he met her gaze and began to move, slowly at first and then with greater firmness, no longer hesitating.

Moaning his name, she dug her hands into his buttocks and brought him closer, bowing her body to meet his strokes.

His pulse thundered in his ears, and his blood surged through his veins. He paused long enough to wrap her legs around his waist so he could reach even deeper.

Relentlessly, he thrust. "You're mine," he whispered against her neck.

"Yes."

He caught her mouth with his and rocked against her rhythmically until he felt the first pulse of her orgasm. He started to thrust hard and fast, slamming into her. The contractions built, and her body convulsed around him, a satiny, steely fist.

Two more all-consuming strokes, and pleasure raged through him. A raw groan tore from his throat. Locked deep inside her, he became a part of her. Shuddering, he growled out his release.

His vision blurred, and he caught a flash of her people and his through the ages.

****

She'd never looked closely at a naked man before, had certainly never had a bedside view. Norah eased the bathroom door shut behind her and tiptoed toward the bed. Her pulse raced, and heat rose on her cheeks.

Asleep and sprawled on his back with his strong arms and long, powerful legs spread wide, Jackson took up most of the queen-sized mattress. Um, um. What a gorgeous man. So why was she standing here with her hands clenched together like the frightened virgin she'd been until so very recently? She finally had a chance to do some catching up.

She shrugged off her terry robe and let it pool at her feet. Absolutely bare-assed, buck-naked, and blushing like a ripe plum, she eased onto the bed. Lying on her side next to him, she took a slow breath and held her palm an inch above his tanned chest. Heat radiated from his body.

With the lightest touch she explored his taut shoulders, traced the definition of his biceps, felt the hardness of bone beneath muscle. Dark stubble shadowed his jaw and neck, rough and raspy against her fingertips.

A diamond of curly, dark hair grew over his sternum, narrowing to a thin line down his flat, muscled abdomen. Her hand brushed the smooth skin of his hipbones and his navel.

Lower, his penis lay in a nest of crisp hair, still surprisingly long and broad, but looking almost vulnerable at rest. She wanted to stroke the tantalizing flesh, but something held her back.

Resting her cheek on one elbow, she drew in a deep breath of his wonderful warm, sexy scent. Light headed, she shivered with a delicious sense of excitement and anticipation. With possessiveness.

Thick whorls of hair grew around each of his flat, male nipples. Would he enjoy her caresses as much as she liked it when he touched her breasts? She traced the brown circle with her finger. The skin beaded, so she flicked a nail back and forth over the center. Yes. She grinned.

With a sleepy noise, he stretched an arm around her and drew her upper body part of the way onto his chest. He tucked her head into the hollow of his shoulder and snuffled against her hair. Such an endearing sound.

Pressed against his length, skin to skin, his heat seeped into her. Her muscles relaxed into shimmering mush, and dampness bloomed between her legs. A mischievous urge grabbed her, and she licked the nipple closest to her, circling with the tip of her tongue, just like she'd done with her nail.

He stirred, and in a heartbeat, he changed. To her surprise, within a split second, his penis grew erect.

Grew huge.

Grew longer and even broader, thrusting up toward his navel.

His gray eyes opened, and he gave her a gravelly chuckle. "Like what you see?"

Caught by his intense gaze, she stammered, "I-I just…"

"Go ahead. Touch." He kissed her palm and drew the tip of one finger into his mouth.

Her stomach fluttered, and her pulse started to race.

He moved her hand lower and curled her fingers around his penis just below the bulbous head. "Mmm. Feels good."

Fascinated, she stroked gently. The skin moved, slipped over the steely shaft. She ran her loose fingers down his velvety length and traced a large vein back up, measuring his rapid pulse. She cupped his sac carefully, feeling the shape of his testicles through the loose, hair-roughened skin.

She circled his shaft with her fingers and stroked, tip to base.

Hissing out a breath through his teeth, he let her explore, but lifted his hand to her face. He brushed his fingers over her cheeks, her eyelids, traced her brows and nose and lips. After a moment, he cupped his strong hand behind her head. "Kiss me, Norah."

But she just kept up the rhythmic, gentle strokes, fascinated. "I like touching you."

He thrust against her palm once and rolled to face her, but didn't dislodge her hold. Suddenly his lips were everywhere, kissing and tasting each part of her face. Her neck, ear, cheekbone.

Finally his tongue circled her mouth. He sucked her lower lip between his and nipped gently with his teeth. His hand found her breast and stroked her nipple.

Her breasts swelled and pebbled. Sweet internal pressure built and the hidden places in her body throbbed.

She drew in a shuddering breath and stroked him again. This time a drop of moisture beaded on the tip of his penis. She spread the warm liquid all over the head.

Closing his eyes, he groaned. His strong hands smoothed over her body and lightly squeezed her bottom. "Come here." Rolling onto his back, he lifted her on top of him, with her legs straddling his hips.

He wound her braid around his hand and tugged her down until her lips met his hungry mouth. When his crisp chest hair teased her nipples, they rose and ached. He licked and bit lightly, then drew her tongue into his mouth. Cupping her bottom, he pressed against her.

Her legs spread wider as he rubbed his hard shaft over the moist folds between her legs. Sharp arrows of pleasure pierced the sensitive flesh. "Oooh."

He thrust again, holding her firmly while he stroked her nub with his steely penis.

"Oh. Oh, my." Her heart beat fast and heavy. With every short, sharp thrust, luscious tension built until sweet contractions throbbed through her. With a moan, she squirmed and tried to work him inside her, but he held her still until the tremors stopped. "That was very nice."

"Almost too nice." He kneaded and massaged her bottom before releasing her. "Rise up on your knees." He must have seen her frown, because he added, "Trust me. Protection comes first."

Norah balanced with one knee on each side of his hips. Her sex, weeping with her own moisture, felt open and exposed in the chilly air. Vulnerable and needy.

He stretched sideways, grabbed a condom from his bedside table and covered himself. "Your breasts are so beautiful." He cupped her breasts and caught her nipples between his thumb and first finger.

Each pinch and tease pulled at her center, but she needed him to fill her. "I want you, Jackson. I feel all swollen and liquid inside, but I ache with emptiness, too."

"Good. Brace your legs farther apart." He touched her with the tip of one finger and circled her nub, in an agonizingly slow, gentle motion. His busy fingers explored her folds, toyed with her. He drove her up, almost to the peak, but each time she reached for her release, he eased off.

The tension coiled tighter. Her legs began to shake. "Jackson—"

"Take me inside, sweetheart. This is your show." His voice had a rasping, intense quality that sent tremors through her.

She guided him to her opening and sank onto him, barely an inch. The broad head of his penis parted her folds and sent such delicious licks of pleasure through her body. She could hardly bear the sensation. He barely fit. She bit her lip, hesitating. No tearing pain had hit her yet this time, but her sex felt sensitive and maybe a little raw. He was huge.

Jackson's breathing grew labored. He groaned, shuddering under her and pressed his thumb against her nub. "Move slowly. Your muscles will relax."

Delectable little throbs pulsed through her, and she opened, adjusting to him. When she lifted up and sank onto his shaft again, more of him slipped inside. She shuddered, but not with pain, just glorious pressure and tension that grew with each stroke.

Finally she managed to take in all of him, and he was seated deep. She moved faster, chasing her release. Each flex of her knees brought him against the entrance to her womb, and he flicked her nub again and again.

A blissful coil of sensation burst inside her. She arched her back and moaned.

Grabbing her waist, he shoved her down hard while his hips jackknifed.

Her body exploded with waves of pleasure. The ecstasy went on and on. Built. Swamped her.

Too much, too strong, too intense. Screaming his name, she collapsed against his chest.

****

Forget the thunderheads massing over the valley below. The sky had never looked this blue. Norah took a deep breath of fresh, clean air and exhaled. Every time she took a step, muscles she'd never noticed before pulsed with lovely, unexpected tenderness. She couldn't wipe the broad smile off her face, couldn't help beaming at the beautiful world.

She glanced at Jackson, walking beside her up the

steep stairs. What a wonderful man to share her life with. She squeezed his hand. "Jackson, I—"

He drew her against him and kissed her breath away. Then he tipped up her chin. "Much as I'm tempted to head back to the hotel, we need to talk to Sheriff Wood and focus on Josh's trail. Besides, you're probably pretty sore."

A blush heated her cheeks, and she dropped her gaze. "A little. But, um, the second time was even better than the first. How about tonight?"

"Good plan." Jackson drew her toward the next set of stairs. He raised their joined hands to kiss her knuckles. "Happy?"

"Very. I feel ecstatic, delirious, gloriously in love." She squeezed his hand. "I phoned Amber while you were asleep. She can't wait to meet you."

Chapter Thirteen

Jackson's insides dropped to the gravel road and rolled around in the dust. His heart drummed in his ears. Suddenly Norah expected orange blossoms and stepfathers. What the hell had he gotten himself into? "What...uh..."

His cell rang. A reprieve. He paused in front of the door, dragged the phone from his pocket and checked the display. "It's Nate Kapulani. Why don't you go inside and wait." Should be safe enough for her to stroke the sheriff's ego. If anything important had come up, Wood had his cell phone number. "Yeah. Check in with Wood. I'll be right there."

"Sure." She had a little frown between her brows, but she lifted the door handle and stepped inside.

Thank God. He could use a break from sexy, spooky, naïve Norah. Flipping the phone open, Jackson held it to his ear and cleared his throat. "Marino."

"Need an update. Caught up with Swank, yet?" the captain asked.

"Got some good leads. Norah's in talking to Sheriff Wood now." Rubbing his forehead, Jackson took a couple steps along the gravel shoulder edging the road. "What's new on your end?"

"Forensics matched the skin fragments under Tyrell's fingernails. Swank left DNA traces in Stacy Kwail's apartment."

"Good. That's good." Jackson paced in front of the station, his steps jerky. "Murder one?"

"And rape. Coroner found puncture wounds and DNA evidence on Stacy Kwail."

His neck and shoulder muscles twisted into steel cables. Pursing his lips, Jackson kicked at the gravel. "Well, hell."

"Jana was already pretty broken up about Tyrell." Anger colored Kapulani's voice. "If my wife caught Swank, I think she'd carve him into little tiny pieces, hold the anesthesia."

"Can't say I blame her." But after she got a play-by-play from Norah, Jana might start slicing on him. Jackson stooped, picked up a rock, and tossed it up and down in his hand.

"Judge Pascal contacted the county there. They issued Arizona warrants."

"Good. I want to put Swank away permanently."

"Keep me posted, Marino."

"Will do." With a heavy heart, he flipped his phone shut. First priority? He had to free Josh from that low-life. But his edge had been blunted by everything that had happened in the past twenty-four. He struggled to set aside the grief. The frustration.

The guilt.

Hell. Wincing, he hurled the rock down the barren slope. He'd taken advantage of Norah, and now he'd face the consequences. No question, he'd taken her innocence.

But that whole lost-it-when-he-played-the-oboe crap was bogus. Who knows? Maybe she'd have recovered her so-called gifts if he'd kept his pants zipped and thought with his brain instead of his freaking gonads.

Taking a deep breath, he studied the tiny, brick church across the street. A few minutes of peace and quiet might help clear his mind and sharpen his instincts. Help him damp down the remorse clawing at his insides.

No. He didn't have time. He had to get back on the trail. Fast.

Climbing the steps of the police station, he caught a glimpse of pink out of the corner of his eye.

He pivoted and met his Nonna's gaze. His jaw dropped.

What the hell?

Pearls, cardigan, a pillbox hat perched on dark hair styled in an old-fashioned French twist. Her pink dress belled out by a dozen petticoats, Nonna stood in front of the little church. Her dark eyes glittered, and she beckoned to him with one white-gloved hand, turned and slipped inside.

His heart pummeled the inside of his ribs, and his face congested with fury. Some sick fuck thought they could play him for a patsy.

Jackson raced across the street. He'd catch the sucker in the act and shut down the charade. Jerking open the sun-bleached wooden door on the old building, he stomped inside.

Empty. No noise. No movement. How did that woman vanish so quickly?

Jackson searched the tiny sanctuary but didn't find a trace. No one behind the altar. Side doors locked. Confessionals empty. The only signs anyone had been here recently were the red glass lamp that glowed above the old-fashioned brass tabernacle and the row of candles flickering in a rack to one side.

Fisting his hands on his hips, he blew out a long breath.

Suckered. But this time Norah wasn't center stage in the magic show.

He looked up and frowned at the old pressed tin ceiling. The bright turquoise and gold paint was jarring. Place looked more like a freaking bar than a church, except for the roughly carved wooden altar figures.

Slipping into a pew, he closed his eyes and speared his hands through his hair. Frustration spewed bile up the back of his throat.

Gentle pressure brushed across his shoulders, and a hint of vanilla teased his nostrils. A chill crept up his spine and raised goose bumps all over his body. He squeezed his eyes closed .

The fucking church was empty. He'd checked.

His grandmother's soft chuckle seemed to echo in his ears. *"Jackie? My little man?"* Soft, cool lips pressed against his cheek. *"Relax."*

His heart hammered, and he hitched in a ragged breath.

Impossible.

Petticoats rustled. The padded kneeler beside him creaked.

Cold sweat trickled along his spine, soaked his polo. He could swear he heard Nonna's ivory Rosary beads clatter against the pew.

Nope. Couldn't happen. With a force of will, he shuttered his mind.

Shit. He had to look.

Nothing.

A curious spasm clenched his chest. Relief or

disappointment?

He shivered and closed his eyes again. The last forty-eight hours had shaken his world like a 7.0 magnitude earthquake. Nonna made the most loving ghost he could imagine, but she still scared him spitless. And she'd have paddled his ass for what he'd done with Norah.

He leaned forward and covered his face with his hands. Ten Hail Marys would hardly make a dent in his penance. Maybe a thousand? Sixty gazillion?

A noise from the front of the church caught his attention. A short, chubby priest in black vestments and old-fashioned horn rimmed glasses stood near the communion rail, watching him.

Jackson rose. "Morning, Father. The door was open, so I…" followed my grandmother's ghost inside. He shook his head. Yeah, right.

The bald man waved a hand and smiled broadly. "Of course. But you look troubled."

Jackson forced a lopsided smile. "Guilty."

"Come here, my son, and talk to me. Sometimes a friendly ear can help." With a groan, the priest sank onto the altar steps in a puddle of black vestments. "I think I'm wearing out. These old bones make it hard to move around nowadays."

Jackson sat on the edge of the bottom step. Leaning against the white railing, he stretched his legs in front of him and crossed them at the ankles. Where to start? He looked down at his hands and went with the basics. "I'm a cop from California, following a kidnapper. Just heard from my captain. The suspect is wanted for two murders, another kid he snatched, and a woman."

A frown creased the old priest's forehead. "What a

terrible shame. It's always hard when someone is mistreated instead of cherished, especially when you think you should have stopped the evil."

"Yeah."

"Realistically, could you have prevented the killings?"

"Guess not." Jackson cleared his throat and started to rise. "I…uh…thought a couple minutes of peace might help me stay focused during the hunt."

"Good idea. But what else is weighing on your mind? I'm always happy to hear a confession." The priest laid a cold, pale, almost weightless hand on Jackson's arm.

The hairs on his nape lifted, and his hand jerked away before he could stop the reaction. His skin crawled like a battalion of ants had marched up his pant leg and fanned out over his body. Could this guy see right through him? Read his thoughts? "Might not be a great idea, Father. It's been eight or ten years."

"Then this is an excellent time."

Jackson squirmed inside, but he cocked his head and covered his embarrassment with a wide grin. "Not sure I'd remember all the moves anymore. Besides, I've been a busy boy. Neither one of us has all morning."

The priest chuckled. "You might be surprised at how fast the memories return. But no matter. Why do you feel guilty?" Through his thick glasses, his brown eyes looked alert and aware and empathetic.

"I'm divorced. Long time ago. The bishop married us with all the trappings, but she, my wife, got a divorce just as if our marriage never happened. I never thought I'd, uh…" Never thought he'd seduce a virgin who was raising a kid and spend the morning fucking her senseless. Worse, he'd slobber all over himself to get back inside her sweet body as fast as he could roll on a fresh condom. Ugly guilt coiled and writhed inside him. He squeezed his eyes shut, wishing for one of Norah's so-called re-dos.

A door squeaked at the rear of the church. He looked up and scrambled to his feet.

Norah called softly, "Jackson?"

He stepped forward, watching her walk toward him, carrying a piece of paper, not a bouquet, but his throat clogged anyway. "I was talking to the priest." He gestured behind him at the altar steps.

Her brows drew together. "The priest?"

"Yeah. I'm sorry. I didn't catch your name, padre." Jackson swung around and gaped at the empty steps. "He was here just a second ago. Short, well fed, glasses. Where'd he go?" He pivoted, looking for a hidden doorway, and then threw up his hands. "The guy vanished."

She handed him the paper. "Did he look like this?"

His eyes widened at the blurred image of the priest he had spoken to. The gist of the flyer sank in. "The church is haunted?"

"Appears so. He was the pastor in the forties and fifties. Looks like you might have reason to change your mind about ghosts."

Jackson stared at the picture and gritted his teeth. "This some kinda stupid hoax?"

She frosted him with a glacial look. "No. But let's talk about ghosts later. We need to head to Verde Valley, now. The sheriff there reported a possible sighting."

Struggling to change gears, he asked, "Of what?"

"A gambler complained about a smart-mouthed boy causing a ruckus."

****

Squeezing the steering wheel with one hand, Jackson turned toward Norah. "Sheriff Wood insisted George Kwail would show at the trading post today."

Norah humphed and crossed her arms in front of her chest. "Waiting for George Kwail was a stupid waste of time."

"He's probably our best witness."

"But it's late afternoon, and we've accomplished exactly nothing. Josh is in grave danger."

"That's why we're gonna wait."

Her eyes took on a glazed, unfocused look, and her mouth opened, but she didn't say anything.

Upset? Ya think? No need to read her aura, but if he could there'd be puffs of angry smoke billowing out her ears and sparks flashing from between her clenched teeth. "Norah?"

No answer. He rotated his shoulders and stretched, softening his tone. "Look, what are the odds? That kid at the casino probably had nothing to do with Josh."

"Grandfather disagrees," she snapped.

Fresh moist air gusted through the open window behind him. A chill raced down his spine, and he shivered.

"Don't you dare roll your eyes at me after you stomped in and grilled Sheriff Wood about that damned sighting instead of trusting me."

He leaned his head against the headrest and massaged his scalp. "Nothing personal. Always check my sources."

"So now I'm just another source?" Red slashed

across her cheekbones, and her tense jaw jutted forward.

"Like Wood said, you misunderstood. The sighting's no big deal. The casino is on the reservation, and there are hundreds of kids in the area who fit Josh's description. You're grasping at a mirage."

"I see," she said with a frigid snort and tossed her head.

Jackson pinched his nose.

"You've delayed me once too often, Detective. Start the car now, or I'll get the local cops to help me instead." She grabbed for the door handle.

"Just relax, okay?" Why not listen to a ghost? He'd had flakier informants than her dead grandfather, and he'd already heard from two other specters today. Before lunch.

"The Casino's just down the road. We can come back and talk to Kwail later. Someone at the Casino might actually know something." Jackson ground the engine and pulled onto the street.

Five minutes into the silent ride, he shot a quick glance at Norah. The brew in his stomach gurgled, like he'd chugged two quarts of hot sauce.

She faced forward, her spine rigid and jaw set. Every time they hit a pothole, her fists bounced on her knees.

Pretty sure she wasn't stuck on happily-ever-after scenarios right now, but they hadn't settled anything. What if he kissed that pout off her sexy lips?

Nah. Bad move. Thinking with your gonads again, Marino.

****

Choking, Norah batted at the foul, smoky haze. Her

eyes watered, blurring her view of the crowded Casino lobby. The huge windowless building flashed with light and color and noise. Above the teeth-grating roar of voices, bells clanged and buzzers screeched.

One wrinkled old man wearing a toffee colored toupee and a shirt covered in beer logos poked a slot machine. He glared at the digital readout and took a drag of his smoldering cigar before hitting the play button again.

She shook her throbbing head. "The house always wins. Don't any of these people do the math?"

"Nope. In here they don't even keep track of the time," Jackson answered, his voice rough with a sharp, impatient edge.

Norah shivered. Besides the pandemonium, the underlying atmosphere grated on her raw nerves. Jarring, jagged auras clashed against her mind and screamed misery. A faint psychic reek like rotting flesh permeated everything. She wrinkled her nose. "What a disgusting place."

"You wanted to come here. Let's talk to the manager and then we can leave." Jackson cupped her elbow and nudged her forward gently, his touch at odds with his gruff tone.

Giddy warmth bubbled through her and insulated her from the worst of the psychic chaos. Wordless longing rose and constricted her throat. She wanted to turn into his arms and bury her face against his chest, listen to the rhythm of his heart and see if his pulse still raced when he held her. But he'd made it very clear he didn't trust her.

A cold, flat numbness sapped her strength and painted her world gray. He'd enjoyed her body. He'd stolen her heart. He'd destroyed her gift. But he didn't even trust her.

How could he reject the connection, the commitment they'd made? She blinked several times. Jeez, this morning her emotions were as volatile as swamp gas.

Maybe she'd just moved too fast, made too many assumptions. She had to know and moping certainly wouldn't win her any answers. As soon as they were alone, she'd straighten her spine and ask him where.they stood.

Absorbing the trickle of protective strength from his hand, she let him guide her through the maze of machines and into the elevator. With her heart pounding, she took a deep breath and turned toward him. "Jackson, I need another two minutes to talk."

His head jerked. He met her gaze and stabbed one hand into his hair. "Sure. Guess I do too." But just as the metal doors started to close, another couple squeezed in.

Norah shut her gaping mouth and frowned.

The tanned middle-aged man was medium height, but built like a professional linebacker. Inside his loud, unbuttoned Hawaiian shirt, thick gold chains tangled in his black, curly chest hair. He swiped his access card for the penthouse floor and cinched the bleached blonde teenager against the tented bulge in his white silk pants.

Wearing leather slave stilettos and a low cut, too-short black latex excuse-for-a-dress, the girl hung all over him, giggling. With her tongue and nails in constant motion, she ground her pelvis against his crotch and moaned.

Norah averted her gaze, but her face heated to a

furious shade of red. In the side mirror, she saw the man's hands cup the blonde's bottom and flex, his chunky diamond signet sparkling. He thrust against the girl, and her skirt rode up.

Black thong. Tanned butt. Norah's stomach lurched, and she squeezed her eyes shut. Oh, my God. Talk about too much information.

When the bell chimed for the second floor, she blindly elbowed past them and out the doors. Rounding a corner, she leaned against the wall and caught her breath.

Jackson moved in front of her silently. The warmth from his body surrounded and protected her.

A moment later, she peeked open one eye. "Couldn't those two have waited until they reached their room? She acted like a wild animal in heat."

He shrugged. "Just a working girl plying her trade."

"Of course, a prostitute." A flood of embarrassment rushed through her, and she swallowed convulsively. How could any woman, take a stranger's money for something so intensely intimate?

He winked. "Bet she'll catch a big tip."

Frigid pain slashed her heart, and her pulse tripped. Did Jackson expect that kind of blatant, easy sexuality from her? Shit. He must. But when they'd made love, she'd been clumsy and a little awkward. Her first time had hurt, and she hadn't been shy about letting her pain show. But she'd also let him know when her eyeballs exploded with pleasure.

Had Jackson back-pedaled on their relationship because she didn't really satisfy him? Had her golly-gee-whiz-let's-check-out-the-naked-man act bored him? She rubbed her forehead with one hand.

"Stop worrying about those two. I'll report them to Sheriff Frederick." His face still held the hint of a smile, and his eyes sparkled. He drew her away from the wall with his big, warm hand on her waist and inclined his head. "Come on."

"Okay. Sure." Drawing in a much-needed breath, she tamped down all the doubts and fears rioting in her belly and fell into step beside him.

He stopped before a door marked Manager and knocked twice, but didn't wait for a response.

She trailed him into the brightly lit office.

A spent-his-life-at-a-gym bodyguard type swaggered toward Jackson and blocked their path. "Whatcha want, buddy?" Slicked back dark hair, broad face with deep-set black eyes below his thick unibrow. Massive neck and shoulders stretched a charcoal sharkskin suit and black silk sport shirt. Aggression and fear pulsed in his bloody orange aura.

Giving the guy a mild, non-threatening smile, she dropped her gaze.

But Jackson reacted differently. Like Alice on mushrooms, he'd puffed up until his shoulders and elbows occupied almost half the room. His aura blazed, and the air took on the distinct odor of testosterone.

The bodyguard's hands fisted. His jaw joints protruded, and the blood vessels in his neck bulged. He closed the distance and stared at Jackson, nose to nose.

Jackson whipped the badge from his back pocket and flashed it. "Sheriff Wood in Jerome sent me. Need a word with your boss."

Her pulse roared in her ears, but she upped the wattage of her smile and moved a little closer. "A child is missing. We'd really appreciate—"

The bodyguard's snort interrupted her. "California, huh? Get outta here. Mr. Smith doesn't have to see no smart ass cop from California." He dismissed them with a flick of his huge paw.

Jackson's eyebrows rose and his gray eyes glittered. He stood even taller. "His choice. Smith can talk to us now, or the sheriff can drag him up to Jerome. Bet that would annoy your boss."

The bodyguard scowled at Jackson for a long moment before he gave a growling snort and grabbed the badge. "Wait here," he barked and disappeared into the inner office.

Jackson's gaze remained glued to the closed door, his expression fixed and intense, from the wrinkled bridge of his nose to his narrowed eyes. The muscles in his jaw and neck and hands were clenched.

Tilting her head to one side, Norah sighed softly. Did she have any real understanding of what drove this man? Sure they'd been intimate, but she'd only known this complicated, driven male a few days. She stared at her feet. Was what she felt love? Or merely afterglow?

A few silent moments later a lean, wiry man with a dark, orangey tan and shock of strawberry blond hair emerged from the inner office.

The nameless bodyguard took up a wide-legged stance, blocking the interior door.

Smiling, the man straightened his Armani jacket, returned the badge and offered Jackson his hand. "Officer Marino. Welcome to Verde Valley Casino. Name's Smith, Vince Smith, General Manager."

Jackson introduced Norah, but Smith just nodded in her direction, keeping his full attention trained on the cop.

She curled her lips into a wry smile. "It's a little public out here, Mr. Smith," she prodded. "Could we speak in private?"

"Love to, but I'm having some work done in my office. Contractors left a dusty mess." He glanced at her and tapped one foot. "Tell you what. Let me buy you a cup of coffee. This time of day the restaurant's usually dead."

Chapter Fourteen

The restaurant looked like a herd of fifty-seven Chevys had been massacred for their tail fins and tuck-and-roll seats. Norah grimaced. Stuck in a corner, the fifties-themed buffet overlooked the casino floor downstairs. *Jailhouse Rock* wailed in the background.

Vince Smith pointed to a chair near the entrance, but Norah walked right past him. She sat with her back to the low planter box edging the restaurant. From this angle she could watch the elevator.

Jackson slid in next to her.

With a wry grin, Smith sat across the chrome and turquoise Formica table and tapped his watch. "I have an appointment in about ten minutes. What can I order for you?"

"Nothing thanks. Won't keep you long." Shaking his head, Jackson waved off the waitress and pulled out an envelope. "Have you seen either of these people recently?"

Smith picked up one photo and stroked his chin. "Gina? Sure. Real Looker. She worked here off and on for around five years. Waitressed and put on a campy fortune telling act. The old farts loved her."

"What about him?" Jackson trained his gaze on the manager.

Smith's Adam's apple bobbed. He loosened his collar with a finger. "Not sure. The face seems vaguely familiar."

Liar. "That's Kenny Swank," Norah ground out. "Gina's husband."

"Yeah, I think you're right." Smith scratched the side of his mouth. "Kicked him out of the Casino when security caught him pulling a scam. Haven't seen him in at least six or eight months. Gina disappeared, too. Never even gave me notice."

"We're also looking for a twelve-year-old boy." Norah slid Josh's school picture forward. "He'd have been here in the last few days."

Smith's eyes widened like a flashbulb had gone off. He tamed his guilty expression into what could have been concern and studied the photo. But his gaze slid sideways off the picture, and his breathing shifted to fast and shallow.

Her heart bumped. He was definitely hiding something.

Heaving a huge sigh, Smith shook his head. "No. Don't think I've seen any kids in here since school started." His manicured nails twitched, and he adjusted his bolo tie. The intricate turquoise inlay of the snake motif flashed in the florescent light of the restaurant.

"You never saw him?" She shoved the picture closer. "Shaggy dark hair and unusual golden eyes? Almost five feet tall?"

Smith curled his lips into an ingratiating smile and shrugged. "Kids are allowed in the game room, but not the casino."

Jackson cleared his throat. "According to the sheriff in Verde Valley, this morning one of your customers reported a juvenile causing a disturbance."

"That?" The manager snapped his fingers and

rolled his eyes. "I'd forgotten all about it. No big deal. One of Marguerite's kids. She's my lead croupier on day shift. Her nine-year-old is a real troublemaker. Ditched school and caused a ruckus. His father had to pick him up and carry him out."

Norah twisted her hands together. More lies.

Smith stood but didn't meet her narrow-eyed stare. "If that's all, I'm late for my appointment."

"Okay." Jackson slid a card across the table. "Give me a call if you see Josh or the Swanks."

With a grimace, the manager pocketed the card, pivoted, and hustled toward the exit.

She sucked air between her teeth to keep from screaming at his back. "Smith lied to us," she hissed. "Josh was here, and that creep saw him."

"Course he did."

She squirmed in her seat and let out an exasperated noise. "So we need to search his inner office right now."

"No way."

"He's hiding something in there, and we need to find out what."

Jackson's brows drew together. "No question. But breaking and entering is still breaking and entering."

"But Josh doesn't have much time."

"No buts. We're both officers of the court. Let's wait. See what Smith does next. If he leaves, I can follow him, or better yet, come back with the sheriff and a warrant."

She touched his arm. "If we need help from local law enforcement, let's call now. That arrogant thug is the key to finding Josh, to breaking open the whole case."

"All the more reason to secure the evidence strictly by the book."

She started to speak, but her cell phone buzzed and she dug it out of her pocket. The phone rang again, and her blood pressure climbed. "It's Amber. Sorry, I need to—"

Jackson closed his hand over the phone before she could answer. "No, Norah. Hold on."

"Let go."

Buzz.

"No. Call her back in a minute. We need to talk first."

"But—" The ringing stopped.

"She'll leave a message." He took off his watch, fiddled with the controls and handed it to her. "Hit the timer and call it my two minutes."

Norah's stomach curled into tiny little knots.

"This morning you jumped the gun when you talked to Amber about me. I don't want her hurt."

All the blood in her body flamed her neck and cheeks and pieces of her shattered heart lodged high in her throat. After what she'd sacrificed, could she bear to listen? Rather than look at him, she traced the turquoise arrows on the Formica table. "Of course not. Neither do I."

"Look, when a kid's involved—" He broke off abruptly. Then he grabbed her and kissed her.

"Hey. What do you think you're doing?" She stiffened, pushing against his shoulders. Her pulse rattled in her ears.

"Quiet." He whispered next her mouth. "Smith and the bodyguard are by the elevator."

With her face half an inch from his, she froze. His

heavy-lashed dark gray gaze pierced hers. In a split second, he seemed to probe her deepest thoughts and fears, twisting her inside out.

He ducked his head into the curve of her neck and encircled her in his arms. His warm lips caressed her neck, and her heart jumped three enormous beats.

A quiver pulsed through her, and she closed her eyes. She couldn't do this, but her body and emotions were at war. She took a deep breath to wall off her feelings.

"They're gone." He relaxed and scooted away, leaving her with a chilly sense of loss.

She peered over the planter box, searching the casino floor. Smith and the bodyguard emerged from the elevator bay and hurried toward the exit. "Now's our chance to check out his office."

Jackson scowled and grabbed her arm. "Not going to happen."

"Look, the bodyguard's gone, but there's bound to be someone handling the phones." She stood, untied the blue scarf from around her neck, and stuffed it into her jacket pocket as she walked.

"Norah!" Jackson growled, following her out of the restaurant.

With her head held high, she marched past the elevators. In front of the manager's office she turned and faced him. "Trust me. I can do this."

He dropped his chin and shook his head, his eyes dark as thunderclouds.

"Stand by the door and stall Smith if he returns." She patted his cheek. "I'll keep everything very safe and very legal."

Jackson rubbed his neck and let out a frustrated

grunt. "Be careful."

Adrenaline pumped, sending her pulse into triple digits, but she took a deep breath, opened the door and strolled inside.

A receptionist with short, spiky, red hair sat behind a desk examining her long black-tipped nails. The pale mounds of her large breasts nearly burst from the deep vee of her sequined top, and her pouty, collagen-enhanced lips were an intense, shiny tomato red.

Norah gave her a friendly grin. "I just, uh, you know, visited Vinny in his office and I think I left my scarf."

The young redhead frowned and hesitated, her vacuous brown eyes round and troubled. She rose and tottered toward Norah on six-inch platform heels.

Norah twirled a strand of hair around one finger. "I wouldn't bother you, but it's Dior. My boyfriend bought it for me last summer when he took me to Paris."

"Paris?" The receptionist crooked her head. "Oh, wow."

Norah leaned closer, thankful the girl couldn't hear the thunder of her heart. "He'll kill me if I lose it," she whispered in a help-me-out-girlfriend way. Then she chewed on her lip and winced. "And he doesn't know about Vinny."

The girl swallowed, and her brow furrowed. Her lashes fluttered. "I'm not supposed—"

"Please?"

"Well I guess you could take a quick peek." She plucked a keycard from the pocket of her short skirt and unlocked the door.

"Thanks, sweetie. I'll be sure to tell Vinny what a

huge help you were."

"Um." Twisting her hands together, the redhead checked over her shoulder.

"Or would you rather I didn't?"

The girl let out a sigh and opened the door.

"Then it's our itty-bitty secret." Norah patted her arm and stepped into the room.

A wallop of energy slammed her, and she covered her mouth to muffle a gasp. She breathed in carefully, but her lungs contorted. Shelf after shelf held ancient artifacts any museum would prize. For a moment she just gaped. No wonder Vince Smith didn't want a cop in here.

Even though her belly still roiled, she glanced around the room with what she hoped was nonchalance. Her muscles were so tense, she ached all over.

Tomb robbing was illegal in Arizona. Most of these incredible treasures must have come from the black market. She shuddered, imagining the desecration behind this display. The petroglyphs alone would earn the thief a long term in jail.

"Do you see your scarf?"

"Um, right. Well, let's look. We were sitting over there." Palming the scarf, she reached into the side crevice of the Italian leather sofa and waved it with a flourish. "Look. Here it is."

"Oh, good."

Norah grinned at the girl and casually draped the blue silk around her neck. "I'm so relieved."

Ignoring the girl's nervous gesture toward the door, Norah edged closer to the display. "Isn't this the most amazing place? I've been trying to talk Vince into selling me this Anasazi piece for an absolute age, but he won't budge on the price. I love the turtles." She pointed to a large black and white pot and sighed longingly.

"He likes that stuff a lot." The receptionist mouthed a fingertip. "He says it's worth big bucks, but I can't help being kinda creeped out. Yah know?"

"I'm not surprised, since most of these pieces are grave goods."

The girl shivered, and her face went a sick, ashy shade.

Norah gritted her teeth. What did all this have to do with Josh? Had he been in here? Seen the artifacts? Touched them? Well shit. Of course. What better motive for kidnapping a boy with his unique talents?

"I guess I'd better scoot." Norah twittered. "My boyfriend's waiting, and I can't afford for him to get suspicious. But don't you worry. I won't say a thing to Vinny. Not a peep."

"Thanks."

Norah turned to leave, but a small basket on the corner of the desk compelled her to reach out and touch.

"Ma'am. Please don't…"

She ignored the receptionist and reached for the intricate and beautiful basket.

"You need to go."

Even before Norah touched the basket, power beckoned. She curved her fingers around its beautiful shape and closed her eyes.

The vision rushed toward her, surrounded her. The man she'd seen before. The shaman. His golden eyes focused on her, and he held out his hand.

Fear streaked down her spine like a lightning

strike. Her lungs seized. She stumbled backward, but couldn't let go. "No. I can't."

The Magician took hold of her, and his greedy spirit snaked into her soul.

She struggled to strengthen her shields, but they were useless. He batted them away like a pile of toothpicks. She couldn't resist him.

"Take the basket. Bring it to me."

She felt her hand tuck the basket into her pocket. Her body turned, and her feet shuffled toward the small bathroom at the back of the room. She closed the door behind her. Flicked the lock.

Someone shouted at her, pounded on the door.

She fought against the overwhelming compulsion, tried to scream for help. Only a faint garbled noise choked from between her lips.

Her hands opened the bathroom window. Electricity zapped her fingers, but no alarm bells rang. She scrambled out onto a ledge.

Her body shinnied down a slick drainpipe and dashed across the parking lot toward the open desert.

Thunder rumbled in the distance.

Cold drops of rain splattered on her face, but didn't break the spell.

****

Jackson jiggled his foot up and down on the ace of spades. He'd counted all the cards in this stretch of ugly maroon carpet twice. Huffing, he pushed away from the wall. Norah had been in that damn office too long. He was an idiot to let her try anything this crazy.

He should have kept her talking until she actually listened, maybe even heard his reasons for taking some time while they grew their relationship. Made her understand his heart couldn't survive another bullet-train marriage that derailed into a pile of smoldering freight cars.

A short, busty redhead burst out the office door and looked around the corridor frantically. Her face was vampire pale, her eyes, gigantic.

The skin on his neck and shoulders crawled and adrenaline pumped through his system. Straightening, he took a step in her direction.

She must have spotted him, because she gasped, and her complexion went even whiter. She hotfooted back into the office, slamming the door behind her.

But why didn't Norah come out when that woman did? Shit. What the hell did Norah do?

He let out a rolling snort and headed along the hall. So much for safe and legal.

The elevator chimed.

No chance he'd reach the office first. He faded back around the corner and ducked behind a ragged palm with cigarette butts sticking up from the dirt. Not so obvious here, but he still had a clear line of sight.

Vince Smith and his bodyguard hit the carpet running, their expressions fierce.

Jackson's heart clenched, and his muscles turned to sludge. Fuck a duck. Norah must have caused some major mayhem. He raked his fingers through his hair. Focus, Marino. Gotta think. Choices? Barrel in after them, 9mm in hand and risk a firefight?

His hands shook, and his body wanted to wade in and fight for his woman. Backup. He needed local backup if things went to shit.

Taking a deep breath, he called Doug Fredericks at Verde Valley PD and briefed him in a few terse sentences. Two squad cars were on the way.

Jackson drew his weapon and checked the load.

The office door slammed open again. "You stupid bitch! Why the fuck did you do that?" Smith bellowed.

A slap rang out, followed by a muffled female cry.

"I gotta go find Swank. Don't let anyone in. You hear me? No one or you're dead." Smith bolted out with the bodyguard close on his heels. Their flushed faces wore pissed off expressions. Smith didn't just poke the elevator button, he pounded, went for the TKO.

Jackson watched them go, but his forehead wrinkled, and his shoulders knotted. He tucked his weapon into his holster. Didn't make sense for Smith to say all that in front of Norah. Where was she? Had she been hurt.

With his heart pounding the inside of his ribcage, he jogged toward the office and rapped on the door. A sniff and muffled sob were his only answers.

Didn't sound like Norah. He knocked again. "You okay in there? I'm kinda worried, sugar."

"I'm fine. Go away."

"Sure sounded like some rough stuff went down. What if I came in and checked?"

"No!"

He massaged his jaw joint. How should he finesse this one? He drew his thumb and forefinger around his open mouth. "Say, was that blond guy your boss or your boyfriend?"

"Both."

"Cute little redhead like you? You don't deserve to be knocked around, even by a high roller." He put some honey in his voice and lowered the volume. "Yeah, you sure deserve better."

"No kidding."

"Come on, sugar, give me a break. Just can't stand to see a good woman mistreated."

She sniffed again. Through the door, he heard shuffling and a quiet rustle, like she'd scooted up close. "But I—I can't let you in."

"Why don't you just show me you're okay?" He added in a gruff whisper, "Don't make me camp out here all night, sugar. Don't want your boyfriend to get the wrong idea."

The door opened a crack, and the woman slipped out into the hall.

His hands fisted.

Her eyes were red and as swollen as her ballooned lips. Mascara trails soiled her cheeks. She'd have one helluva shiner by morning.

She wiped her nose with the back of her hand and swallowed. But when her chest heaved, she almost achieved a major wardrobe malfunction. "See. I'm fine. Really. Vinny might have a temper, but I deserved a wallop from him this time."

Jackson tipped her chin with one finger and avoided staring at the two flesh-covered silicon mounds that threatened to fall out of her top. "Sweet little thing like you? What did you do to piss him off? Nothing worth that big old bruise, I'll bet." Why the hell hadn't Norah heard him and reacted?

The redhead shrugged and stepped away from him, staring at her shoes.

"I'm Jackson. What's your name, sugar?"

"N-Natalie."

"Pretty name for a gorgeous girl." Draping an arm

across her shoulders, he pushed open the door and herded her inside. "Now let's find you a tissue, Natalie. You can dry those beautiful brown eyes while you tell me what happened."

"You have to leave." She stiffened, and her gaze darted frantically around the office. "I can't let you in."

"Too late. But no one's gonna know." His muscles cranked tighter, but Jackson guided her to the sofa, giving her a wide, sheepish grin. No noise from the inner office. Where the hell was Norah? "See, I'm looking for my fiancée. She came in here hunting for her scarf. You help me find her, and Smith will never be the wiser."

The redhead hitched in some air, her boobs jiggling. "She's…she left. You just missed her."

Gone? His heart raced like a setter after a squirrel, but he chuckled softly. "Come on, Natalie. I'm a nice guy, but I don't appreciate bullshit."

"Really. She left maybe ten or fifteen minutes ago." She bit her knuckle and winced. Even though her gaze remained steady, she had to be lying.

"I was outside watching this door the whole time. She's not under the desk. Why don't you make it easy on both of us? Where's she stashed?" Ditching the grin, he rose and stalked across the office to the inner door, glaring at her. "Inside?"

"No. I never let anyone in Mr. Smith's office." This time, the redhead's features were out of sync. Wide eyes, lips flapping, then forced into a smile. Her toes were turned in, and her fingers twisted into a triple sheepshank. *Liar.*

Jackson held out a hand. "Key," he barked.

"I told you. I can't."

"Your choice, Natalie. I'm going to search that room. Think Vince Smith will notice if I splinter this nice door?"

She squeezed her eyes shut, balled her fists and hunched forward, letting out a high-pitched squeal. Next she'd stomp her feet.

"Running out of time."

She flounced over to him and handed him her key card. "Hurry up. See for yourself."

He pushed past her into a room full of what had to be illegal artifacts.

But no Norah.

The bathroom door hung ajar, and he stuck his head inside. Acres of mirrors. Gold and crystal fixtures. Gold-veined black marble floor, walls and countertops. The window stood open.

Frowning, he stalked back to Natalie and grabbed her by the arms. "What the fuck happened to Norah?"

Just as the woman opened her mouth, a low moan seemed to float through the opposite wall.

Jackson's head jerked toward the sound.

A rustle.

Something thumped.

The paneling looked solid, but there had to be a hidden doorway.

Footsteps pounded down the hall and clomped into the outer office.

Pivoting, Jackson drew his gun and braced. His heart pounded like an automatic weapons barrage, but his hands were steady.

"Oh, my God! Vinny will kill me." The redheaded receptionist squealed and raced into the bathroom, slamming the door behind her.

A series of knocks rattled the outer office doorframe. "Police!"

"In here, Fredericks." Jackson holstered his 9mm and shook some of the tension out of his arms.

The Verde Valley Sergeant entered Smith's office, trailed by two uniforms. His gaze swept the room full of ancient artifacts, and his jaw dropped. "This place is obscene. A fucking fortune in contraband."

One lanky patrolman, dark-haired and dark-eyed with Geronimo's cheekbones, tucked his thumbs into his duty belt and whistled. "Hot damn. We can finally nail Vince Smith for trafficking."

His sandy haired, freckle-faced buddy with the linebacker's neck elbowed him, grinning. "Yeah and ain't it nice to just stroll right in?"

Doug Fredericks crossed his arms over his chest. "Get on the horn, Starr. Need a photographer and the CSI team in here pronto. O'Sullivan, get moving on that warrant for Smith," he ordered and turned to Jackson. "Where's Ms. Redfox?"

A sense of urgency slammed into him like a .45 slug hitting Kevlar. Jackson flexed his fists. "Don't know. She came in here forty-five minutes ago and never came out. I heard some suspicious noises from the next room. I'm afraid Norah could be hurt."

"What would she be doing—" A muffled moan and rustle interrupted Fredericks.

An adrenaline rush doubled Jackson's pulse rate, and all four cops turned toward the section of paneling.

Fredericks scowled. "What the hell? Anybody know how to get in there?"

"Break through the wall? Receptionist invited me in here and then ducked into the bathroom when she heard you guys knock."

The door clicked open, and Natalie peeked out. "I told you, your girlfriend left."

"Then who made that noise?" Jackson barked, his expression steely.

"I-I don't know. Mr. Smith took away my keys to his private quarters"—she sniffed and rubbed her cheek—"after he hit me."

Fredericks reached her in three quick strides and turned her chin toward the light. "You willing to press assault charges, ma'am?"

She paled and gulped. "Uh, I don't know. Vinny would be really mad."

A weak, whining groan filtered through the wall.

Jackson's spine stiffened ramrod straight. His nostrils flared. The local cops were dicking around with the dumb-as-a-bag-of-silicon receptionist, while Norah moaned in pain just yards away. "Handle that shit later. Get me inside."

"Well, there's a button under my desk that slides the—"

"Move!"

Natalie teetered to her desk and bent over, flashing the room.

Jackson winced and shook the image from his mind.

Oblivious, she pushed the button and straightened. A wall panel slid aside revealing a door with an electronic lock. "Like I told you, I don't have the key."

"Missing woman. Suspicious noises. Probable cause where I come from. Wanna lend a shoulder?" Jackson asked.

The Verde Valley cop gave a quick nod. "On my

mark. One, two…"

They hit the secret door together. It shuddered and splintered around the locking hardware. A couple quick kicks and they were inside.

"Norah?" Jackson called into the silence. Icy prickles ran over his skin. He focused on a closet backed against the office and yanked it open. The rank smells of urine and feces stung his senses, and his head jerked back.

A child lay hogtied on the floor in a puddle of his own filth. His shredded T-shirt revealed angry bruises and three clusters of cigarette burns on his arms and back, some healing, some still fiery.

"Josh?" Kneeling, Jackson removed the restraints and brushed the boy's hair from his face before taking a pulse. Slow and irregular. Skin clammy. Jackson lifted his lids. His eyes were rolled back in his head.

Josh twitched, deeply unconscious.

"Call an ambulance. We're losing him," Jackson ordered. "Then light a fire under that judge and score a warrant, now. I'm gonna tear this fucking place apart."

Chapter Fifteen

Norah's heart pumped madly in her chest as her possessed body sprinted across the highway. The lights of an eighteen-wheeler slashed through the darkness and reflected off the damp, slippery asphalt.

An air horn blasted.

Her muscles jumped. Nausea stabbed her stomach and burned her throat.

Brakes squealed, tires slid, and metal crunched. She scrambled down the embankment bordering the highway and landed in a gully.

Lightning flashed overhead and thunder growled. Rain pelted her face.

Her body straightened and surged forward. Mesquite scratched at her hands. Creosote tore at her clothes, but she loped relentlessly toward an unknown goal. The Magician's voracious spirit drove her through the desert. He gloated like some crazy scientist from a seventies B film. He'd built an impenetrable psychic barrier in her mind, severing all her ties to her spirit guide and freedom. He controlled her every muscle, enslaving her.

The Magician avoided the scattered, lighted dwellings along the road. Avoided anywhere she might have attracted attention, maybe gotten help.

A huge dark SUV crawled along the road bordering the flat expanse of desert. Her skin roughened with goose bumps, and she flopped to the ground. Searchlights played over the desert, silhouetting the spiny ocotillo above her.

The Magician held her flat for endless minutes. Her pulse throbbed in her temples, and insects crawled beneath her.

When he yanked her to her feet, her stomach rebelled. Bile surged into her throat, and she heaved. She brushed off bugs. Her skin itched, and she wanted to scratch until she was raw all over, but her fingers refused to move.

From within the tiny, walled-off prison inside her brain, she gathered strength and waited, like a cougar stalking a buck. She focused on the cadence of her steps, picturing herself in purple velvet robes, a hypnotist swinging a pocket watch before the ancient sorcerer.

Keep your eyes on the shiny, spinning gold and relax.

Left. Right. Left. Right.

Concentrate. Let your mind rest easy.

Left. Right. Left. Right.

You're safe. You have absolute control. You can afford to relax.

Left. Right. Left. Right. His mind beat in time with hers.

Like a giant, flaming battering ram, Norah slammed her spirit against the polished granite wall that held her captive. The barrier shuddered and bowed. Her prison boundaries shifted. Widened.

She fired rapid, laser-sharp mental barrages at the shield but couldn't quite break through or wrest control of her legs and arms.

Lightning crashed directly above her, and the scrubby pine on her right erupted into flame. Thunder roared. The air crackled with electricity.

Her blood rioted in her veins. She aimed a caustic mental fireball at a thin spot in her prison wall.

The Magician's control faltered for a split second.

With a giddy burst of joy, she forced all the air from her lungs and held her breath.

A dozen steps later, dizziness overwhelmed her. Fluorescent spots swam through her vision. She tripped and tumbled into a culvert half full of run-off from the storm. Pain stabbed through her. Sharp rocks bruised her knees and hands and every muscle screamed.

But the Magician seized her diaphragm and tugged. Another frigid blast of air seared her nose and throat.

Despair and frustration clawed at her insides. A scream welled up, but couldn't escape. She wanted to lie there, turn her face into the dirty water and drown.

But her body rose and waded out through knee-deep water. Shivering with cold, she jogged on. At least she'd expanded her awareness and controlled a bigger chunk of her mind and her body. She gloried in the tiny bit of freedom she'd wrested from the Magician, but passively allowed him to move her forward. She had to find shelter. Hypothermia was a real danger.

"There is safety ahead. I must have your help. Will you trust me?"

Norah didn't answer, just reinforced her mental shielding.

Lightning struck to the east over the mesa. The glow briefly lit the thick layers of clouds, and the low hills ahead glinted white through the drizzle. Salt?

"Yes. Our wealth was from salt. We traded with

other peoples far to the north and south. For turquoise. Obsidian. Gold."

Left. Right. Left. Right.

"Trust me." His control eased.

Her abused muscles ached, but she trudged on, moving closer to the hills. Her shoes squished with each step.

She ducked under a barbed wire fence and crunched across soft, sandy mounds that sparkled like snow in the lightning flashes. Ahead, a boarded-up mine had been gouged into the side of the hill.

Her knees trembled, and her mind screamed danger. But she picked up a long, galvanized pipe and used it to pry at the rotted boards that blocked the entrance. Rusty nails creaked and popped.

Lifting one side of the board, she peered into the blackness. Another lightning strike lit the night, thunder boomed over the valley, and the drizzle turned into a downpour.

"Go in."

Norah squeezed through the opening and into the mine, yanking the board into place behind her. Every hair on her nape stood erect, but at least she wouldn't get any wetter and could rest out of the wind.

The Magician's control winked out, and she stumbled. She still wasn't alone in her mind and could sense his presence, but she bent over, hands on her knees and caught her breath without any resistance from him. After a moment, she straightened and squared her shoulders.

Keeping one shaky hand on the left wall, she followed the narrow main path as it climbed down and curved twenty or thirty feet into the hill. Her pulse slowed, and her eyes adjusted to make out some shapes in the darkness.

At a wide spot, she sat and took off her soggy shoes. She set them beside her, pointing toward the entrance. She sure wished she still had that cardboard energy bar with her and maybe a bottle of water.

Shivering, she removed her jacket, intending to shake off the rainwater, but stopped. Twisting the sleeve, she sucked some of the moisture into her mouth. The cool liquid tasted stale, but she sloshed it around her mouth before she swallowed. Bliss. Unfortunately she had nothing to collect it in. Her fingers brushed against the basket in her pocket.

The Magician's spirit invaded her mind, more gently this time. Warmth filled her from her bones to her chilled skin.

"I would show you my story," his deep voice said in his ancient, melodic language and somehow she understood.

Norah crossed her legs and centered her mind, holding the basket close to her heart. She cracked open her inner vision.

Drums pounded from far away, like a ricochet echoing through a narrow canyon. Firelight crackled in an open pit, and smoke that smelled like juniper made her eyes burn.

An elder in a loincloth and high, buckskin boots sat near a small river, warming his hands over a crackling fire. Many lines scored his face and framed his mouth and eyes. He wore a totem necklace on his bare chest. A fierce carved turquoise cat radiated power. Eagle feathers were woven into his long, gray-streaked braids.

"Will you hear my story, daughter? Know me?"

She flung open her senses and let the Magician slowly retake control of her thoughts.

The drums filled her ears, drove her heartbeat, heated her chilly limbs. She stood in a dark cave. Awareness of the web of desert life filled her thoughts. Knowledge of the people who had once flourished here filled her soul. Sadness filled her heart, and she wept for the death of their great leader.

****

More dirt covered the Magician's still face with each drumbeat. The fine grains sifted around his body, pressed on his chest and filled his mouth and nostrils, but he did not gasp for breath.

The drums faded and well-earned darkness enveloped him. Staff in hand, cat totem around his neck, he rested, at peace with the guardian spirits, his spears and wands and baskets arranged beside him in precise display. With these ritual tools, he could serve the People from the next world.

His shade faced west toward the sacred mountain and followed the serpent on the cornmeal trail.

But after many seasons passed, a presence brushed against his awareness. In the soft twilight of the cave, the Magician's spirit stirred.

His apprentice squeezed through a cleft in the stone and crept toward his resting place. The young man's face was anxious under a thatch of dull hair. The Magician saw fear in his eyes and pitied him. But why had the apprentice disturbed the sacred kiva?

Puzzled, the Magician noticed the man's sunken cheeks. Open sores marked his face. A taint had crept in, poisoning his people. Had they taken forbidden *water from the bottomless well? Fools!*

Whispering hurried prayers, the apprentice snatched the cat talisman from his grave.

Violation!

Lightning knifed through the Magician's consciousness. The vortex surrounding him jerked to a halt.

"Do not disturb me," his spirit thundered, shooting jagged waves of power into the chamber.

Eyes wide with terror, the apprentice cringed, but dropped to his knees and pawed through the grave. Dirt scattered in every direction as he uncovered a basket of seed corn. He shoved the basket into his deerskin bag and dug deeper, exposing a water pot.

"Do not disturb me."

Each loss punched another ragged hole in the Magician's power and goaded him into a silent scream. A serpent coiled deep within his breast, but could no longer strike.

The apprentice glanced from side to side and shivered. Goose flesh rose on his skin. He grabbed a bone flute and placed it in his sack, then edged backward through the crevice, dragging the bag with him.

The Magician could only draw on small remnants of his power. His bones lay scattered in his desecrated grave. The People were unprotected.

****

Jackson tamped down the impatience simmering in his guts. He loosened his fists, un-kinked his fingers, and took another sip of the brewed-to-sludge hospital coffee.

With his big brown eyes glazed and droopy, the kid

across the table slouched in his seat and gave a giant yawn. Josh pillowed his sagging head on one arm and nodded off in the middle of chewing a forkful of hash browns.

Trays clanged, and the breakfast crew clunked pans and utensils. Most people seated in the cafeteria wore wrinkled scrubs and weary expressions. The smell of pine disinfectant warred with the aromas of fried bacon and half-burned coffee.

Jackson shifted in the plastic chair. Yeah, he and Norah had managed to rescue Josh. Chalk up one huge success for the A team.

But Norah had gone missing, and somehow he'd gotten stuck feeding the boy when he itched to be out on the desert hunting for her.

Pursing his lips, he leaned his chin on his hand. Why had the woman abandoned her purse, stolen a basket and climbed out the freaking bathroom window?

His phone rang, and Jackson groaned. Great. The captain. Now he'd have to explain why the Verde Valley PD was out combing through the cactus for Norah, and he was sitting on his ass chewing pancakes.

"Any news?" Nate growled. "When Norah didn't call Amber last night, the kid cried herself to sleep. Jana's freaked."

Jackson's stomach contorted. Norah gone. Now Jana on the rampage. Plus a hysterical little girl who'd lost her mom only a year ago. He shivered. "She's still missing. Damn woman just disappeared. Local cops are on the case. They're rounding up the usual coyotes, but Smith and his bodyguard still haven't been apprehended."

"Can't you track her?"

"Don't know where to start beyond the Casino's ten-acre parking lot. Cloudburst last night washed away any chance of picking up her trail."

"Shit. Any other witnesses?"

Jackson rubbed his hand over his face. "Besides that silicon-brained hooker-wannabe? Just a beer-soaked-bubba driving truck. Swears he saw a woman run across the highway. The idiot jackknifed his rig trying not to hit her."

"Could he be telling the truth?"

"More likely the empty twelve-pack behind his seat was to blame." Jackson cleared his throat. "Josh is awake."

"One good thing. Get his story and call me. Soon."

Jackson hung up and gave the boy a gentle pat on his good shoulder. "Come on, Josh. How about another drink of soda? Doc said you could use the sugar."

"Hum? Oh, sure." Josh sucked a couple mouthfuls through his straw and let out a burp. "Excuse me." He squirted more ketchup on his greasy fried potatoes, doused the mountain with maple syrup, and stirred.

Ugh. Jackson pushed away his tray.

Josh shoveled in a mouthful. "So, uh, where's Ms. Redfox? You didn't answer me."

One hand curled into a fist again. Jackson flattened his fingers and scrubbed them up and down his leg. "Don't know, exactly. She smashed a pot in Vince Smith's office and then disappeared with some valuable antique basket. No one's seen her since."

Josh chewed, his expression morphing from half-asleep to thoughtful. The kid met his gaze with a loud gulp. "Um, she didn't break the pot. I did. It was a fake."

"Okay."

A flash of pain crossed the boy's face. He rubbed his sprained shoulder through the sling. "No one would listen when I said Uncle Kenny murdered my mom. He hurt me, so I told those stupid creeps lies about Spanish gold."

Jackson's eyebrows rose, and he grinned, watching the kid fidget. "Good time to lie. Sounds like you've got more story to tell."

"Maybe." Josh cocked his head, but kept his eyes level. "Sgt. Marino, do you know which basket she took?"

"Receptionist called the thing a seed basket. Had a rattlesnake design. Apparently Smith paid some tomb-robber-masquerading-as-an-archeologist big bucks for it a couple months ago. Why do you ask?"

"Tell you in a minute. This might sound kinda weird, but do you know if Ms. Redfox ever saw, uh, ever talked about ghosts?"

Jackson started and sat up a little straighter. Suspicion prickled the back of his neck. "Ghosts? What's the tie in to ghosts?"

"Well, when my Uncle Kenny made me touch a basket like that with Sinagua designs, I saw an ancient spirit." Rubbing one hand across his mouth and chin, Josh cleared his throat. "Actually the Magician kinda snatched hold of my mind, and I wondered if he might have, uh, grabbed Ms. Redfox."

A shiver stabbed the base of Jackson's spine and laddered up his backbone, spreading frost. "What do you mean?"

"The basket belongs to the Magician. He wants it back."

With his stomach writhing like a den of snakes, Jackson took another slurp of coffee. Not an answer. He let the silence between them grow.

"He took control of my body so I'd bring it to him," Josh blurted. "But then Uncle Kenny drugged me again, and I went to sleep."

"Okay. So you think this Magician might have overtaken Norah instead?"

Josh nodded, and his shaggy hair flopped over his forehead, covering his eyes. He swiped the mop aside. "Her gifts are different than mine, but she's really strong. So is the Magician. Old, but really strong."

Shit. Fuck. Piss. Why did that make so damn much sense? Jackson pushed back and rubbed his fingers over his stubbled chin. She'd said an elder had tried to grab her at the museum, but he hadn't listened. Norah had latched on to him and fought off the spook. But in Smith's office, he hadn't been within reach to serve as her personal panic bar. Jackson drummed his hands on the table. "Tell me how your gifts work."

"When I touch something like the basket, I always sorta know stuff." Josh's face screwed up into a puzzled frown. "But the Magician is different. Powerful. It's more like he haunts the things he used to own."

Jackson licked his lip and chewed on one corner. He didn't much like the idea he'd gotten some quality face time with two ghosts yesterday. Thought gave him the heebie-jeebies all the way to his toenails, but no point wasting time denying what his senses had told him.

Or what Josh was saying.

Okay, so now he'd listen. Maybe the kid could help find Norah. He'd run a little test and see. Jackson looked around the room and finally patted the Formica in front of him. "Show me. What can you sense about this table?"

Frowning, Josh laid his hands flat. After a moment, he shook his head. "Too many people have touched it. All I see is a mash up of grief and fear and pain."

"Okay." Jackson rummaged through his pockets. What did he have on him? Grinning, he reached under his shirt, unlatched his St. Christopher medal and passed it over. "Can you read this?"

Taking a deep breath, Josh reached for the gold chain and let the medal clink onto his open palm. "You've had this since you were very young. Like second grade?"

"Yeah." Was that the whole show? With an encouraging nod, Jackson crossed his arms and waited.

Josh's eyes closed, and his face went slack. "A boy with dark curly hair wears his brand new suit. He's happy and smiling, but his bow tie strangles him, and his hands sweat, and the step beneath his knees is cold and hard."

Frowning, Jackson stayed silent.

"Lots of people watch him, and his heart squeezes in his chest. He looks up at another man, young and thin, and his hair is pale, and his eyes are blue and they twinkle. The man wears a long dress. No, a robe, with a green sash across his shoulders that trails down his chest. They're in a big room with candles and flowers and soft lights. A church."

The skin on the back of Jackson's neck crawled. He ran a hand over one ear and stretched the lobe a couple times. Still, the kid could be bullshitting.

"A woman brings the boy chocolate cake. His

mouth already tastes like crackers and wine and he's proud and happy, but he wants a taste of the chocolate cake, and his mouth waters. Her smile is wide, but her eyes brim with tears, and she sniffs and hands him a package. The medal is inside." Josh swayed forward in his seat and gave a low moan.

Jackson scooted the cola out of the way and reached to steady the boy.

"The woman's hair is black, streaked with gray, and twisted up under a little round hat with a funny lace veil. She wears a pink dress and high heels and a white sweater clipped together with a string of pearls." Josh's face softened, and his lips twitched. "She kisses his cheek and ruffles his hair, and she smells very good. She smells like love and sugar cookies."

Eyes wide, jaw gaping, Jackson rubbed his forehead and exhaled slowly. "My first communion. How could you possibly know?"

Josh opened his eyes and blinked, the wistful smile still on his face. "Our kitchen used to smell like that before Mom got sick. Did your grandma bake cookies for you?"

Jackson swallowed past the boulder in his throat. "Yeah."

"You still miss her." The smile vanished. "Her heart didn't work right, did it? She died a few weeks later, and you think of her every morning when you put on the medal."

A whole new set of creepy crawlies boogied over his skin. Jackson couldn't restrain a shudder, couldn't force an answer out between his dry lips. He could only nod mutely.

Josh sat very still for a long moment and then

nodded, more to himself than to Jackson. "I think I know someone who can help us find Ms. Redfox."

Blinking rapidly, Jackson raked a hand through his hair. "Right. Sounds good. Who?"

"My dad's cousin. George. He's a shaman. The Magician says this morning he'll be at Newspaper Rock to start the equinox ceremony."

Chapter Sixteen

Norah's tongue stuck to the roof of her mouth. Her pores oozed salt, and her empty stomach gurgled and growled and threatened spontaneous combustion.

Dawn light filtered through the boarded up entrance and made the mine tunnel feel even more claustrophobic. She stretched her sore muscles, flexed her calves and rolled her shoulders.

Last night's marathon across the desert had been a workout from hell. She forced a chuckle. At least none of that white chocolate mousse would end up padding her hips. With one hand on the wall of the salt mine, she felt her way back toward the entrance.

The Magician brushed ghostly fingers over her shoulder. *"Beware. Go slowly."*

Shivering, she paused and listened.

"There aren't any footprints up this way," a deep voice shouted outside.

"It rained last night, you stupid fuck," Vince Smith growled, his voice flat and sarcastic.

Her heart raced, but she squinted through the break in the boards. They'd followed her. Fifty yards away Vince Smith and his bodyguard stood in the bright dawn sunlight. No way could she sneak past them. Smith would find her in here, hurt her and take the basket.

She didn't dare move the boards closer together,

either. If she tried to close the gap, they'd creak and give her away.

"She's just a woman. She can't have gotten this far in that fucking storm," the bodyguard argued.

"We looked everywhere else on this side of the highway, checked all around the casino, even on the Rez." Smith kicked at a pile of rocks, sending salt splattering into the air. "But the bitch hasn't surfaced. There aren't that many places to hole up in this fucking wasteland."

"A trucker reported seeing a woman cross the highway. Maybe she hitched a ride."

"In that downpour? More likely she's road kill. But I gotta be absolutely sure. Besides, I want my God damn basket back." Smith adjusted his matte black designer sunglasses. "Glare's getting to me. Check all the mine tunnels, Benny. I'll wait in the car."

She zipped the basket beneath her jacket and hurried back into the blackness of the mine. If she crept silently, perhaps they wouldn't notice her, even if they did look inside this tunnel.

Footsteps crunched closer across the salt.

Terror speared through her, stealing her breath and clogging her dry throat. She eased past the wide spot where she'd slept, but the deeper she went the more the mine tunnel narrowed. The walls closed in, and the ceiling height angled lower until she couldn't stand straight. The passage became a cramped, terrifying crawl space.

Hunching, she felt along the damp walls and found a break in the timber supports about waist high. She squeezed through and curled into a ball in the thick darkness.

With a loud creak and pop, Benny the bodyguard wedged the entrance open. Dust and salt particles danced in the shaft of light. "Oof. Kinda tight quarters in here. Gives me the fucking creeps."

Her heart throbbed in her ears, but Norah held absolutely still, didn't dare peek between the rotten, splintered timbers.

"Nothing in here. I'm going to close this one up, Vinny. Don't want nobody getting in." The boards creaked again, and the shaft of light winked out.

When Benny banged on the old nails, the mine echoed and shuddered, and she covered her head. Salt rained on her, choked her, but at least that gorilla hadn't found her.

Every one of her muscles was shaking. She tried to swallow despite her parched throat. Nothing. Her jacket had dried overnight and was crusted with salt like a giant hot pretzel.

Outside the mine, the crunching footsteps and shouted curses continued. Would they ever give up?

With her arms curled around her body, Norah rocked back and forth where she lay. If she stayed in this ancient death trap alone much longer, she'd go totally crazy and run out screaming into Smith's hands. She opened her mind a tiny crack, but she couldn't reach Grandfather.

She tried to hold on to her sanity, picturing his lodge when she was a child. A thread of curiosity rose inside her. Last night she'd fought so very hard to free herself from the Magician's grasp. Could she risk asking a question? She sat and braced her back against the wall.

"Magician? Elder? I'd like to know more of your

251

people. Why did their lives move from plenty to famine?"

"In my youth, life was good. Our people had strong leaders, water, food, healthy children." He held out his hands. *"Do you wish to see?"*

After a moment's hesitation, Norah nodded and opened her mind further.

Her spirit transported to a deep valley between two sandstone mesas. Bright yellow and gold cottonwood leaves stirred in the breeze. A herd of deer grazed in the distant meadow.

The creek rushed around her feet, tumbling over rocks slick with moss. She picked her way toward the bank past a silver-bellied trout swimming along the bottom.

She stepped out of the stream into knee high grass and a family of quail rose from the brush, beating their wings. She drew a deep breath. The air was clear and clean, scented with herbs and grasses. The trees rustled, the running water sounded like music. A golden eagle drifting on a thermal air current cried. Peace surrounded her. Every sound had a natural origin important to the people.

The Magician waited by the cliff face, sipping water from a black and white figured pot. He rose and beckoned.

She followed him, scrambling over the piled boulders and leaping from rock to rock. As they scrambled down the canyon, she struggled to keep up with the man's long, sure- footed strides.

She paused to catch her breath and studied the pictures carved into the black-stained walls. Animals hunted by the Magician's people. Big horn sheep and deer. Coyotes roamed. Snakes wriggled up the walls and into crevices followed by a shaman dancing and waving a staff.

An engine turned over in the distance and brought her back from the light trance. Norah opened her eyes.

The car roared away. Then silence.

She squirmed back out into the main tunnel and crept toward the entrance. Weak light trickled through the battered lumber. She pushed against the board she'd removed the night before, but it wouldn't budge.

Her heart squeezed in her chest. Trapped. Tasting bile at the back of her throat, she swallowed her terror of this closed-in-coffin-of-a-mine.

She slammed against the wood with all her might, but it wouldn't give way. She needed a lever, something to pry with, but all the timbers inside the mine were old and rotten. She tried one anyway, but the wood splintered under the pressure. Grunting with effort, she kicked the entrance boards again and again, fruitlessly.

Exhausted, she crawled back to the wide spot and swiped at her tears with gritty palms. Her mouth and eyes stung with salt. She let out a great heaving sob and listened to the frantic beating of her heart.

Was that faint sound water dripping further back in the mine? She held her breath and strained to hear.

The noise was elusive, intermittent, but real. She bit her lip and crawled back through the opening in the timbers where she'd hidden from Smith. On her hands and knees, she crept a few feet further into the mine and faced a narrow passage.

"Yes. This way is clear," the Magician whispered in her mind.

Her pulse pounded with sickening force, and her stomach jittered at the prospect of that tiny space, but she had to try. She wriggled on her belly into the passage. Her shoulders and hips rubbed against the sides as she scooted forward.

Oh, God. Oh, God. Oh, God.

Terror cramped her muscles and froze her brain, but she closed her eyes and inched along, closer to the water. She had to keep breathing.

About ten feet in, the shaft widened gradually. A few more feet and she could rise to her knees. She felt along the ceiling, and her spirit lightened. Keeping her hands in front of her head, she moved carefully toward the sound of water, her steps slow and deliberate.

This far back, the walls of the mine were damp to the touch. A drop landed on her hair, and she turned her face upward. The water trickled down her nose and over her parched lips. She shifted and opened her mouth. When the next salty drop hit her tongue, she let the trickle cool her burning throat. But it didn't slake her raging thirst.

Through the darkness ahead, dim light glistened on the slick walls. A dizzy sense of glee zinged through her. She couldn't touch the ceiling here. Was it an upward tunnel? A skylight?

Escape?

She managed a toehold on one sloped wall and dragged herself to within a dozen feet of the opening. A smile teased her parched lips.

Her eyes adjusted to the dim light. A piece of flint had lodged into one wall. She pried it free and used the notch for a handhold, pulling herself higher. Behind her, water dripped steadily onto the floor. Balancing carefully, she dug into the wall above her and carved out a narrow shelf.

She heaved herself up and braced one hip on the shallow ledge with her feet dangling. Pebbles rained into the pit below her. She reached up and started to dig again. Her fingers ached. Dust clogged her throat. She yanked some tattered rushes protruding from the wall, and they crumbled into ash.

With filthy hands, she shoved away the loose debris. She climbed onto the wider shelf, only a few feet from daylight. Almost there. She couldn't quite reach the tiny opening even if she stretched.

When she checked to make sure the basket was safe in her pocket, her flint tool slipped from her hand.

She automatically grabbed for the stone and nearly fell. But she scrambled for balance and hugged the wall until she could catch her breath.

After a moment, she patted the shallow indentation, searching for another tool to widen the hole. She found a smooth timber about eighteen inches long with a knob on the end. Stretching up, she poked it through the opening. Rock and dirt showered her, but the fissure widened.

She glanced at the shelf beside her, and the blood drained from her face. Every hair on her body lifted and she breathed in great, ragged gulps. In the bright sunlight she stared into the eye sockets of a skull.

Stifling a scream, Norah shrank away, almost falling back into the mine. She looked at the tool in her hand, and her goose bumps grew goose bumps. A long bone. Trembling, she placed the femur beside the skeleton with a murmur of thanks and fled into the morning light.

When she stood, her legs buckled under her, so she crawled away from the pit.

****

Kenny wrapped a rubber band around the last stack of hundreds. Slouching on the orange plastic dinette seat in his camper van, he ground out his cigarette and sucked on a cup of lukewarm coffee. Sweet. Fifty grand all piled up nice and tidy.

But nowhere near enough. Nowhere near what he deserved.

He rubbed the rough stubble on his chin and stretched a kink out of his back. Dim morning light shot between the camper's front curtains. He pushed one aside and stared across the high, barren desert. His treasure lay buried somewhere close. He could smell the fucking gold.

Gina snored like a jet engine. Always did when he doped her. He stowed the money under his seat and leaned over the bed, watching her sleep.

She smacked her lips together and turned on her side exposing bite shaped bruises on her naked tit.

His pulse tripped, and he grinned. Finger marks on her neck, too. Yeah, he'd hurt her last night, but she'd begged for the punishment. And he'd made her come screaming a dozen times.

The bitch was fucking lucky, and she knew it. They'd chased all around this God-forsaken desert yesterday. How many snake infested, flooded washes had they searched? And all for nothing. But today he'd give her one more chance.

"Gina. Wake up."

Shifting her hair to the side, he scraped his whiskered chin over the soft skin beneath her ear.

"Gina."

Frowning, she batted at him and shrank away. "W-What?"

"Get the fuck up. It's light. We gotta get moving."

She rose part way on one elbow, but slumped back on the pillow like her head weighed a ton. "What time's it?" Her voice slurred.

"Almost 6:30."

She let out another long moan, and he gritted his teeth. "Get out of bed. We're leaving in five minutes," he said very calmly.

She went still. Her eyes peeked out half-open lids, and she headed for the can.

Warmth spread through his chest. He crossed his arms and nodded. Progress. She was learning not to argue.

"Don't wear those fucking sandals again. We got ground to cover," he shouted at the thin door and stowed the journal in his jacket pocket.

She mumbled something but came out dressed and almost presentable. Skin tight jeans, sneakers, but no bra. Her hard nipples poked against the thin T-shirt material.

His cock throbbed. Should he fuck her first? No, he'd make her wait. "Come on." He grabbed her hand and turned toward the door. But she twisted free, and the pissed-off look on her face stopped him.

Angry heat rushed up his neck. "What the fuck?"

She narrowed her black eyes to slits and planted her feet. "I want to go get Josh."

Hit her? No, jive her along. He let out his breath slow and even. Remember, one more chance. "Told you. He's staying with Smith while we look for the treasure." He drew out the word in a low, sugary voice, letting a come-on-baby twinkle light his smile and eyes.

But she crossed her arms and covered her boobs. "He could help us find the petroglyph."

"Nah, he'd just get in our way. Let him play with his friends."

"But—"

"Watch it, Gina. I told you Josh is safe with Smith and his boys." He drew in a silent breath through his nose and fisted his hands behind his back. He itched to backhand her, but she was the key to finding his treasure. That is if the idiot ever remembered which fucking canyon her grandma had lived near.

"Find the fucking cat, find the fucking treasure." He smiled and added through clenched teeth, "Then you can mother the fucking kid all you want."

"I can spot a liar, too." She turned and flounced toward the bed.

The blood in his brain ignited like a welding torch, and his vision blurred to red. When had she become such a fucking smart-ass? Fine. Punishment first.

He stomped after her, grabbed her by the hair and twisted. Hard.

When she cried out, he wrapped an arm around her middle and yanked her against him. No way he'd let her abandon him for some worthless runt. He'd kill her first.

"Kenny! No!" She struggled against his hold.

His balls tightened. His cock hardened. He jerked her around and jammed his face against hers. "Josh is safe. For now."

She whimpered.

He yanked again, and tears dripped from her bloodshot eyes. "But I will wring his scrawny, good-for-shit-neck if you don't find my treasure."

Chapter Seventeen

Norah cowered behind the dumpster. Her body, held by the Magician's paralyzing grip, curled around a pilfered bag of stale sourdough and a half-empty water bottle. Inside her chest, her heart thumped faster than she could jitterbug.

The back door of the roadside café squeaked open, and the cook peered out, wiping his hands on the grungy apron covering his beer belly. He took a quick stroll around, walking within five feet of where she hunched. But he clomped right past.

If she could knock over that beer bottle on the ground, the noise would surely grab his attention. Focusing all her energy on one hand, she strained against the Magician's control.

She couldn't manage even a finger twitch.

In her mind she screamed, "I'm here! Look around and see me! Help me!"

Nothing.

The thirty-something man had last night's stubble prickling his weak chin and brown hair tied back in a tail. Dark circles bagged under his bloodshot eyes. Scratching his cheek, he yawned and dug in his shirt pocket for a pack of cigarettes. He lit one, took a lung-scorching drag and faced the screen door. "Nothing out here now, boss. Musta been those damn cats again."

A voice grouched through the door, but Norah

couldn't make out the words.

"All right, all right. I'm coming. Who cares if their freaking bacon's burnt?" The cook ground out his smoke and, with one last glance around the area, stomped back inside.

The Magician pulled a psychic puppet string, and her body straightened. *"Hurry. Move this way. Quietly."*

Norah heaved a gigantic mental sigh and edged around the open dumpster. Her hand snagged a bruised green apple as she crept past. At least her stomach wouldn't chew on itself anymore.

Her feet followed the damp path beside a creek that trickled down the middle of a wide, sandy wash. A squad car swooshed by in the distance. Her heart wrenched, but her body just loped along, hidden in the arroyo. Could they be searching for her?

Step by step, she left the café, the road, and the town far behind. Soon the streambed widened and half a dozen channels flowed between deeply carved, sandy banks. The Magician pushed her along until she reached a stand of cottonwood trees. She scrambled out of the wash and sank to the ground inside the small grove.

The Magician crammed a chunk of dry sourdough into her mouth.

"Water first. Please," she choked out around the crumbs. When his control relaxed, she spat out the bread and drank deeply from the bottle she'd scrounged. Tepid, stale, but the liquid felt wonderful to her parched throat.

After gnawing the apple to the core, she finished the bread and filled the empty plastic bottle from the free flowing stream. She tucked the bottle and the bread she hadn't eaten into a satchel she'd made from her jacket and rinsed the salt and sweat off her face and neck.

"Hurry," The Magician poked her mind again and jerked her to her feet.

Grimacing, she looped the sleeves of her makeshift backpack over her shoulders and adjusted the knot. She trudged forward, even though every muscle ached. Blisters on her heels, one calf cramping, her hips and lower back were sore from last night's unending, pounding steps.

Her heart thudded behind her temples, but the sulfuric rage at the Magician's invasion had dulled into aching, smoldering frustration. His dominating presence was so very different from Grandfather's touch, even at his most demanding. Less enigmatic, but more controlling.

More powerful.

Vastly more exasperating.

Pain shot through her lower back, and she groaned. *"Damn it! I can't keep up this pace."*

The Magician eased her into a power walk.

Her arms pumped with each awkward step. The makeshift pack straps rubbed against her shoulders, and her back twanged. Torture. She was the Magician's slave.

Okay. Think. She couldn't block him out entirely, no matter how hard she struggled. Her body ached, partly because he'd pushed her so hard for so long, forcing her limbs to repeat movements that were unnatural for her. Unnatural for anyone with a female center of gravity.

She shoved at him with her thoughts. *"Look. If I promise to follow your directions, to help you, will you release me? At least give me the freedom to move on my own?"*

The space within her mind expanded, and she blew out a breath. *"Thank you."*

"This way."

"First give me a minute to stretch."

Rotating her neck one last time, she turned north and followed the stream. The sun cast long, cold shadows to her left. Following the Magician's more subtle guidance, she forged steadily uphill toward the black mountains in the distance. The red cliffs from his visions loomed in front of her. She hiked into the canyon filled with cottonwoods and lush grass.

No homes, no people lived along the banks of the creek. No chance to seek help.

Surrounded by towering sandstone cliffs, the narrow patch of sky above her was vivid blue. But rain-filled clouds hovered on the horizon. She grimaced and pushed her matted, salt-encrusted hair off her damp forehead. In a flash flood, this narrow canyon would be a death trap.

She rounded a bend and stopped. A soggy mess of brush and fallen trees blocked the path ahead.

The Magician nudged her into the streambed.

Norah picked her way along a line of the slick, mossy rocks. One stone wobbled under her shoe, and she lost her balance, but caught herself before she fell backward into the rushing water. Her insides twisted. She waited with her arms wrapped around her waist until her pulse slowed.

As she walked, the creek ran deeper, faster.

On the east bank, a shadowed path emerged from the undergrowth. She scrambled up onto the uneven trail.

A dozen paces later she put her foot down next to a stick. The stick moved. Her shriek echoed off the wind-carved walls, and her heart thundered in her throat while the small black snake wriggled under some brush.

A deep chuckle echoed in her mind, "The serpent was harmless."

Tears stung her eyes. Her hands trembled as she swiped them away. Sullen anger rose in her chest. *"I hate snakes."*

Grinding her teeth, she leaned forward with her hands on her knees and examined the petroglyphs etched into tall sandstone cliffs that had been blackened and stained by countless floods. The snake figures all wriggled upstream. With a shudder, she trudged along the trail.

Below her, the stream had become a river that gushed and raged between the narrow canyon walls. Debris floated in the churning water. The icy wind bit through her clothing. More rain must be falling in the mountains. She climbed a steep cascade of broken rocks, but couldn't scale the concave, fissured overhang.

"Hurry."

The river, choked with debris, now flowed shoulder deep from wall to wall. Still rising, the frigid water lapped over her shoes and soon rushed around her ankles, chasing her along the upslope.

Near her hand, a stylized snake was etched into the rock wall with its split tongue pointed at the sky.

"Hurry. Climb up"

Shivering, Norah gritted her teeth and inched higher along the steep walls, using the fissures in the rock and narrow toe holds. The roar of rushing water deafened her.

Numb from the cold, her fingers slipped. She landed against the trunk of a fallen sycamore, all the air knocked from her lungs. She dragged herself up into a crevice and lay gasping. The metallic taste of blood filled her mouth, and she touched her swollen lip.

Resting against the damp walls while she caught her breath, she shook out her aching arms. The river twenty feet below formed a raging torrent through the rocky canyon.

Hidden in the shadowy cleft of the rock, a third snake wriggled up the cliff toward a huge petroglyph of a cat. The centuries old saber tooth glared at her, with fierce claws and sharp teeth like those in the Magician's necklace.

"I led you here for a reason. Dig."

Her heartbeat quickened. Beneath the cat and mostly buried in gravel lay a large white stone unlike the dark rock of the cliffs. She brushed her fingers across the smooth surface. A marker, placed there by human hands?

Pulse racing, she squinted at the rock. Yes. A carved snake.

Balancing on the narrow ledge, Norah dug at the sides of the stone with her fingers. She shoveled away the mucky gravel until she finally wiggled the heavy rock free and then heaved it into the water churning below.

A deep, dark hole gaped in the limestone.

She scrunched her eyes shut. *"Snakes?"*

"No living ones."

With her face squeezed in a grimace, Norah reached into the pit. She wrapped her fingers around a bundle hidden beneath the marker.

On her hands and knees, she unwrapped stiff shreds of old leather and held up a small, black and white pot painted with a snake motif.

"The dragonflies never drank at the bottomless well."

"What?" Another bloody enigma. The past few days, she'd had lots of questions, but very few answers from the ghostly old men in her life. Time to try a different approach. Exhausted and filthy, she cradled the ancient pot in her lap and heaved a sigh. *"If you have more to tell, I will listen, elder."*

"Yes, daughter." A warm thread of approval colored his mental voice. *"The Cat Clan People worked together to divert and save river water to irrigate the fields. Men dug in the mine for salt, precious to other tribes who traveled far for trade. Women harvested the agave, the golden saguaro and the prickly pear. During my life, I cautioned the People. I warned my apprentice not to yield to temptation, not to drink the water. The well was tainted, poisoned by evil spirits."*

"Is that what happened? Your People were poisoned?"

"Over time. For a few seasons, the rain god tested them and refused to send the rain. Crops withered. The People became frightened.

"Is that when the Apprentice stole your things?"

"Yes. He was lazy and arrogant. He thought if he possessed my tools he would be so powerful he could ignore the spirits. But the old ones are very wise and

always watchful."

"What happened?"

"At his direction, the People used poisoned water from the well to irrigate the crops. I could not stop them. For a season, his trickery seemed to work. Then the children sickened. The hunters and women became weak."

Probably arsenic, like the so-called Montezuma's well. Norah glanced out over the desert landscape. The shadows were shorter now. On the next outcropping across the river, an ancient dwelling had been built in the cliff overhang with rough sandstone walls. Small windows and doors were gouged into the rock.

The Magician followed her gaze. *"This was my home."* His voice sounded so lonely.

She swallowed the bitter taste in her mouth.

"My People have not lived here for many years. I could not protect them."

"Could you now? Is that what you want?"

A long moment passed before he spoke again. *"My life was over long ago, and I am very tired. But if I had my sacred tools, I could protect them while I teach a new Magician. An Apprentice. Someone who could lead the People in this new time."*

Norah fingered the tiny water bowl, and a shiver raced through her as fast and cold as the river below. *"Josh."*

"The boy is of my blood."

In her mind, she looked into the Magician's tortured face, and her breath caught. Of course. The same amber color lit his eyes. *"But I don't know where Josh is."*

"He will come if I am ready, but we have little

time. I must have all my missing tools for my power to return."

"How long?"

"Until the sun casts light upon my grave." He *pointed to the high mesa across the river. "Midday."*

The tall mesa to the north looked blue in the morning sun. Her throat seized up. No question, she'd never reach her destination by noon unless she got moving.

Taking a deep breath, she shrugged off her makeshift pack and checked inside. Both the basket and pot were safe, packed in soft green cottonwood leaves and wrapped inside her blue scarf. Reaching for the water bottle she'd scrounged, she took a drink and dribbled a little over the gouges in her hands, hissing at the sting.

She set out at a controlled jog. Her immediate goal? The silhouette of a twisted piñon barely visible ahead. She'd always loved to run. Once her muscles loosened she covered the rough ground along the canyon rim with ease.

She probed for her grandfather's presence. No. Still blocked. Her mind felt strange and empty without his touch. Even the Magician remained quiet. For the moment she was alone.

The desert seemed immense. Silent. Spooky.

People had lived and died in this valley for many centuries. The long gash of narrow canyon on her left cut her off from the distant cliffs she'd have to scale. But first, she had to find a way across the flooded river. No time to wait for the waters to retreat.

The wind gusted at her back as she loped past the piñon toward a clump of agave plants. A quarter mile further, the canyon veered west, and the distance between the two mesas narrowed.

She slowed. Careful to avoid loose gravel, she looked over the side. The river still churned and boiled. But just ahead, a large pine had fallen across the river twenty feet below the canyon rim. The broken tip was wedged against the opposite cliff face just above water level and lay across the wide trail. This crude bridge looked like her best shot at crossing anytime soon.

Following a deer trail, she dodged around a stand of scrubby juniper and slid, butt first, into a damp crevice above the river.

Her pulse pounded in her ears as she scrambled up the tangled tree roots. She used the strong limbs for balance to climb over the fresh jagged splinters where the tree had split. The odor of doused campfire filled her nose. From the burn marks on the wood and the surrounding rocks, it looked like the tree had been struck by lightning.

She rocked back and forth on the pine and then bounced a couple times. Seemed stable.

She took three deep breaths and swallowed past the giant lump in her throat. Dodging branches that swiped at her face and snatched at her hair, she picked her way across on her hands and knees.

Thud!

Debris in the roiling water smashed against the tree trunk. With a loud crack, the pine groaned and shifted.

Heart hammering against the inside of her ribs, she flattened and clung to the battered tree.

Her body shook. Cold water soaked her clothes and sprayed her face. She inched along on her belly until she reached the far bank.

She bolted forward on wobbly legs. A surge of joy bubbled through her. She burst out laughing. Her sticky hands smelled like pinesap, and the scrapes on her palms burned like crazy. She'd never in an eon get her jeans clean, and she was cold and wet and sore. But she was across that damn clutching, raging river.

She stretched her back, rolled her shoulders and trudged off again. Every blast of wind set off shivers. The seams of her water logged jeans rubbed against her thighs as she jogged along the precarious path.

Chapter Eighteen

Over fifteen hours ago he'd bitten his tongue and watched Norah march into Smith's office. Fifteen hours in which he'd wished a zillion times he had her back, safe. Jackson's chest contorted, and something unpleasant squeezed his heart. Fifteen hours since he'd known for sure she was still alive.

His dry eyes felt gritty, and his hand wasn't absolutely steady, but he shoved his espresso into the cup holder, breathing slow and deep, and deliberate. The hunt was afoot. "Ready to find your cousin George?"

Josh buckled his seat belt and pointed north. "Yep. Newspaper Rock's that way."

How the hell did the kid know? Restraining a headshake, Jackson drove out of the hospital parking lot and onto the side street. He drove through the early morning in silence, edging around the country town of Verde Valley.

He slowed outside the Casino's huge, neon-lit parking lot. Three, no four squad cars still blocked the entrance. Fredericks and his crew had spent the night tearing the place apart. No sign of Norah, but they'd scored a fortune in contraband: drugs, illegal antiquities and Smith's stable of under-age prostitutes.

Josh made a noise of revulsion. "Thanks for getting me out of there. But don't worry. We'll find Ms.

Redfox today."

A trickle of adrenaline cleared Jackson's mind and centered his thoughts. His white-knuckled grip on the wheel relaxed. "You bet."

Sunrise lit the sky with streaks of hot gold and orange and red. The mountains cast long shadows on the desert floor. Crisscrossing a running stream, Jackson headed almost due north through the expanse of flat, open desert.

At an un-posted junction, Josh pointed northeast. A dirt road wound past stands of creosote and spindly, spiky cactus. The SUV bounced along the rutted track and forded a flooded wash. The bullet-pocked sign read, "Beaver Creek."

Almost three miles of bumps and grinds later, they reached a chained metal gate marked "V-Bar-V Ranch." Jackson's stomach twisted. "Looks like the parking lot's closed."

"It's okay. Just pull off over there. The Forest Service gives my tribe access for rituals and stuff. Come on." Josh jumped out of the car and ducked under the rusted fence.

Jackson stomped on the parking brake and followed. Apprehension twitched in his belly like a pissed-off rattlesnake and not just from the apology he owed Norah. He tamped down a raging thread of panic.

Maybe Norah was here, and she'd somehow connected with this shaman guy, George. Shared the sunrise and some spooky root-and-twig tea. Maybe she was waiting for him, smiling and ready to listen. He pursed his lips. No. Didn't feel right. No way this would be over so easily.

Josh scuffed along the muddy, washed-out trail and

approached a large, flat-faced black rock with a crack running up the middle.

Hundreds of petroglyphs crowded the face of the huge stone, visible even in the slanting light. Ancient graffiti. So dense and layered that Jackson's gaze kept shifting to another square spiral or heron or space-helmeted stick figure.

A rustle caught his attention. A man, dressed in a denim shirt and jeans with a big silver buckle, sat in the shade of the rock. Mid-fifties. Hefty yet powerful. Intelligent face. Leather thongs and eagle feathers tied his long salt and pepper braids. He wore wide turquoise and silver bracelets, and a multi-string necklace with carved cat fetishes. Chunky rings crowded his knobby brown fingers.

Jackson's jaw clamped shut. No Norah anywhere.

"Hi, Cousin George." Josh gave a brief, nodding bow. His hair flopped onto his forehead.

As he stood, the man's tanned leathery face broke into a smile with deep creases bracketing his mouth. "I've been waiting for you." A couple inches shy of six feet, he kicked the dust off his worn cowboy boots. Then he settled his gray felt cowboy hat lower on his brow, shielding his eyes from the glare.

Jackson put out his hand and stepped closer. "Jackson Marino, Sereno PD." When their hands touched, a chill caught him between the shoulder blades. The man's body seemed surrounded by ancient ghosts.

"Detective," George said and turned to Josh. "I brought you some food, cousin. Come. Sit in the shade while I tell you a story."

Muscles aching with tension, Jackson scanned the

area, still hoping for…what? For Norah to walk up and give him a big kiss? "Business first, Kwail. I'm looking for Norah Redfox. Have you seen her?"

"Seen? No, not exactly." George bent and dug in his rucksack.

Jackson's fingers clenched against his thighs. "What do you mean, 'exactly'?" he growled.

But the man ignored him and handed Josh a familiar looking fast food bag.

The kid grinned and sat under a nearby Palo Verde tree, holding his sore shoulder steady. Paper crinkled. Within seconds Josh had a red and yellow cardboard box out and open and had stuffed half the breakfast sandwich in his mouth. Egg yolk dripped down his chin, and he licked his fingers.

George chuckled while the boy wolfed the other half. "How long since you've eaten?"

"An hour," Jackson answered dryly.

"But before that, Tuesday, I think." With a loud slurp, Josh sucked the plastic juice bottle dry.

"Kid's had a tough time." Jackson tucked his thumbs into his belt loops. "Now about Norah Redfox—"

"I have some supplies in my truck." With an old man's grunt, George rose slowly to his feet. "Stay here. I'll be back in a minute."

Controlling an urge to roll his eyes, Jackson watched Josh plow through a second sandwich. In the middle of a huge bite, he stopped chewing. "Hear that?"

"Just the wind."

Josh shook his head, his brow wrinkled. "No. A rattle." The boy's eyes widened with surprise, and then he nodded.

Cold prickles crawled through his gut. Jackson reached for his weapon, scanning the ground. "Snake?"

"No. The Magician's spirit is near." Josh stood, squared his thin shoulders, and stared hard, his expression intent and his eyes unfocused. The kid looked just like Norah when she said she was listening to her grandfather.

Jackson's fingers edged closer to his holster. Sure. Shoot a ghost? Excellent tactics, Marino. His hackles rose. He dropped his hand and stared at the ancient sorcerer. Tall, carved cheekbones, gray braids tied with leather. His deeply tanned, scarred chest lean but muscled. Wearing a loincloth, he carried a staff with snakes carved into the wood. The dead, ancient sorcerer radiated power.

George clomped back around the huge rock. He put down a plastic carryall and moved silently to Josh's side. "Did the Magician speak?"

Josh turned and whispered, "Do you see him, too?"

"I can hear his rattle, sense his presence. Sometimes I see him as a shadow," George said.

"I can hear him speak, but I don't understand his words." The boy shivered. "He's pointing there."

Jackson stared at the monolith covered in mysterious etchings. The ghost vanished.

The boy sighed, and his body relaxed. "He left." The kid ran over and examined one design closely. "He pointed to this mountain lion."

"You and the hunter have a journey ahead," George said, his tone low, but riddled with suppressed excitement.

A frown tightened Jackson's jaw. His heart bumped. "Where?"

"You must follow the Magician."

"Where do we start?" Josh's voice jumped an octave, and his fingers rubbed nervously across his mouth.

"I can lead you for a short distance. From there we will learn the next step."

"Why a mountain lion?" Jackson probed.

"That was his clan. Our clan. North of here a large petroglyph marks a sacred place."

Jackson cocked one brow and scrutinized the older man. "Is Norah there?"

"Perhaps." George's eyes slewed left. With a shrug, he put a hand on the boy's shoulder and guided him to the shade.

Grinding a fist against his palm, Jackson bit his lower lip and followed. He needed more than vague hunches. He growled under his breath and put a hand out to block the man. "Listen, Kwail. Who's this Magician? Why did he kidnap Norah?"

George stopped and settled gracefully onto the ground, crossing his legs. He drew Josh down beside him and gestured for Jackson to join them. "There is a legend among our people."

Jackson's pulse doubled, and adrenaline pumped into his limbs. He needed answers, fast, not long-winded stories to repeat around the campfire. "Tell Josh your story some other time. We need to find Norah fast. She's in danger."

For a long moment, George sat silent with his eyes closed. Jackson's blood pressure climbed.

Then George shook his head. "She's safe at present. The Magician guards her on her quest."

Jackson let out a long, frustrated hiss. The guy

would take his sweet time explaining, no matter what. Arresting him for obstructing justice would waste even more time. Not much he could do but listen. Jackson folded his legs and thumped his butt onto the ground.

With a knowing smile, George turned to Josh. "Long ago, in the time of great plenty, there lived a powerful shaman of the Cat Clan. The Magician spoke with the gods and rain fell on the valley. The People were blessed with plentiful game, lush crops, and many children. Because of his power, the People flourished and built great cliff dwellings, traded salt, grew wealthy."

Yeah. Yeah. Jackson picked up a twig and poked it into the sand. Dust scattered.

"But as with all men, the gods called the Magician to the next life. When he died, he was a very old man. His People buried him with his hunting arrows, his pots and baskets of herbs, and the powerful magic tokens he had used to bring them prosperity. The People prayed he would still help them from the next world."

Jackson drew a cat face with vicious, saber-tooth tiger fangs. Frowning, he brushed his hand through the dirt to erase the lines.

"Long ago, the Magician's grave was hidden in a most sacred place. Even now, the kiva can only be found when the sun god allows a chosen man to see the way," George intoned in a singsong voice.

Jackson doodled a spiral design. He squinted. Where had he seen that picture before?

Eyes wide, Josh bent forward. "Have you been there?"

"Only to the marker." George leaned his back against the bright green tree trunk. "For a few seasons the People prospered. But then the summers turned hotter, and the crops withered. The children grew thin, and hungry, and died. Enemies crowded into the valley, searching for game. In the time of plenty, hunters had found elk, deer, buffalo. Now the People ate only rabbits and snakes."

Jackson shifted and rotated his shoulders.

"Before he died, the Magician had trained an Apprentice. The worried elders told him to perform a sacred ritual and ask the Magician for help. The Apprentice, now a grown man with a wife and child, feared the powerful Magician, but he also feared the elders, so he obeyed. He went to the Magician's burial site and waited on the high cliff by the solar calendar."

"Did the Magician come?" Josh asked.

George shook his head. "No. Thunder roared and lightning seared the night sky. Terrified of the storm, terrified he'd angered the Magician, the Apprentice ran blindly and fell from the mesa."

The twig snapped in Jackson's grip. "He died?"

"Yes, but an elder found him first, broken but still alive, and heard his story. Years before, when the suffering first began, the Apprentice had broken into the sacred site and stolen four magical tools. Two he lost, one he kept for himself. Hoping to bring rain, he buried the third, the stolen water bowl, near the river."

"But he only wanted to help."

"Yes. But in his arrogance, he lacked patience, lacked respect for the spirits. After his crime, the people's suffering grew. Some died, some moved north, but soon the People of the Valley were no more."

Josh rose to his knees and rubbed his hand over his face. "How do you know all this, cousin?"

"The story was told to me when I was a boy, just as I repeated it to you. Shaman to Shaman, the words have not changed in over seven hundred years."

"Why tell me?"

George's glittering black eyes honed in on Josh. "You are different. Chosen. For many hundreds of years no other shaman has seen the Magician's face. But today he appeared to you."

Josh shivered. "I'm a shaman?"

Jackson's goose bumps matched the boy's. He rubbed his hands over his arms.

"You've always been a shaman."

His expressive face clouding, Josh shook his head. "But I don't understand what the Magician wants."

George rested his hands on the boy's head. "You will return the water bowl to the sacred kiva." He turned to face Jackson. "The hunter will accompany you."

Jackson stood and brushed the dust off his jeans. "Helluva story."

One gray eyebrow rose and then dropped. "A skeptic."

"A cop." Jackson punctuated his reply with a stiff jerk of his head. "Now give me a straight answer. Where's Norah?"

"You will need what I have for you." George pulled a length of thick rope from his carryall and handed him the coil.

"Planning a little climb?"

"You aren't surprised?"

Jackson clucked his tongue against his teeth. "What else have you got?"

"A first aid kit and short wave radio."

Chapter Nineteen

Kenny gunned the engine and skidded onto the narrow, unpaved road. The truck tires kicked up dust and gravel through the open window. Grit crunched between his teeth. "You sure this is the way?"

Gina pushed hair out of her eyes. "We're on the right track now, I'm sure. I remember Grandma helping me wade across the river over there. We stopped to splash in the water because it was so hot."

A stick on the road suddenly raised its head and coiled. He stomped on the gas and roared toward a five-foot long diamondback. The front and then the back tires bumped over the snake.

"Ew!" Gina screwed up her face.

Kenny checked the side mirror. A buzz rushed through him. The rattler's guts had squirted out, but the head section still squirmed, fangs thrashing the air for a target. "This time of year, stupid snakes should be hibernating."

"No. September's still too warm."

The satisfied feeling in his chest vanished, and his jaw clenched. Nagging bitch just wouldn't keep her mouth shut. He'd have to punish her again, but not until they found the treasure.

The track got rougher, narrower. Dodging boulders, he fought to keep all four wheels on the road.

"Take a right." She pointed up a steep fire road.

He made the turn but sideswiped two giant sword plants. The barbs screeched against the rear fender.

Five minutes in, she held up a hand. "Can you slow down? I don't want to miss the tree."

"You're asking for it, bitch," he muttered under his breath. But he stopped, revving the engine.

With a dirty look, she stuck her head out the window and pointed to a huge, dead tree. "Yeah, this is the place. My grandmother's house was just beyond that sycamore. That one with all the lightning scars."

"Damn well better be." He pulled over.

"We have to go the rest of the way on foot. The petroglyph is along that canyon about a mile upriver. I'll—"

"You'll stay put. I can get it."

With an irritating smirk, she handed him the journal and crossed her arms. "Super. After you find your way down the canyon wall, follow the middle stream. Past the stand of piñon pines, take the right fork."

He shot her a warning glance, and his hands itched to close around her throat. No. The phony, lying bitch still served a purpose. He gave her back the damn book. "Fine. Show me. But stay outta my way."

She trailed him the short distance to the cliff edge, where he studied the churning floodwater fifty feet below. "How the fuck are we going to get through that? The treasure had better be worth it, bitch."

Gina sucked on a water bottle. "Flash floods don't last long. Come on. We can climb down here."

Fifteen minutes later, they stood on the bank, breathing hard. The water had gone down some, but branches still choked the fast flowing river, and the mud made walking tricky.

His shoe slid across a wobbly rock, almost dumping him into the raging water. He dodged another slime-covered tree trunk and checked over his shoulder.

Arms flapping like a pathetic dodo bird, Gina balanced on a rounded stone, slick with green sludge. "Look, Kenny. Over there," she giggled and hopped lightly to the next.

The red walls of the canyon did have old drawings on them. Big deal. A bunch of stick figures hunting with bows and spears. Dead animals. Kindergarten crap.

"The saber tooth should be around the next bend," she called, her voice high and so damn cheerful.

Kenny grunted and waded into a deep puddle. Mud squelched under his feet and sucked at his shoes. Squinting into the sun, he found the cat on a protected wall ten feet above the flood line. Wouldn't call the drawing a work of art, but the curved fangs were fucking impressive. He whistled with satisfaction. Vince would pay big bucks for this sucker.

Gina walked up behind him and stared over his shoulder. "Cool claws, huh?"

"No shit." Yeah. He could hire a couple guys to pry it off the canyon wall and lug it out.

"Told you I could find the right spot." Gina threw herself down in the shade of a twisted cottonwood and took a sip of water.

Kenny scratched his head. "Yeah, you did, but so fucking what? Why's the damn cat in the journal? I don't see any treasure."

She shrugged, looking stupider than usual. "You're the one who wanted to come here. I can't help it if you don't find anything."

Anger sizzled his blood. He drew in a few breaths to regain control. Not. Now. Focus.

He scanned the area. Fuck. Nothing but mud and waterlogged plants. He kicked at a couple stones below the cat and fisted his hands on his waist. The canyon walls were still shiny a good six feet up. Everything dripped. "Musta been a real gully washer. No way to know if anyone's already been here."

"Who do you mean?"

"Nothing."

Kenny sloshed backward into the middle of the stream. Bracing his legs against the rush of cold water, he studied the rock wall around the cat. Halfway up a large snake drawing slithered toward a shaded spot in the rock. Looked kinda familiar.

Hurrying back to shore, he grabbed the journal out of her hands. "Gimme that." He checked one page and thrust the leather covered book into his pocket, smiling.

"What did you find?" She tugged on his arm.

He didn't answer, just shook her off, and dug his fingers into a crack on the canyon wall. After a few slips and scrapes, he pulled himself onto a ledge twenty feet above the river. Gasping for air, he planted his feet on the narrow outcropping.

Gina shielded her eyes from the glare. "Do you see anything?"

"No."

But a fresh looking hole had been dug into the cliff. Heart pounding, he reached inside the recess.

Empty.

Damn. Someone had been here and stolen his treasure. He batted the loose rocks over the edge, and they took a second to reach the ground.

"Hey! Watch it!" Gina squealed, dodging the fall out.

He snickered and kicked some more loose.

"Kenny! Be careful," she whined.

He got to his feet and looked upstream. The river was blocked by huge stones and massive tree stumps. Never get through that way. The thief musta gone up.

Kenny sighed and continued his climb, his muscles straining. Fucking good thing he'd kept up his workout. But when he topped the ridge, his heart pounded.

The morning sun had warmed the desert. He stared into the distance, sweeping slowly across the expanse. There. Movement.

His pulse still raced. Something, someone moved against the far ridge. Too far away to see clearly, but moving fast toward the mountains to the north.

Well, hell. A woman? His heart banged in his chest, and he couldn't catch his breath. That woman. What the hell was that fucking Redfox bitch doing out here?

Grinding his teeth together to keep from shouting, Kenny shaded his eyes and scouted the terrain. No houses, no roads, no other people. She was at least a couple miles ahead and on the far side of the canyon. No way could he catch up, even if he did get across. Gina better know a short cut.

He climbed down, sliding on his ass the last ten feet.

She dodged out of his way, chewing on her lip.

"Come on," he growled and stalked along the riverbank toward his truck.

"Kenny! Tell me what you saw up there." Whining

like a kicked dog, Gina caught up with him.

"What did I see?" When he grabbed her, she let out a shriek.

"That woman. I saw that fucking woman." Spit flew in her face. He shook her. "She stole my treasure, and she's headed for more."

"But how—?"

"That spooky little shit musta told her where to look." He fisted his hands in Gina's shirt and pushed his face up close to hers. No. Not yet. "She's heading for the western mesa. You're going to show me how to get there. Fast."

White faced, Gina cringed, but nodded. Silent for once.

Releasing her with a shove, he pivoted and stomped away down the ravine.

"Wait a minute. This is too hard. I can't keep up." She plopped her fat butt on a wet log and dumped the sand out of her shoe.

"I don't have time for your crap." Drenched and puffing, he yanked her arm and shoved her ahead of him. "Move, or I'll leave you behind."

"Okay, okay." She hopped on one foot, struggling back into the shoe.

"How do we get across the river?"

"From here?"

"No, you stupid bitch, from Mars."

Her eyes slid sideways like she was gonna make up something. "Uh. Well."

He grabbed her neck and squeezed. "The truth, Gina."

She swallowed, and her bruised face paled to an interesting shade of yellow green. "There's no bridge.

We have to go back to the junction. Then make a right instead of going straight."

"How long?"

"Not too far. We can probably make the junction in half an hour. But why do you want to go out that way? There's nothing there but some old ruins." She tugged on his arm. "Come on, sweetie. We can look again this afternoon. I'm tired. And dirty. Why don't we go back to the Casino? That was a really nice room."

Spots crept across his vision, flooding everything with a red haze. He shook his head, but the stain behind his eyes blocked the sunlight. Cold sliced through his limbs, and his hands trembled. Gina had earned whatever he gave her. Always whining, always squealing like a fucking pig. Wasting his time. His talent. His money.

Gina's fault that damn woman got here first and was miles ahead of him.

Gina's fault he had to hike all over this fucking desert for nothing.

Gina's fault he didn't have the treasure.

His treasure.

Gina would pay.

Pulling the Colt .45 out of his belt, he stepped back and blasted her.

She fell, her mouth wide open, and her arms grabbing at her belly.

An adrenaline rush lit up his brain and surged straight to his cock. Goddamn that felt good. Like cool water had washed over him.

His vision cleared, and a huge grin curved his lips.

Gina dropped to her knees with a shocked look on her face. She flapped her mouth like a fucking fish, but no noise came out.

"Nice change, sweetheart." His pulse slowed. His muscles relaxed. He stood over her and smiled while blood seeped between her fingers.

He wanted to shoot her again. Feel the kick from the gun, smell the powder.

But the noise, even out here in this god-forsaken-wasteland, might draw the curious.

Or the cops.

He leveled the gun. Fuck 'em. He could reload.

Chapter Twenty

Jackson rode shotgun, jostling along the canyon rim in George Kwail's decrepit rust-bucket Jeep. Below them, Beaver Creek had transformed into a roaring flash flood. He shivered. Hope to God Norah wasn't caught in that maelstrom.

Louder than the groaning engine, the wind whistled through the open sides. His ears and cheeks burned.

George hit a pothole. The Jeep bounced at a crazy angle.

Jackson's butt left the seat and for a second, all four tires spun in the air. He grabbed the roll bar and clenched his teeth.

Belted in the jump seat behind him, Josh squeaked. Then he laughed like a kid on a roller coaster.

Hard not to crack a smile. Jackson glanced at George Kwail.

A grin lit the older man's face, too. He eased up on the throttle to snake through a couple large boulders that almost blocked the road. "The site isn't too far from here."

A gunshot cracked.

The bottom dropped out of his stomach like he'd fallen into a cold, dark pool. What the fuck?

A second report echoed through the canyon about a mile ahead. Jackson's hand curled around the roll bar. He bent toward George. "Can you tell where that came from?"

The man's face had gone pale and rigid around the mouth. "Too damn close to the petroglyph."

Jackson's throat slapped shut. Cold sweat broke out on his forehead and pooled under his arms. "Shit. Norah?"

"Can't tell you, detective. I'm driving," George said through gritted teeth. "Want me to pull over and ask the Magician?"

"No. We need to hurry."

The Jeep lurched forward again with a teeth rattling jolt. Bracing his feet against the floorboards, Jackson wiped his slippery palms on his jeans, counting the seconds.

Maybe three quarters of a mile ahead, a cloud of dust raced toward them.

Squinting, Jackson strained closer to the pitted windshield. The distance closed fast. The blur solidified into a black camper van. A quarter mile off, the truck veered at a ninety-degree angle, away from the ravine.

Josh pounded on his left shoulder. "That's Uncle Kenny's van!"

George slowed a fraction. "Want me to follow?"

A frisson of alarm smashed up his spine and lit up every nerve in his body. Jackson shook his head. "No! Norah might be hurt. Check the site first. We can radio in the Swank's truck."

"I didn't see Aunt Gina. Hope she's okay." Josh worried his lower lip between his front teeth.

They bumped over another mile of mud and gravel and rocks.

Tire tracks stopped just past a stand of smashed up silver agave. "Looks like Swank parked here. Can we go much further?"

Brows scrunched, hands white-knuckled around the wheel, George shook his head. "Not even in this baby. Too narrow." He stopped with the grill against a huge boulder and yanked on the hand brake.

Jackson jumped out and jogged toward the sound of water. Debris and broken branches clogged the narrow ravine, blocking the flow of water into several large pools. Run-off gushed at his feet.

"Looks safe to head upstream," George called from behind him. "Most of the flood has passed."

Jackson waded into the icy creek and clamored over slick boulders. His feet were soon numb, but he hurried ahead. "How much further?" he shouted back at George.

With Josh's help, the older man ducked under a fallen pine. "Around that curve. Keep going," Kwail wheezed.

"We'll catch up," Josh said.

Jackson leaped from rock to rock. Damn slippery, but faster than wading through the muck on the bank. He climbed on a high boulder in the center of the creek and shaded his eyes. "Norah!"

"Nor-rah. Norah. Norah." The sound bounced off the narrow canyon walls and echoed into nothing. A shiver crawled over his skin.

He listened for a reply. Dammit! Be here, woman.

Nothing. Nothing but his own heart pounding inside his ribs like a son-of-a-jackhammer.

He let his shoulders sag.

Someone moaned, faint, but close. Or was it just the wind?

Josh scrambled up beside him and cupped his

hands over his mouth. "Aunt Gina?"

There was that sound again. Jackson slid into the stream and splashed to the far side.

Gina Swank looked even thinner than the pictures from the hospital camera. Her face covered with bruises, her clothes soaked with blood, she'd curled on her side in the mud. She'd been shot. Twice. But only the belly wound looked serious. He ripped off his sweatshirt and applied pressure.

The woman moaned, moving her head from side to side. She'd lost a lot of blood.

"I'll get the first aid kit from the truck." Josh offered and turned back the way they'd come.

"No. Got it here," George puffed, moving fast. He shrugged off his pack and dug out a navy blue box.

"Got that short wave, too?"

George called for help on his radio.

"Grab one of those compresses, Josh." Jackson inclined his head. "Hold it on her leg over the blood. There ya go. Good job."

"Is she gonna be okay?" Tears muffled the kid's voice.

Jackson didn't look up. "You're helping. Just keep the pressure on."

George knelt beside them. "Got hold of Rocky Hummel. He's got a Life Flight chopper ready, but it'll take a while."

"Can you handle this Kwail? I need to go after Swank. If he'd shoot his own wife, no telling what'll happen if he catches up with Norah."

"What about the Magician? Do we need to find the pot?" Josh asked.

George's brow wrinkled with deep furrows, and he

stared at the cliff. "Nothing there."

"Did Uncle Kenny steal it?"

Gina sucked in a breath through her teeth. "Woman. Kenny saw her."

The blood drained from Jackson's brain. Adrenaline surged, and his muscles hardened to flint. Time slowed. He felt like he'd shatter if anyone spoke too loud or crowded too close. Standing, he shoved away the blazing fear.

George held up the keys to the jeep. "Take these. And take Josh. You have to reach the solar calendar before midday."

Josh glanced at the barely conscious woman. "But—"

"She'll be fine." George drew a quick map in the sand and gave Jackson simple directions. "Be sure not to miss the cutoff. It'll save you at least twenty minutes."

"I hope Uncle Kenny doesn't know the short cut."

George positioned his hands to apply pressure. "I can take over."

Jackson eased his hands off the bloody bandages and stood, giving the map one last glance. "What the hell is a solar calendar?"

Chapter Twenty-One

Norah shivered. What she'd give for dry shoes and running clothes.

In the distance a gunshot cracked.

A chill of fear flickered through her and roughened the skin on her neck and arms. She flattened against the cliff, scanning the desert. Probably just a hunter. Nothing to do with her or her quest.

A second retort echoed off the canyon walls.

Her pulse jittered, but she hurried along the trail.

Was Josh okay? What about Jackson?

The Magician had insisted the boy was safe but wouldn't give her any details. Ironic. Now she'd welcome the ancient puppet master back for a breaking news update. She chuckled, imagining the somber, powerful Magician sitting behind a microphone, wearing a tousled blond toupee and bleached smile.

Hopefully Jackson had found Josh. But had her big, tough, sexy, love-you-but-only-on-the-sly cop arrested the Swanks? Or were the two shysters and that nasty crook, Vince Smith, still on the loose? She shivered. Should she expect a black SUV full of villains to appear on her heels any second?

From the very beginning, Grandfather had insisted she needed Jackson to succeed at this task. But where was that skeptical idiot now? She snorted. Masterfully handling all those pesky details while she endured her lonely marathon.

Another question whipped through her brain and twisted her stomach. She stumbled and slowed. How would her life change after this made-for-the-wide-screen adventure ended?

She pulled a rude face and dodged around a saguaro. Its huge human-like arms cast long shadows, mocking her when she desperately wanted the comfort of a hug.

Face facts. Based on her grand total of two or, depending on how you counted, three experiences, sex could be incredible. Transforming. Pretty damned knock-your-panties-off and singe-your-toenails magical.

While she'd love to slink right back into Jackson's bed for a couple more rounds, or maybe a couple dozen, she was raising a very vulnerable child. Her first concern had to be Amber. She should finish this quest and refuse to see that no-woman's-gonna-hogtie-me cop ever again.

Norah sighed, and her tongue tangled with the wounded heart beating in her throat. No question, she'd have to face Jackson. Eventually, she'd have to tell the stupid cop she forever and always loved him.

What would he say? She hissed out a breath and trotted across a dry wash.

More important, what would she do when he stammered, "Well shucks, ma'am," kicked a rock and walked away?

The sun bleached desert sand reflected the glare, and she blinked moisture from her eyes. Her spirit felt as heavy as one of the mammoth boulders up ahead. She'd been a naïve fool.

But she jammed the ache into a dark corner of her heart and concentrated on the monumental assignment she'd been given. Glancing over her shoulder, she checked the angle of the sun. Close to 11:00? Maybe later. She hoped she was wrong, but she picked up her pace and ran a little faster.

A large, undermined cliff shadowed the area ahead. A spring seeped from the limestone and puddled in a depression beside the wide trail. She'd love to lie down and wallow in the water.

No time.

Noon. She had to be on the mesa top before noon.

Feeling like the March Hare, she paused to refill her bottle from the spring. Tracks marked the muddy edge, some of them large. Animals accessed the water here, too.

An itch tickled her shoulders. Feeling watched, she glanced around. From the shadows under the cliff shelf, dark, square-cut windows looked back at her.

She stopped in surprise. Although tumbled-down rock littered the area, the overhang mushroomed back, hiding an ancient cliff dwelling. Doors and small windows had been built into the stone. Most of the entrances were up high, because the people used rope ladders to climb in. But one trail led to a low opening. Sipping her water, she peeked through the doorway.

Ghostly firelight flickered inside the kiva. Gooseflesh rose on her skin. Spirits flowed all around her, mesmerized her. Her heart thudded faster. The room felt cool. Damp. Like she was underground.

Gently, her consciousness shifted. The ruined city looked different. Whole. Vital and alive.

Not hijacked this time, rather welcomed to a world

that existed in parallel to Grandfather's spirit lodge.

The air smelled different. Cleaner, fresher, but full of human sweat and sacred herbs, and the sweet smell of the child in her arms.

In a very different body, Norah sat on the hard packed dirt floor of the low-ceilinged room with the other women of the tribe.

The Magician's topaz eyes glowed in the firelight. He raised a small reed flute to his lips. Music poured from him. Magic flowed and ghostly fingers traced her spine.

A naked child tussled with his brother. A woman, ripe in late pregnancy, ground corn and sang softly.

The rich smell of roasting meat filled her nostrils. Her mouth watered, and her stomach rumbled.

A look of longing flickered over The Magician's leathered face.

"Your family?" she asked.

"Yes."

The vision wavered and dissolved into fallen stones and crumbling adobe.

Empty.

Barren.

Norah's eyes stung.

Shaking his head, the Magician led her outside to a stand of ripe, purple hackberries.

Norah cracked open the prickly berries and sucked the pulp. The distinctive bittersweet taste stung her tongue and filled her mouth. She scavenged the brush for another mouthful of the pungent fruit. Not roasted wild boar, but still necessary fuel.

"You must go."

She filled her pockets with hackberries and jogged

away from the dwellings. Half-running, half-walking, she moved along the path again.

Rounding a sharp corner, she skidded to a stop.

Gravel rained over the end of the cliff trail and fell off the shelf into the nothingness a thousand feet below.

Chapter Twenty-Two

Damn it. Where's that fucking junction? He'd been past this rusted piece-of-shit trailer twice in the last ten minutes. Kenny wiped the sweat out of his eyes with his sleeve and whipped the truck into a U-turn, heading back along the two-lane dirt road the way he'd come.

He hit eighty, but once he started up the hill he had to ease off. Yeah. There. That's where the road forked. This looked right. He wasn't too late. He'd score the gold. "Won't I, Gina?"

With a big, dopey smile, she nodded her agreement and laid a hand on his thigh.

He laughed again. She looked damn good. Younger. Firmer. All tits and big brown eyes. "We can go someplace. Together. You can take real good care of me."

Gina licked her lips. Her mouth looked moist and red. Totally fuckable.

"Yeah. Someplace nice. Maybe Mexico. You'll like Mexico. Lotsa cheap drugs down there. But I'll have plenty of money. Plenty of money to spend on whatever I want." He didn't look over, but with her silence she let him know she agreed.

"Gotta find the treasure. Gotta find it first," he muttered through clenched teeth. "That Redfox bitch knows where the gold is. Yeah. Find her. Follow her. Make her hurt until she tells me where to dig."

The thought sent pleasure sizzling through his brain. He closed his eyes for a split second, savoring the buzz.

The truck bounced over a large rock. The bottom scraped. Hard.

A jacked-up SUV coming right at him blew its air horn.

With his heart racing like he'd smoked a whole bag, Kenny yanked the wheel and pulled back onto the road. He hung his hand out the window and flipped off the asshole. "Big fucking horn, limp little cock."

He sucked in a couple quick breaths to slow his pulse. Man, he could use another snort. His hands shook, and he was sweating like a pig. But he couldn't stop. Not now. They were too close. "Get me a beer, Gina."

He looked sideways. "Gina?" She wasn't in her seat. Where'd she go? "Gina!"

But the bitch didn't answer. "Where the fuck?"

The only sounds came from his tires bumping along the gravel road. The engine rumbling. The wind whistling past the open window.

Oh, yeah. Now he remembered.

Her shocked look.

Her blood gushing through her fingers.

Adrenaline pumped through his body again.

Grinning, he swung the truck around the next curve. The barren desert floor and layers of mountains spread out in front of him. But in the distance an old Jeep climbed the steep switchback, leaving a long trail of dust.

Angry heat stole across his face, and a red haze fuzzed his vision. "No!" He stood on the gas pedal. The truck fishtailed, but he yanked it back under control.

He ground his teeth until they ached. Vince. Was Vince after the treasure, too?

No, couldn't be. Vince would never drive a piece of junk like that.

Could it be that fucking cop? Yeah. The Redfox bitch musta clued him in.

A rut in the road turned his wheels to the right. The truck lunged into the drainage ditch and smashed against a tree.

The blaring horn brought him to his senses. His head ached where he'd whacked it against the steering wheel. Blood trickled into his right eye.

He blinked to clear his vision. The Jeep had disappeared.

"No time. No fucking time," he screamed, pounding on the dashboard with both fists. His voice sounded harsh, far away, like he was yelling through a tunnel. But he threw the gearshift into reverse and spun the wheels until he finally caught some traction.

One mile ahead the road forked. He skidded to a stop, holding his throbbing head between his hands. A cloud of red dusted the truck, and a trail of blood trickled down his cheek. He wiped his sticky fingers on his jeans.

What had Gina said? A right? No. Stay straight toward the tallest mountain.

From the seat beside him, Gina cackled like a cartoon witch, pointing a long claw at the blood dripping off his forehead.

He swiped the gash. Pain stabbed his skull, and lightning flashed behind his eyelids. Hissing, he reached for her neck with both hands.

Came away empty.

But her taunting laugh filled the truck and scraped against his raw nerves.

He covered his ears but couldn't shut her out. She'd abandoned him for that runt. Why wouldn't she just leave Josh the fuck alone?

Every muscle in his body cramped. He wanted to jump out of the truck and run away screaming.

But he was too strong, and he deserved better. He deserved his treasure.

Kenny sat very still and tried to think. His skull burned like his brain was stuck in a vat of dry ice. But he could work this out.

Okay.

More dust to the right. He'd follow the Jeep and take what was his.

****

They could be in hell, for all Jackson knew. He hadn't taken his eyes off the grimy, tooth-rattling road in almost an hour. His arms ached from fighting the ruts where the rain-soaked soil had dried to cement.

The vegetation had changed from mesquite and Palo Verde to wind-blown piñon and scrubby juniper. How could anything grow in this moonscape?

He glanced at the passenger seat. "Still sure we're headed in the right direction?"

Josh let go of his death grip on the armrest and pointed to the odd shaped volcanic cone rising from the desert floor. "Yep. That's the Sacred Mountain."

"Is that good?"

"Means we're almost there. George said the turnoff was a mile ahead."

"That could take all day on this road." Jackson

dodged another pothole the size of Utah. He grimaced. "No dust in the air. No one's driven this road recently."

A deer darted across the track. Jackson swerved and slammed on the brakes, throwing them both forward.

Feet wedged against the dash, Josh braced.

Jackson drummed on the steering wheel while a pair of fawns bounded after the doe. Once they'd passed he popped the clutch and started uphill. "Sure hope we find Norah."

"She's real nice. Ms. Redfox, I mean. I like her, too."

Too? Suddenly, the inside of the old Jeep was hot and prickly. Jackson stuck his head out his open window. Fresh air whipped through his hair and cooled some of the sweat off his face.

Taking a deep breath, he pulled his head back inside. "Yeah. She's special."

"It's okay, you know. My mom always looked like you do when she talked about my dad."

"Looked like what?"

"You know. Goofy. Dreamy."

Jackson let out a hoot and some of the dead weight lifted from his sternum. "How'd you get so smart, kid?"

Josh shrugged.

Jackson gave the boy a pat on his good shoulder and stared ahead. Poor kid. Parents dead. Nobody to watch over him except a pair of con artists. Where would Josh end up? Some foster home? Probably not the best place for a spooky kid.

Then there was Amber. Mom dead. No father in the picture. Taking responsibility for a kid was a huge, scary commitment, but Norah had adopted Amber, given her a safe, healthy home. What would happen to her if Norah… He tried to swallow the rhino thrashing around in his throat, but made a choking sound instead. When he'd called Nate back, he'd talked to Amber, helped calm her down some, but the kid was freaked. Understandable.

"You okay?"

"Fine." He gunned the engine to climb the next set of boulders.

"There." Josh shouted. "By the big pile of logs. That's the short cut."

With a barrage of gravel, Jackson skidded onto an even rougher road, little more than a trail winding through a forest of agave plants. "Some short cut."

"Cuts off another mile."

Fifteen minutes later, they slewed around a corner onto a dusty plateau. The track ended near the canyon's edge.

Jackson yanked the parking brake and jumped out. A crumbling chimney rose amidst the burnt-out ruin of an abandoned shack. The bleached skull of a cow stared up at the sky through empty, hollow sockets.

Shuddering, he checked his watch. Half an hour till noon.

"George said to climb down near the leaning pine."

A couple hundred yards away, a huge ponderosa clung to the rocks. "Must be that one. Hold on a minute." Jackson dug in the cluttered space behind his seat. Pulling out a pair of beat-up cowboy hats, he plopped one on Josh's head before putting on the other.

"Thanks. The sun's kinda bright, huh?"

"Yep." Jackson led the way down a slope of crushed granite and up over a slight rise. No footprints.

No trail to follow. The rhythm of their steps, the occasional birdcall, and the scratch of a lizard were the only sounds.

The base of the pine clung to the edge of the mesa. With one hand on the trunk, Jackson peered over, and his heart bumped in his chest. The river below had carved a deep gorge. On both sides, canyon walls rose nearly two thousand feet from the dark green wash on the valley floor.

Josh edged up next to him and let out a long whistle. "Want me to go first?"

"Nope." Past an outcropping of granite, Jackson sidestepped his way down the steep trail but kept one arm out to guard Josh. The kid seemed sure-footed, but no point in taking chances. Avoiding the prickly pear and cholla, Jackson dodged through the loose gravel slide.

Twenty feet down, they reached a three-foot wide ledge and maneuvered between boulders and cacti until they'd worked their way around the first bend in the cliff. Jackson kept his eyes on the ground ahead and didn't look over, but vertigo still roared in his ears. Helluva long way down.

Josh balanced on a big rock on the trail and pointed overhead. "That's the cool petroglyph. The one George told us about with the animals passing through to the next world. Must have been hard to draw them up that high."

Jackson squinted at the herd of etched animals running across the face of the red cliff. At a huge fissure in the rock, they seemed to change form and fly off the ground. Clever artist.

Moving along the ledge, he searched the walls for

the solar calendar. But in the flat midday light the designs faded into the rock face.

Ahead the ledge had eroded where a twisted, ancient juniper grew out over nothing. How would he ever get Josh across that big gap?

His heart did a sudden twist. Was Norah coming? Had they missed her? George had assured him she would be here at noon. Jackson checked his watch. Fifteen minutes 'til and no Norah. He scanned the horizon and the trail behind them. How else could she get here other than the route they'd taken?

He looked down and blew out a breath. No way. Only a mountain goat could climb that cliff.

Across the canyon, two eagles circled on up-drafts, hardly moving their wide wings. He swallowed the prickly lump in his throat. If only he could see through their eyes. Maybe then he could find Norah and tell her how he felt.

In the quiet, the noise of a chopper echoed up the steep canyon. Good. One problem solved.

"Hear that? The helicopter is coming for Aunt Gina." Beaming, Josh hung out over the edge of the cliff.

Jackson grabbed the kid by the scruff. "Be careful. Okay? I need to get you to Norah in one piece. Not splattered all over the base of this cliff."

Chapter Twenty-Three

Dead end. Either she'd have to retrace her steps past the ancient city or climb the cliff. In the meager late morning shadow, Norah picked up a small leaf and tossed it into the air. When the leaf fluttered up to the rock above her, her brows drew together. What on earth?

The leaf floated still higher. She stepped back a few paces and studied the wall face, then shook her head. No way could she scale that precipice.

"You must."

"Climb up there? You're joking. I get dizzy on the bathroom stool."

No response.

She sat under a wind-twisted pine and moaned. Resting her chin on her hands, she looked out over the canyon.

A thousand feet above, an eagle glided on the thermals. Its call reverberated against the striated rock, and its mate replied. They danced in easy circles, spiraling higher into the clear desert air.

She rose and paced in front of the tree. *"I'd need to be Spiderwoman to make that climb."* Had the Magician listened? Could he catch her mental picture of the comic book superhero?

Clouds cast purple shadows over a rough trail that wound through the rocks. She scanned the face of the cliff. It wasn't absolutely sheer. There were handholds. Maybe she could.

"You must. I will help."

She pinched her lips together and studied the path, memorizing the turns and landmarks she would need to locate while she climbed.

Left at the large juniper with the broken limb. Right where the rocks turned from red to gray. She craned her neck backward and hissed. So damn high.

Norah stepped carefully around a clump of tall century plants that littered the outcropping. Their sharp, spiny leaves grew upward like silver swords.

Heaving a sigh, she began.

A hundred feet up, she hugged the cliff and rested. Her hands had blisters. Her knees shook.

Up. Look up. Not down. Only a few more feet to the first ledge and she could stop and catch her breath.

She reached for the next handhold, but stabbing pain cramped her arm. Her toe slipped. She cried out and grabbed for a dead branch. The rough bark gouged into her fingers but the roots held. Dust showered down and choked her. She closed her eyes until her pulse slowed.

"I know the way. Don't fight against me this time."

Norah gritted her teeth. *"Fine."* She allowed the Magician control of her arms and legs.

Right toe here, left hand there.

Easier.

The Magician drew her up the rock face. Moving with new surety, she climbed onto the first ledge and collapsed in the shade of the broken juniper. Bleeding. Exhausted. Boneless. But alive.

She heard the whoosh of strong wings. The eagles

still soared above her. She finished off her stash of hackberries and her last gulp of water, and let out a long sigh. What she wouldn't give for a tall glass of iced tea or even one of those mouth-burning green beef enchiladas.

A tiny blue-bellied lizard watched her from a rock. When she twitched, it ducked back into the crevice. She was alone. Sitting on a cliff a hundred yards below her goal. Too far to climb up, too far to fall.

Her heart felt huge and heavy, like her chest might explode. What she wouldn't give to hear Jackson's voice. See his smile. Feel his arms around her, his hands and his mouth on her body.

She leaned back and drew her knees up into a ball. *"I don't have the strength to go further."*

"You must."

In the distance, the whoop-whoop of a helicopter broke the silence. Trying to spot it, she braced her foot against a boulder, but the rock gave way and fell down the cliff. The noisy helicopter hovered somewhere over the canyon behind her while the rock crashed and tumbled, finally hitting the valley floor. She quivered.

"I won't let you fall."

Who else did she have to trust?

"Yourself."

She faced the rock and crawled up the next segment. Her hands and feet placed themselves. Her body moved steadily upward. The mesa top was close now. She let out a small chuckle. Maybe they could do this together.

Her arm muscles screamed with exhaustion, but Norah dragged her two-ton body onto the narrow ledge. Covered in sweat, she lay gasping on the sun-warmed rock. Her heart thundered beyond painfully in her chest.

Dizzy from the height, she closed her eyes and inched away from the edge.

****

Jackson scratched his stubbled chin and surveyed the three-foot gap in the path. An ancient juniper growing out from the cliff had eroded the ledge to nothing. Twenty feet ahead, the path narrowed to the width of a goat track and disappeared around a granite outcropping.

The gnarled evergreen, its massive trunk twisted like a bundle of rope, jutted skyward like a massive erection. Jackson pursed his lips. Along the shaft spiky needles and berries the size of golf balls poked through a mat of dusty spider webs.

"Man, I kinda wish we had cousin George's rope." Josh squinted at the tree. "How we gonna get across?"

"Good question. You think the solar calendar's on that side?"

"I'm pretty sure it's somewhere close." Josh pointed at a small, waist-high carving on the far side of the juniper. "I think that's a drawing of the Magician."

Shading his eyes, Jackson leaned into the blazing midday sun.

"See? He's holding a staff and wearing a feathered headdress."

Could be the figure of a man. Jackson rubbed a palm over the back of his sweaty neck. "Okay. Good sign. But what about that solar calendar?"

"There must be other petroglyphs by that crevice, but I can't see them from here. If you lift me up on the tree trunk, I can jump to the other side."

Jackson restrained an urge to yank the kid further

away from the edge of the cliff. "You sure?"

"Positive." Josh straightened to his full height, his mouth drawn into a stubborn line. "If you won't help, I'll try by myself."

Ice twisted Jackson's belly. "Okay. Okay. Stand right by the edge and put one foot on my knee."

Josh braced his legs, and Jackson boosted him onto the tree. The kid straddled the trunk like it was a fat-barreled pony and scrambled off the other side. "Easy. Are you coming?"

Jackson vaulted onto the juniper with both palms flat and swung his leg over. A breeze caught the brim of his hat. It flipped off and spiraled down the cliff face. For a dozen heartbeats he just sat there breathing hard with his legs hanging into space. His ears roared even though he hadn't looked down, but he climbed onto the path.

Flat on his belly, Josh frowned at the etched figures covering the sandstone wall. He traced the small drawings with his index finger as if reading a story. He looked up and shook his head. "The calendar's not here either."

With a sigh, Jackson looked back at the juniper. "Then what next?"

"I guess I could ask."

"Huh? Ask who?" Jackson swallowed past the creepy sensation filling his throat. "The ghost?"

Josh dropped to his haunches and sat cross-legged in the dirt. He nodded silently.

Jackson lifted his shoulders, but stopped in the middle of the shrug. What was that scratching sound? An animal? What kind of creature could climb this cliff? With one finger, he signaled Josh to remain still.

Breathing. Heavy breathing. Nearby.

His brain raced and adrenaline spiked. Something scraped against the cliff. A shoe? Gravel trickled down the cliff into the canyon. He reached for his gun.

"Darn it! Almost there," Norah muttered.

Relief, elation and, admit it sucker, a blazing hot blast of love washed over him.

"Woof. Alley oop!" she said.

Twenty feet ahead, where the path bent, a hand reached around the granite boulder. Jackson's pulse broke into a sprint. A warm heaviness invaded his chest. Smiling like a fool, he squatted and pressed his fingers over the kid's open mouth, shaking his head gently. Not the time to distract her.

Norah edged around the outcropping. Her belly pressed against the canyon wall as her feet shuffled along the narrow ledge. She'd tied her jacket into a carryall on her back, and her hair and clothes were filthy with dust, and mud, and twigs.

She was the most beautiful sight he'd ever seen. All he could think to do was to grab her in his arms and never let go. Body vibrating with tension, he waited.

Finally she stepped all the way onto the path and heaved in a huge lungful.

"Hey! Right on time, pretty lady." He chuckled, and then let out a relieved sigh.

Gasping, she turned and staggered toward them. "Jackson? Josh?" Her huge mahogany eyes met his as a true smile curled her lips.

Delicious tension coiled inside him. His own grin had to be wide enough to expose his wisdom teeth. But he didn't care if his feelings were written on his face in big black letters.

He swept her close and nuzzled her neck. The softness of her breasts pressed against his chest sent a giddy sense of joy bubbling through him. She smelled wonderful. Fresh and salty, like the desert. Like Norah.

Why had he hesitated, even for a second? She was his, the love of his life, the other half of his soul. Absolutely nothing like his grasping, greedy princess of an ex-wife. If Norah wanted orange blossoms and stepfathers, he was all for the program. Soon. He linked his hands behind her waist and kissed her fiercely. "Careful, sweetheart! Long way down."

"No kidding, it's a long way. But for me you mean a long way up. My nails will never be the same." She brushed one battered hand over his cheek.

Her soft touch warmed him to his toes. Then his brain kicked in, and his jaw dropped. "You can't mean you climbed up all by yourself."

"The Magician helped me. I'd never have made it alone."

"Glad he did." Jackson gently stroked the corners of her mouth with his thumbs, closed his eyes and lowered his lips toward hers.

Josh cleared his throat.

Dragged back to the present, Jackson pressed a quick kiss to her nose and loosened his hold.

She angled her face to one side and slipped out of his arms. A frown creased her forehead. "Josh, are you all right?"

The kid took in a long, slow breath and turned his topaz eyes to her. "Much better. But it's almost noon, and we haven't found the kiva."

Norah checked the position of the sun. "I'd guess the solstice is about ten minutes away."

An insistent itch, like a parade of mosquitoes, stung Jackson's spine. His frown deepened. He kept his eyes wide, searching for danger. Exposed, vulnerable, only one-way in or out. Not the most defensible position. He grimaced and drew his weapon.

Norah shook her head. "There's no danger from the Magician. He just wants his tools returned."

"I'm not worried about the ghost," Jackson growled.

She touched his arm. "What's the matter?"

The mosquitoes had put on steel-toed boots. "I have a bad feeling. We need to finish and leave."

"There's a little crevice on the other side of that outcropping. Maybe we'd be safer there."

"Feels right. Lead the way."

With Josh between them, they eased back around the granite boulder.

The path widened a little and under a sheltered overhang, water dripped from somewhere back in the crags. Jackson welcomed the coolness. Plants grew in the narrow fissure. Prickly pears bowed from the weight of red fruit. He glanced at Norah. "What do we do?"

She hesitated and then turned toward the boy. "Josh, the Magician speaks to you. Ask him where we should go." Her voice was low and breathy.

The kid scrambled into his cross-legged pose and closed his eyes.

The golden eagle keened overhead.

Ignoring the goose bumps racing up his arms, Jackson concentrated on sweeping the area. So far they were alone.

"Now we wait." Norah folded her legs beneath her,

sitting next to Josh in the shallow recess. She took on a peacefulness that unsettled him. How could she be this calm?

Jackson flattened against the rock wall but kept his eyes and ears tuned to the highest sensitivity.

Josh's face lightened. "Can you hear that?"

She tipped up her head and then nodded. "A flute."

Jackson strained toward the sound. Had to be the wind whistling through the rocks. Cool, ghostly hands brushed the nape of his neck. A spirit moved nearby. A very old spirit.

Feeling cornered, he paced the narrow space. Like this eight hundred year dead shaman would just float by and draw a map.

Hyper alert, Jackson checked both directions. Swank was still out there. Somewhere. The crazy con man was dangerous.

Creeping back around the granite boulder, he paced toward the juniper. The danger he sensed came from this direction, but he couldn't see anything from here.

With a grimace, he holstered his weapon and crawled onto the giant juniper. He leaned through the thick tangle of branches to check the far side of the ledge.

Nothing. He placed his palms to make the leap and took a deep breath.

"Hold it right there."

Jackson froze. His heart beat like an artillery barrage, and adrenaline raced through his system.

Swank pointed a hand cannon at his chest. Too close to miss. But the big guy looked fagged-out, red-faced and sweaty. His clothes were damp and grimy, caked with mud from the knees down. The guy also looked mean as a rabid mastiff.

Swank waved his gun. "Hand over your piece."

Balancing himself on the branches hanging out from the cliff, Jackson unbuckled his holster and heaved it at the con artist.

Swank grabbed the gun and backed away.

"I need to climb down." Jackson swung his right leg over the juniper and scooted closer to the roots, facing Swank straight on.

"No fucking way. Stay put, or I'll shoot. Where's the boy?"

Jackson's insides twisted, but he looked Swank straight in the eyes. "I sent him back to Verde Valley with Norah," he barked, hoping Norah and Josh would hear.

Swank wasn't buying his lie. "There's only one way off this fucking mesa, you asshole. I'm not stupid."

With his gaze on Swank, Jackson carefully lifted his hands off the scabby tree trunk and stuck them in the air, re-centering his weight. If only he could reach that rock by his knee.

He tried to look chagrined and gave a dramatic shrug. "Josh knows a back way down. Round that corner."

The eagle screeched again and dove at them.

"Behind you!" Jackson pointed.

For a split second, Swank raised his arm, protecting his face.

Jackson grabbed the rock, heaved it as hard as he could and then flattened against the rough bark.

With a deafening blast, the branch near his head splintered. His heart faltered, and his blood ran to ice.

Frantically, he groped for another.

In slow motion, the trunk cracked under his weight and broke away. Terror numbed his brain. For an instant he was weightless before slamming into rock below.

Pain.

Then blackness.

Chapter Twenty-Four

Her heart slammed into her throat. Norah rushed toward the precipice where the broken juniper hung and screamed Jackson's name.

Nothing.

Grief overwhelmed her, blanked her mind. Her heart ached like it had been ripped from her chest. She couldn't, wouldn't look down. At the bottom of the cliff, silver agave grew like a forest of sabers.

Waving his gun at her, Swank grinned.

Fear sliced through her belly, but his pistol shook as he picked his way toward the jumble of branches, his movements jerky. His blond hair stuck up at odd angles, and blood spattered his T-shirt.

Her heart pumped ice water into her veins, and she shivered in the midday sun. Even at this distance, he stank of madness. She backed up a step, shielding Josh between her body and the cliff.

"Give me the kid. He's mine. The treasure's mine." Swank's crazed blue eyes hardened to flint. "You can't keep what's mine."

The cold spread to her bones. Her mouth felt too dry to speak. She shook her head, and held Josh behind her. Her hands trembled, but she stuck out her chin. "No."

Swank's mouth twisted into an ugly sneer. His left eye twitched. "You can't lie to me. You came here to steal my gold, but you can't have it. You hear me, Josh?"

"But I lied, Uncle Kenny. There's no treasure, no gold," Josh said with a determined edge to his voice.

Swank's face flushed. He swiped at the trickle of blood oozing onto his forehead and waved the gun. "Bullshit. I ain't leaving without my treasure. Don't care what I have to do. Don't care who else I have to kill. It's my gold." He gave a shrill laugh, his eyes wild and unseeing.

A scraping sound behind the man drew her gaze. Breaking into a cold sweat, Norah gasped. A snake with a body thick as her arm slithered out from under the exposed roots of the juniper.

Mute with horror, Norah watched the sidewinder zigzag along the cliff face.

The snake coiled behind Swank. Its tongue tested the air, seeming to taste the psychopath's muddy aura.

The reptile swayed.

The long, segmented rattle on its tail vibrated.

Swank batted at his ears, his head twitching sideways. "Fucking bees. They're everywhere."

Stammering, she pointed at the cliff.

Josh got the words out first. "Hold still, Uncle Kenny. Rattler."

Swank laughed and waved his hand above his head. "Right. You think I'm some fucking idiot—"

With a warning hiss, the snake launched off the cliff and drove its fangs into the man's neck.

Swaying, he clawed at the snake, his face glow-in-the-dark purple.

He tottered and then plunged off the edge. His terrified shriek echoed from the canyon walls as he fell.

Norah looked over the cliff and bile rose at the back of her throat.

Impaled on the agave far below, spikes protruded through his limp body. He was dead.

Close to the juniper stump, Josh peered over the outcropping. "There's Mr. Marino. He's on the ledge down there."

A rush of relief surged through her. She leaned over the cliff, clinging to a branch. "Jackson?" she yelled.

No answer. He lay on a narrow shelf about ten feet below the path. His chest lifted.

He was still breathing.

Her heart started to beat again.

"There's a way down." Josh helped her to her feet. "There's a toehold a few yards back."

With a quick plea to the Magician, Norah led the way. The shaman's gentle touch steadied her hands and feet while she climbed down.

The pool of blood under Jackson's head terrified her, but his pulse was strong. She checked for broken limbs.

"Jackson," she begged and cradled his hands.

He spoke before he opened his eyes. "I'm okay."

"Thank God." She sat back on her heels and felt a tingle of joy flow through her veins. Finally she could breathe.

She helped him sit up and dug in her makeshift pack for something to staunch the flow of blood.

When she touched the wound with her scarf, he flinched and grabbed her arm. "Swank?"

"He can't hurt us."

"Can you make it up to the path?" she asked

Jackson. "Or I could go for help and leave Josh here."

"My head's pounding, but the rest of me is in one piece. Come on, Josh. Want to help me out?" Jackson rested one hand on Josh's shoulder and the boy smiled.

Norah followed them toward the steep path, but below the broken juniper, something shiny caught her eye. A cat with golden eyes lay half buried in the rubble. Warm pleasure sang through her. She reached down and brushed away the gravel from a small reed flute with intricate inlay and grinned. "Look. This belongs to the Magician. The apprentice must have dropped it in the brush eons ago."

The Magician's gentle laugh feathered through her mind.

Josh stiffened, staring at a large sun symbol etched on a cleft in the rock wall.

"Weird. Do you feel that chill?" Jackson shook his head. "My head is still ringing from the fall."

Josh turned toward them and smiled. "He's here."

Then the Magician stood before them. She had never seen him so clearly. He was tall, with strong arms and legs. Dressed in a buckskin kilt, his deeply bronzed skin held the scars of a lifetime. He'd painted black smudges under his eyes, and his long silver braids held precious totems.

He carried blue prayer sticks decorated with eagle feathers.

Norah knelt and dug through her pack for the basket and pot. She handed them to Josh along with the flute. "You'll need these."

The boy curled his arms around the treasures. His face went slack, and his eyes rolled back in his head. "He beckons me to the third world. I must bring the basket and bowl. Bring the necklace and the flute. They belong to him. His tools will make him strong, and he will protect the People once more. The People have waited so very long."

Norah's heart thumped in her chest.

Josh stepped into a circle of rocks laid on the ground in front of the wall. The sun crested the cliff. A giant white spiral blazed out, shining as if lit by a thousand watts.

All around them, drawings had been carefully etched into the red walls. Deer, antelope and wolf galloped across the rock and disappeared into the deep fissure. Above the crevice their ghostly spirits soared up and disappeared.

The blue-violet mystery of the place shined like an aura. A deep reverence and sense of peace filled her. She stood.

A flash of light covered the boy, more dazzling than the noon sun.

Jackson reached an arm around her waist and pulled her close.

She leaned her head against his chest and listened to the steady beat of his heart.

Josh smiled back at them, but his topaz eyes held a strange unfocused stare.

The beam of light moved across the cliff, and the slit widened. Josh climbed through the opening.

The brilliant light winked out, and the cliff wall returned to solid rock. The sunbeam continued to creep across the solar calendar.

Shivering, Norah let her shoulders sag and closed her eyes. Her pulse slowed to almost a normal rhythm for the first time in a week.

"Where'd they go?" Jackson's breath stirred her hair, and he rubbed his hand over her arm.

"Into the kiva." She glanced up at him. "Don't worry. Josh will return."

"Cool looking ghost."

Norah narrowed her eyes and took a couple steps away from Jackson. "You saw the Magician?"

"Yeah. He has quite a presence. Big guy. Close to six feet, but somehow he fills more space than he should. Long graying braids, eagle feathers, but the color of his eyes was the giveaway. He's related to Josh."

"I know." She studied his calm expression. "You're not upset about seeing another ghost?"

He brushed off his jeans. "Still damn spooky, but I'll get used to it. Guess I've been seeing them for a while."

She didn't know how to take this admission. A cop, a really skeptical cop, who'd admit seeing an ancient ghost? And he wasn't even freaked out?

Jackson gave her a head-to-toe look that sent hot and cold chills racing over her skin. He focused on her eyes. "Norah, we need to talk."

His aura, visible in the shade, had changed. Still warm colors at the core, but now far more blue-green swirled at the edge and less orange. Most of the brown streaks had melted away.

When he took a step closer, she put a palm flat on his chest. "Not here."

"Here. Now." His voice had a rumbling quality that made her skin tingle.

Terrific. No place to run. No place to hide her heart. And there went her damn pulse again. She stuck out her chin.

He gently smoothed his big calloused fingers over her cheek. "I love you, Norah." His voice was even firmer and deeper, his face unsmiling.

Her stomach plummeted off the cliff behind them, and for a moment she couldn't find any words. She must have looked stunned, because he flashed her one of his blinding, got-you-now-girl grins.

"I…no, Jackson. I've thought about this. The whole misunderstanding was my fault, and I'm sorry. I know I'm naïve, maybe too dumb to live. I should never have expected so much commitment from you so fast."

Silence. He just stood there and waited.

She folded her arms across her chest, cupping her elbows. "As much as I would love to jump back into bed with you…"

A wider grin.

The guy was insufferable. Maybe she should just push him over the cliff.

She clenched her jaw and her fists, and everything else. "I do love you, but I can't risk having an ongoing relationship with you. I have Amber to care for. And I don't know what will happen to my gifts. Everything has changed. I don't even know if Grandfather will return."

He nodded as if unfazed by her arguments. "Norah, I love you and you love me."

The repeated words, soft and warm and genuine, ignited every nerve cell in her body. Could she trust him? She shook her head. "No. You'll walk away again. Someday. I'll do something that freaks you out, and you'll leave. I'd risk my heart, but never a child's.

Never Amber's. She's already lost far too much."

Jackson took her hand and placed it on his chest, nestled under his. The rapid beat of his heart matched her racing pulse.

"I'd never risk a child. Never will. Look, I know you're feeling hurt. I was surprised, no damn it, scared shitless by how I felt about you the morning after. Now I've had twenty-two hours to think since you were kidnapped."

"The Magician didn't exactly kidnap me. He hijacked my body." She balled her fist and pushed back, but he held on.

"Doesn't matter." He drew in a long breath and waited several heartbeats. "I want you. I want us to be a family. A forever family. With Amber and Josh, if he needs a home. Maybe a few more."

Unable to swallow the choke in her throat, she glanced beyond the cliff edge into the pale blue sky. The golden eagles floated together in lazy circles. If only her decision could be so damn easy and natural. She let out a long, painful sigh. "No."

He pushed a strand of hair off her face. "You need time. You need to trust me."

She nodded, unable to look at him. She couldn't let him see the tears gathering under her lowered lids.

He caressed his thumb across her cheek.

She blinked hard, but the tears leaked. Damn. Caught. How idiotic. She was crying because she couldn't have what she really wanted, who she really wanted.

"We can take things slowly, but I'm not going anywhere. And I'll start annulment proceedings, so I'm ready to marry you when you finally say yes."

She met his gaze. His aura, blazing with clear blue-green light. Truth.

He cleared his throat. "One more thing you should know. Amber and I have already talked a couple times."

"What?"

"I helped Nate and Jana calm her down. Amber was worried when you were out running around the desert with that spook."

Norah met his smoky gray eyes. His gaze seemed to reach inside and tug on her heart. Seemed to touch her soul.

Chapter Twenty-Five

"Felt pretty good when you said you loved me."

Norah's face burned from her neck to her hairline, and Jackson shot her another satisfied, I-got-you-girl grin.

"I said that in the heat of the moment."

He nibbled on her ear. "Been a lot of hot minutes lately. Ready for a bunch more?"

Delicious chills rushed through her, and something low in her body melted. Again. And it had only been an hour.

Opening the glass door, he ushered her inside the front entrance to the community hospital. After the roasting temperature of sundown in Verde Valley, the wide, shiny corridor felt cool. When an aide rushed past, Jackson pulled Norah closer to his side.

To change the subject, she hurried ahead and approached the sheriff. "Is Gina doing better?" The wrapped bouquet she'd brought crinkled in her nervous hands.

Leaning against the pale green wall, Wood gave a quick nod and unfolded his arms. "She's out of the ICU. Doc says she'll be fine. Rocky musta pushed that chopper to the limit. He and George saved her life."

Norah peeked through the window into the hospital room. Gina Swank, bandaged and pale, held Josh's hand through the tangled IV lines. Norah couldn't hear the conversation, but Rocky broke out in laughter, and Josh joined in.

Norah hugged the flowers in her arms, and the spicy scent of carnations surrounded her.

"Looks like they're doing fine," Jackson said.

"For such a big tough guy, Rocky looks smitten."

"Says he saved just enough room on his bicep for a tattoo of Gina's name. So what's next?" Wood asked.

"Judge Pascal insisted I bring Josh back to Sereno for a hearing. I plan to ask for temporary custody, but eventually he needs to live here on the reservation." Until then she would have the time to work with the boy to control his gifts. And Amber would enjoy Josh's company.

George Kwail approached from the nurses' station, his face crinkled in a grin. "I'd be happy to take Josh in when he's ready to come home. The tribe will be waiting for our new shaman, but what about Gina?"

The sheriff tipped his hat off his forehead. "She'll have some questions to answer, but Josh insists she wasn't in on the crime."

"Although she kidnapped him, she did try to protect him from his uncle," Norah said. "She even tried to help Tyrell. The judge will take that into account."

Jackson swung a casual arm around her waist. "What about Smith and his bodyguard?"

The sheriff fanned his hat and looked very satisfied. "Verde Valley PD arrested those two thugs a couple hours ago. Feds will pick them up tomorrow. With all the evidence we collected, they'll be out of circulation until they're using walkers."

George pursed his lips for a moment and then

nodded. "The Tribal Council is taking over direct management of the casino. There'll be big changes. Big improvements."

Norah's phone chirped in her pocket. When she read the caller ID, a soft smile bloomed on her face. "Hi, baby."

"Hi, Aunt Norah. Can I speak to Jackson? I want to invite him to the soccer picnic."

Hesitating, she glanced up at Jackson. "The, uh, the big picnic? I don't think so, sweetie. Let's talk some more when I get home."

"Please?"

"Not right now."

Jackson drew his arm around her shoulder. "Amber? Let me speak to her."

Norah's brow furrowed, but he'd already talked to Amber three times. Too late to stuff that genie back in the barn. She shrugged and handed him her cell.

He switched the phone to speaker, and Norah raised an eyebrow. What was he up to?

"Hey, kiddo."

"Hi, Jackson," Amber said coyly, drawing out his name. "Can you come to my soccer family picnic? It's not till next weekend. You'll be home by then, won't you?"

Norah's whole body jittered in place. Her heart threatened to explode out of her chest.

Jackson swallowed, but leveled his determined stare right at her eyes. "I'd love to come to your picnic." With one finger, he drew her chin up and kissed her gently on the lips.

Incredible electricity sizzled up and down her limbs and fried her brain. She kissed him back, even with everyone watching.

Jackson released Norah. His eyes glowed as he brought the phone back to his ear. "Hey, Amber."

"Jackson?" Amber's voice came over the speaker. "Where'd you go?"

"Nowhere." He grinned. "Just kissing your aunt. Say, do they need another coach on your team?"

Norah smelled smoke. She turned, suddenly surrounded by the log walls of Grandfather's lodge. Clothed in a pale beaded buckskin dress, she sat across the hissing fire from him. She crossed her arms. "Took you long enough to show up."

Grandfather shrugged and grinned like a well-satisfied fox.

A word about the author...

Along with teaching, Joy began her writing career by publishing children's historical fiction. Later, she found writing romantic suspense fulfilled her need for travel and romance. She lives with her husband and two dogs near Silicon Valley and the mythical town of Sereno.

Connect with her online and on Facebook.
http://www.joybrighton-author.com

Thank you for purchasing
this publication of The Wild Rose Press, Inc.

If you enjoyed the story, we would appreciate your
letting others know by leaving a review.

For other wonderful stories,
please visit our on-line bookstore at
www.thewildrosepress.com.

For questions or more information
contact us at
info@thewildrosepress.com.

The Wild Rose Press, Inc.
www.thewildrosepress.com

Stay current with The Wild Rose Press, Inc.

Like us on Facebook

https://www.facebook.com/TheWildRosePress

And Follow us on Twitter
https://twitter.com/WildRosePress

www.ingramcontent.com/pod-product-compliance
Lightning Source LLC
Chambersburg PA
CBHW071524260626
47170CB00002B/497